CW01622274

13.10.20
02.11.20
14. OCT 21
14/5/23
16/7/23

LANGPORT

CANCELLED

SOLAN

Please return/renew this item by the last date shown on this label, or on your self-service receipt.

To renew this item, visit **www.librarieswest.org.uk**, use the LibrariesWest app, or contact your library.

Your borrower number and PIN are required.

Libraries**West**

BOOKS

1 3 1777870 6

Published 2019
Joffe Books, London
www.joffebooks.com

© David Hodges

This book is a work of fiction. Names, characters, businesses, organisations, places and events are either the product of the author's imagination or are used fictitiously. Any resemblance to actual persons, living or dead, events or locales is entirely coincidental. The spelling used is British English except where fidelity to the author's rendering of accent or dialect supersedes this. The right of David Hodges to be identified as author of this work has been asserted by him in accordance with the Copyright, Designs and Patents Act 1988

We hate typos too but sometimes they slip through.
Please send any errors you find to
corrections@joffebooks.com
We'll get them fixed ASAP. We're very grateful to eagle-eyed readers who take the time to contact us.

Please join our mailing list for free Kindle crime thriller, detective, mystery books and new releases.
http://www.joffebooks.com/contact/

ISBN: 978-1-78931-162-4

Dedication

This book is dedicated to my wife, Elizabeth, for all her love, patience and support over so many wonderful years and to my late mother and father, whose faith in me to one day achieve my ambition as a writer remained steadfast throughout their lifetime and whose tragic passing has left a hole in my life that will never be filled.

AUTHOR'S NOTE

Although the action in this novel takes place within the Avon & Somerset Police area, the story itself and all the characters in it are entirely fictitious. Similarly, at the time of writing, there is *no* police station in Highbridge. This has been drawn entirely from the author's imagination to ensure no connection is made between any existing police station or personnel in the force and the content of the novel. I would also point out that I have used some poetic licence in relation to the local police structure and some of the specific procedures followed by Avon & Somerset Police in order to meet the requirements of the plot. Nevertheless, the policing background depicted in the novel is broadly in accord with the national picture and these little departures from fact will, hopefully, not spoil the reading enjoyment of serving or retired police officers, for whom I have the utmost respect.

David Hodges

BEFORE THE FACT

There was not as much blood as might have been expected. The sharpened pencil penetrated the cornea of the psychiatrist's right eye and buried itself in the sixty-year-old's brain with the ease of a breadstick sliding into a guacamole dip. Death was instantaneous, of course, and when the body had stopped twitching, it was a simple enough matter to exchange clothes with the victim before hauling the cadaver into the private flat that adjoined the consulting room, closing and locking the door afterwards, and pocketing the key. Dumped in there, it could be days before the body was found, and probably only then when the sweet, sickly smell that accompanied the natural process of early decomposition attracted attention.

George Lupin had been a 'guest' at a succession of mental institutions since early adulthood, before finally ending up at Larchfield Secure Psychiatric Hospital. In fact, at the start of it all, decades ago, the then assize court had obviously intended to throw away the key when they'd passed judgement. By recording a verdict of 'unfit to plead by reason of insanity', they had in effect handed down an indeterminate sentence. Not that that had been much of a surprise to George, who had admitted to the torture of some halfwit kid in a shed at the young offenders' institution, just months after the teenager had been sent there for fatally stabbing a pervert at the orphanage.

Mind you, it had not been too bad in the hospital. Actually, it had been a bit like staying in a hotel. Except for the massive outer wall, the surveillance cameras, electronic gates, tight perimeter security, and the compulsory pharmacological medication, which had at times produced similar psychedelic effects to those experienced by Jack Nicholson's character in the early stages of the film, *One Flew Over the Cuckoo's Nest.*

George had even enjoyed the regular visits of the 'shrink.' It had been fun pretending to respond to the treatment and all that counselling claptrap – deceiving the hospital's naive hierarchy into believing that their pathetic treatment programme had made a difference to one of their most dangerous psychopaths, even though release was unlikely to be an option. Not after what Patient 174 had done.

But then the worst news possible had been delivered by the hospital's senior consultant after George had noticed some bleeding, accompanied by substantial weight loss. A tumour, they'd said; a nasty, aggressive one that was inoperable and eating away at the essential organs, like something out of the film *Alien.* As yet, there was no real pain, just discomfort, but they'd admitted it would come at the end. Their resident psycho had just a few months left, with the grim prospect of inheriting a nice little plot in the hospital's cemetery before Christmas arrived. It wasn't fair. All those years of incarceration and now the final turn of the screw.

What would they inscribe on the tombstone, George wondered? 'George Lupin' or maybe just 'Patient 174', with a date of birth and death, plus the usual 'RIP'? In short, just another deceased inmate passing into obscurity like all the others. No, there had to be something better than that, something more enduring; a reason for society to remember this sad, sick psycho, as they had remembered others who had earned a prominent place in history through their notoriety, like the Moors Murderers or Dr Shipman.

It was then that George Lupin had made the decision to ditch the mind-bending drugs the hospital had been prescribing – to secretly regurgitate the little coloured tablets after they had been issued and consign them to the toilet – before breaking out of Larchfield altogether, to spend the last few weeks that remained giving free rein to the paranoid desires which the medication had so far suppressed.

The whole thing had taken meticulous planning.

First, pre-escape preparation. That had meant deciding on a weapon for what George had in mind. Sharps of any sort were out of the question, so it had to be something that could be adapted. A biro? No, that wouldn't be permitted. A pencil, then? No, the same would apply on this wing, unless … the art classes had been boring, but they had provided access to some basic kit, including pencils; nice, sharp pencils. The dotty art teacher Larchfield brought in from outside the hospital was more concerned with the creative aspects of her role than monitoring the return of the kit she had issued.

So far, so good – the weapon had been obtained. Now for the second part of the plan; a haircut. George had quite long, blond hair, but it needed to be much shorter and of a similar style to the blond hair of the psychiatrist, who was to be Patient 174's ticket out of Larchfield. To avoid attracting attention – any sudden change always aroused suspicion – the trim had to be carried out over a period of weeks. A little bit shorter to start with, so that everyone got used to it, then a bit more and a bit more, until it was done. That meant eating into the last two months of George's remaining life expectancy, but it couldn't be helped and, in any event, it still left enough time for what needed to be done on the outside, so it was worth the risk.

Next on the agenda was the 'going away' outfit. The shrink was about the same build as George, with similar size feet, so borrowing his clothes and shoes after the victim had been dispatched hadn't seemed to pose too much of a problem.

But then had come the difficult part – getting past security – and that meant choosing precisely the right moment. One-to-one psychotherapy sessions were organized on a pretty regular basis and every fourth one-to-one was on the Thursday afternoon, just before shift change, when the 'rock apes' who maintained hospital security were either reporting for duty or signing off, creating mass movement and an element of confusion. The hospital's programme could not have been more tailored to George's plan, coupled with which, the bank holiday weekend was now about to get underway, meaning that just half the regular staff complement would be on duty, with the administration unit already closed altogether.

As a result, no one would be checking up on the Thursday therapy session until much later on the Tuesday morning and, under the innovative regime that had been set up as an experiment at Larchfield (God bless the liberalists), patients on George's wing had much more freedom of movement and association than was the case in other secure units up and down the country. Doors were seldom locked and, apart from the compulsory therapy sessions, there was little physical supervision or individual monitoring, which meant that it would be a while before George was missed.

As for the unfortunate psychiatrist, it was common knowledge that he lived alone in a city semi, 10 miles away, using the private hospital accommodation only when he was on cover duty. In any event, he had revealed to his scheming patient that he was about to go on a week's holiday, so it was unlikely anyone would miss him until Monday week, by which time Patient 174 would be long gone.

Now dressed in the shrink's gear, including the distinctive black Fedora hat and long, dark coat of the true eccentric, and carrying the dead man's red patient file – the Lupin file – under one arm, it turned out to be relatively easy to walk out the front door of the building into the grounds, which were always accessible to trusted patients during the day.

Finding the doc's ancient red VW Beetle in the staff car park was also proved straightforward, as it was always parked in the same place, although mastering the car's gears proved to be a bit of a problem at first. Fortunately, in common with some of the other trusted patients at Larchfield, George had been given the opportunity of learning to drive the hospital's internal flatbed truck, and had used it from time to time to transport bed linen, refuse bins, and garden waste from one part of the site to another, so all the basic driving know-how was there. As a result, when Patient 174 finally pulled away, the process was achieved without too much rough handling and the guard in the gate lodge, who was well used to the good doctor's own ham-fisted driving, even gave a casual, half-humorous salute as the car drove through on to the external service road.

Out and free. The feeling was truly exhilarating. Out and free to do what should have been done so long ago and which a lifetime of incarceration had made impossible, and where better to head for than where it had started all those years ago? The depths of the beautiful Somerset countryside.

But first there was a little job that needed doing. Pulling into the next motorway services and slipping on a pair of thin leather gloves discovered in the driver's door pocket of the VW, George bought a notebook, a pen, an envelope and a first-class stamp from the shop with the dead psychiatrist's money. Then Patient 174 sat down over a cup of coffee in the cafeteria to write a letter, a very special letter indeed.

CHAPTER 1

The spot would have made an ideal set for a spooky Hollywood movie. But it wasn't ghosts that Detective Sergeant Kate Lewis was thinking about as she perched on the edge of the overturned crate in the woodshed. She shivered in the damp rising from the concrete floor, in spite of the heavy coat and thick corduroy trousers she was wearing. Her eyes were glued to the window through a pair of night-vision binoculars, watching for the slightest movement in the supposedly derelict mansion 20–30 yards away across the swathe of moonlit lawn.

Beside her, junior colleague Detective Constable Danny Ferris stretched his heavy frame carefully and rubbed the back of one hand across the stubble on his chin, the rasping sound drawing an irritable glance from Kate.

'Reckon anyone will show, skipper?' he growled, pulling his woolly hat even tighter over his mop of black curly hair. 'Been here for two hours now already and not a dicky bird. Bloody waste of time, if you ask me.'

'Well, no one *is* asking you,' Kate retorted tartly, dropping the binoculars into her lap on the end of their thin leather neck-cord. 'So, cool it and have a bit of patience.'

'Cool it?' he snorted. 'Can't get much cooler in this shit-hole, can we? My friggin' bollocks are frozen. You'd think it would be warmer at this time of the year. Bloody weather is all to cock.'

Kate smiled faintly, unfazed by his colourful language. In her mid-thirties and with over ten years police service behind her – most of them on Highbridge nick's Criminal Investigation Department – there wasn't anything anyone could come out with that she hadn't heard before.

'And what is this drum we're watching anyway?' Ferris went on. 'What was it they called it at briefing – Talbot Court, wasn't it? Fancy name for a bloody ruin. The place gives me the creeps.'

Kate's gaze travelled over the moon-splashed stone walls, prominent buttresses and broken sash windows of the derelict building, and, for some unaccountable reason, she shivered.

'It was once a Georgian mansion, I'm told,' she replied. 'Footmen, coaches and horses – that sort of thing. But over the last two hundred years it's also been an asylum, an approved school for juvenile delinquents, and lastly an orphanage with a very dodgy reputation. The orphanage was actually closed down after a series of nasty incidents, including the murder of a member of staff, complaints from some of the inmates of sexual abuse, and a serious fire which virtually gutted the place.'

Ferris grunted. 'Why doesn't that surprise me? Dirty paedo bastards seem to be everywhere nowadays.' He grinned. 'Talking of which, where's Hayden tonight? I thought he'd be here with us.'

Kate glared at him in the gloom, failing to appreciate his humour when her detective constable husband was the target.

'Sick,' she replied tersely.

She thought of the lame excuse given by her other half that an upset stomach meant he was unable to take part in the surveillance operation. More likely he hadn't wanted to miss the big match on television, she mused unkindly, conjuring up a vision of him slumped in an armchair before a roaring log fire in their little thatched cottage, no doubt warming a glass of wine in his hands.

'He's got the runs,' she added finally. 'Some sort of bug, it seems.'

Ferris snorted. 'Nice. Been trying to poison him, have you?'

'Don't tempt me,' she muttered under her breath, then her focus abruptly returned to the task in hand. 'Watch out, we've got company.'

Raising her night-vision binoculars, she watched as the dark Transit van that had appeared suddenly through the arched entrance gateway pulled up on the gravel hardstanding by the front door of the house and cut its lights. A couple of minutes passed before the passenger door was thrown open and a tall figure dressed in black climbed out, studying his surroundings. Apparently satisfied, he went round to the back of the Transit, to be joined by the driver who unlocked the rear doors and pulled them open.

Kate adjusted the plastic earpiece which linked to the radio pack-set strapped to her chest, pressed the transmit button, and spoke quietly into the mouthpiece.

'Green One-zero,' she announced softly. 'Targets present at front of building.'

The gruff voice of Detective Inspector Ted Roscoe growled back, '*Understood One-zero. Hold your position for present. Report when they enter premises.*'

Kate could feel the excitement welling up inside her as she acknowledged the instruction and she clenched her fists involuntarily in an effort to control the sudden heady surge of adrenalin.

The moon disappeared behind scudding clouds, returning the night to almost Stygian blackness, then re-emerged, flooding the scene with renewed brilliance. The Transit was still there, its rear doors wide open, but the two men had disappeared, and as the fact dawned on her, she saw a glimmer of light in a downstairs window of the house.

'Green One-zero,' she breathed. 'They're in.'

'*Blue tactical units only,*' Roscoe rapped. '*Go! Go! Go!*'

Ferris jumped to his feet, but Kate grabbed his arm tightly.

'Blue units only,' she reminded him. 'They have to clear the building before we can go in. Didn't you listen to the briefing? Patience.'

As Ferris reluctantly sat down again, a stream of armed figures in black military-style uniforms and NATO helmets emerged from woodland on both sides of the house and quickly encircled the building. Seconds later a small contingent broke away from the main group and burst through the open front door, shouting hoarsely to warn those inside that they were armed police.

In just over twenty minutes it was all over without a shot being fired, as two uniformed policemen appeared in the doorway, manhandling what looked like the tall passenger from the Transit out into the moonlight. His wrists were securely handcuffed, but he was struggling violently and snarling abuse at his captors as they dragged him to a waiting police patrol car. Another man, possibly the van driver, was brought out afterwards, though he seemed to have accepted his fate and walked docilely between two more officers to a second patrol car. Then, with blue beacons flashing, both police vehicles turned around in a swirl of gravel and drove back out through the archway, signifying the end of the operation.

Kate waited until she had received the general '*all clear*' message on her radio from the inspector leading the search team before she and Ferris left the woodshed. They reached the front of the house just as an old Honda Civic rolled up, firing plumes of smoke from its exhaust with every alternate beat of its out-of-tune engine.

'Guv'nor,' Kate greeted as the short, muscular figure in the overcoat and pork-pie hat climbed out.

Even from where she was standing, she could smell the stale beer and cigarette smoke off him and she was unsurprised by his non-committal grunt in response. Detective Inspector Ted Roscoe was a good, experienced policeman, but he would never have won any prizes at charm school, and she smiled tightly to herself as she followed him through the front door of the house with Ferris trailing behind, knowing full well from the intelligence they had received where the boss would be heading.

The basement was two levels down – below another floor that had no doubt originally comprised the servants' quarters, plus the wine and food stores and the kitchen. Accessed via an arched doorway in the corner of a large, white-tiled room, which had obviously once been the kitchen itself, it was located at the foot of an iron-railed stone staircase, one that plunged steeply between peeling plaster walls into darkness. Their torches revealed a short passageway at the bottom burrowing into the gloom to their left, and the boiler room they were seeking was directly in front of them, its door standing wide open. The plastic bags were stacked neatly inside, close to a massive rusted boiler, and the padlock which seemed to have been used to secure the door skated into the room under the toe of Roscoe's shoe when he failed to spot it on his approach.

'Must be around half a ton there, guv,' Kate breathed, studying the plastic bags in the beam of her torch, 'and if that really is coke, your snout has certainly earned his bread.'

Roscoe grunted again. 'It had better be coke,' he growled. 'It cost me a bloody big slice of the snouts' fund.'

He straightened and turned to Kate. 'You and Ferris remain here to preserve the scene,' he said. 'No one goes in until SOCO arrive. Got that? I'll get a plod down here to guard this little lot as soon as I can.'

Then he was gone, a fast-fading spot of light bobbing about in a black void almost in time to the sharp tap of his footsteps on the stone stairs.

Kate watched the bobbing light until it had disappeared completely, then turned to Ferris.

'Looks like we'll be here for a while,' she remarked, repressing a shiver. 'Hope your thermals are up to it.'

She heard him sniff.

'Never mind the bloody thermals,' he said. 'I just hope the pair who've just been nicked don't have an army of pals who decide to turn up here looking to make a claim.'

She gave a short laugh, then abruptly swallowed the reply that was on the tip of her tongue and gripped his arm tightly.

'What was that?' she whispered sharply.

'What was what?' he retorted.

She squeezed his arm again and this time he heard it – a scraping sound from somewhere further along the passageway.

'Probably a rat,' he said, but there was a nervous tremor in his tone. 'Can't be anything else – the tactical team checked out the whole place.'

Kate directed her own torch into the gloom, but saw only bare walls and the gashes of two other doorways.

'Stay here,' she ordered. 'I'm going to take a look.'

'What, on your own? Don't be daft. I'm coming with you.'

She muttered an oath. 'You'll do no such thing, Danny. Someone has to stay here to preserve the scene. I'll yell if I need you.'

For all her bravado, Kate felt her stomach muscles knotting as she parted company with her colleague's reassuring bulk, but she pressed on. More scrapings now and for a moment she froze. She could actually feel the thud of her own heart in the claustrophobic blackness and was conscious of the fact that her mouth had suddenly dried up.

She checked the first room, which opened off to her left, but she saw nothing save piles of old, broken furniture, a child's rocking horse, and a stack of tea chests.

She moved on to the second room, which faced her at the end of the passageway. The door was partially closed and its rusted hinges groaned as she pushed it open. The beam of her torch traced a path across the dirty concrete floor, then over the bare brick walls, picking out a stack of mattresses in the left-hand corner and a couple of iron-framed beds with twisted springs pushed up against the right-hand wall. Then, venturing further into the room, she saw something else – a single mattress, with a couple of blankets dumped in a bundle on top, beside a litter of plastic cups and the remains of what looked like plastic sandwich cartons. There was a strong, rancid smell, like urine, and touching the mattress she found it was soaking wet – no doubt from the water which she could see slowly creeping down the lagging of a broken pipe extending from the ceiling to a horizontal section running along the lower part of the wall.

She felt her stomach churn. Someone had been using the place as a doss and the scraping sounds she had heard suggested he was still here, lurking somewhere in the darkness. But where?

A sudden sound behind her and she instinctively spun round, the beam of her torch illuminating a tall figure in a wide-brimmed, trilby-type hat and long, dark overcoat, who had materialized from the darkness on the other side of the door, just feet away.

'And who the hell are you?' she gasped, her free hand diving for the CS gas spray in her pocket.

The figure threw up an arm to shield his eyes from the glare of the torch.

'You okay, skip?' she heard Ferris' voice call faintly from the far end of the passageway.

'I said, who are you?' she repeated, still struggling to extricate the gas spray from the lining of her pocket.

Rimless, gold-coloured glasses blazed back at her in the light of the torch and she glimpsed a thin, pale face, framed by straggly blond hair. Then, to her astonishment, the figure seemed to smile, raising a finger to his lips before suddenly lurching forward and hurling her to one side with a sweep of one powerful arm. She hit the floor with a force that knocked much of the breath out of her body, cracking her head on the concrete in the process, the torch flying from her hand and bouncing away into the gloom.

As she struggled up on to her knees, senses swimming in a sea of pain, she heard running footsteps and saw the beam of another torch bobbing towards her.

'Skipper?' Ferris was panting from the exertion when he reached her side.

'Where'd he go?' she gasped as he hauled her to her feet.

Ferris spotted her torch, miraculously still lit, lying a few feet away and retrieved it for her.

'Where did who go?'

She took the torch from him and directed the beam back along the passageway.

'The blond guy. He vanished – just like that.'

'I heard you yell, but I ain't seen no one.'

'He must have run right past you.'

'Well, *I* never saw him.'

She pushed past him, training her torch on the first room she had checked a few moments before. At first, she saw just the same broken furniture she had noted before, but then she became aware of something else – the rocking horse was rising and falling on its base with the creak of its mechanism, as if being rocked by an unseen hand.

Gritting her teeth, she advanced slowly into the room, the gas spray held out at arm's length in front of her, but there was no need for caution. The bird had flown and she saw how he had managed it.

There was a narrow door in the far corner of the room, half hidden by the stack of tea chests. Further investigation revealed a flight of stairs on the other side, which were found to lead to a scullery at the back of the house, behind the kitchen. Moonlight flooded the room through a smashed window, glinting on the shards of broken glass littering the twin draining boards and stone-flagged floor, while the back door hung open at an angle on one hinge, as if mocking the two detectives as they stumbled into the room.

Pushing through the open door and climbing another shorter flight of steps, Kate found herself standing in a partially overgrown walled yard, littered with broken roof tiles, lengths of lead guttering, and other debris. It was apparent that the ground at the rear of the house was a lot lower than that at the front, and a wide opening to her right, sporting the remains of a high wooden gate, gave access to a lane bordered on the far side by a rhyne – one of Somerset's man-made ditches. Predictably, there was no sign of anyone.

'Bastard's gone,' Kate said savagely, after striding to the gateway and studying the empty lane.

'Reckon he was part of this business?' Ferris asked at her elbow. 'Maybe your feller had been left here by the others to keep an eye on the stash until they could come back to pick it up?'

Kate shook her head doubtfully. 'I don't know. Somehow, I don't think so. He seemed more like a dosser to me. There's a mattress and blanket in the basement, which he may have been using.'

Ferris grunted. 'Funny the search team didn't find him when they nicked the other two.'

She nodded. 'I suspect he was hiding behind the stack of mattresses in the room where I found him.'

'Mr Roscoe won't be happy we lost him.'

She snorted. 'Mr Roscoe is never happy anyway,' she retorted angrily, 'so what's new?'

CHAPTER 2

It was a fact that Detective Inspector Ted Roscoe rarely smiled and, when he did, it looked like a ferocious extension of his usual scowl. With his Stalin-style moustache and bushy eyebrows, the chunky former Marine presented quite a formidable figure, despite his unimpressive stature, and his forceful personality had an intimidating effect on most people who came into contact with him.

Detective Sergeant Kate Lewis was not one of those people. Her vivid blue eyes and pale, freckled face, framed by a mane of auburn hair, may have turned the heads of most red-blooded males and aroused envy in the hearts of most young women denied the looks she had inherited from her late mother, but a book should never be judged by its cover. Underneath was a resourceful, headstrong and stubborn young woman, who was certainly not afraid to stand up to her scowling, overbearing boss. This did not make for an easy relationship between the two and although, deep down, they shared a mutual respect for each other, neither would ever be prepared to admit to it.

There was certainly no hint of this mutual respect when Kate returned to Highbridge police station to find her boss slumped behind the desk in his small office.

'So, you've let the side down again, eh, Lewis?' he growled, popping a strip of chewing gum into his mouth after she had told him about the rough sleeper. 'Let the third member of the gang get clean away?'

She treated him to a laser-like stare. 'It wasn't like that at all, guv, and you know it,' she retorted. 'Anyway, I don't think he was part of the gang. Probably just a dosser who happened to be in the wrong place at the wrong time.'

'What? A dosser wearing a trilby hat? That'll be a first.'

'We found a mattress, blankets and other evidence of a rough sleeper,' she went on with exaggerated patience, 'so it all checks out.'

'He could still have been the watchman, looking after the coke until it was collected.'

'Unlikely, in my opinion.'

He grunted. 'Well, that's all right then, isn't it? If that's the opinion of the force's ace sleuth, Detective Sergeant Kate Lewis, we can all rest easy, can't we?'

She flushed angrily. 'That's not fair, guv,' she snapped back. 'He came out of nowhere and knocked me flat. I cracked my head on the bloody floor too. I could have been seriously injured.'

'Well, you weren't, were you? What do you want, a flippin' medal? And anyway, what was Ferris doing while all this was going on? Having a crap?'

She rose to the bait before she could stop herself. 'With respect, *sir*, you are out of order. DC Ferris was guarding the crime scene, as you had instructed, but he came to my assistance as soon as he realized there was a problem.'

'But your man still got away, didn't he? What did he look like?'

'I didn't get much of a look at him. I just saw a pale face, glasses, and blondish hair. Anyway, I've already circulated what I can remember about him, so maybe someone will pick him up in due course.'

He gave a disparaging snort. 'Yeah, and maybe the Tooth Fairy will leave a couple of sovs under my pillow tonight.'

With a bit of luck, it will be a grenade, she thought grimly. Roscoe sat back in his chair and treated her to a wolfish grin through a wad of chewing gum.

'Go on, Lewis, piss off home and rest that sore head of yours,' he mocked. 'Can't have our top detective suffering brain damage, can we? You can close the door on your way out.'

And she did – with a slam that rattled the whole office.

*

The thatched cottage Kate and Hayden had made their home stood close to the main road on the outskirts of the village of Burtle, within a patchwork of waterlogged fields, criss-crossed by rhynes.

Kate turned the nose of her Mazda MX5 sports car into the gravel driveway at the side of the cottage at just after midnight and sat there for a few moments after shutting off the engine, stretching her aching muscles. It had been a long night and she was ready for bed.

Hayden was still up and waiting for her, his good-natured face, framed by a mop of unruly fair hair, wearing a wide grin as she pushed through the front door and dumped her briefcase on the floor beside the telephone table in the living room. Fresh logs spluttered on the open fire and a bottle of red wine and two full glasses stood on the coffee table in front of it.

'Good result, old girl?' Hayden asked, picking up one of the glasses of wine and holding it out towards her.

She kicked off her shoes and, shrugging out of her coat, draped it over the back of an armchair.

'Good enough,' she replied, taking the glass from him and dropping on to the settee where he had obviously been lounging. 'We nicked two and seized a load of what looked like coke. Unfortunately, one got away, but it's likely he was just a dosser in the wrong place at the wrong time.' She eyed him critically. 'How's the stomach?'

His grin faded to a sheepish smile. 'Oh, a lot better, thanks,' he said hastily. 'Must have been nothing more than bad indigestion.'

She gulped some wine and glanced at the dirty plate lying on the edge of the hearth beside the settee, which bore the remains of what looked to have been a pizza and chips. Still smarting over Roscoe's remarks and keen to take her anger out on someone, she waved an arm towards the dirty plate.

'And of course, a big doughy pizza and greasy chips were the ideal remedy for that, weren't they?' she said with heavy sarcasm.

He looked embarrassed and tried to avoid her stare.

'Er … well, no, but I got a bit … er … peckish after the indigestion went, so I rang Angelo's. Nice youngster delivered it on a scooter.'

She nodded slowly. 'Was that before or after you'd watched the big match or had started on the red wine?' she said tightly.

He glanced at the television screen, then at his glass, but said nothing and she shook her head bitterly.

'You really do take the biscuit, Hayd,' she went on remorselessly. 'You should have been on this operation tonight and while you were lounging here in front of the fire – supposedly sick, yet managing to stuff yourself with pizza and watch bloody football – Danny Ferris and I were freezing our tits off in a sodding shed, with just a flask of coffee to keep out the cold.'

He frowned. 'That's not fair, Kate,' he protested. 'I really did feel ill when you left for the nick at six. I wasn't swinging the lead.'

She snorted. 'Tell that to the Marines, Hayd, and they'd probably shoot you!' She stood up, draining her glass. 'Anyway, I'm going to bed. I'm knackered and I haven't the energy to argue the toss with you.'

She was halfway to the stairs when she turned with a frown of her own, sniffing the air.

‘What’s that smell? It’s like perfume.’ She treated him to a hard stare. ‘Had a woman in here, have you, Hayd?’

His eyes widened and he visibly gulped. ‘Good lord, no,’ he exclaimed indignantly. ‘What sort of person do you think I am? It must have been the pizza girl—’

‘Girl?’

‘Yes, Jackie I think she said her name was. She … she put the pizza in the kitchen for me.’ He choked for a moment. ‘How can you even think something like that?’

Her eyes sparkled. She was pleased she had managed to ruffle his feathers. The lying sod deserved it. Poor old Hayden was the most devoted man she had ever met. Eccentric, pompous, overweight and bone idle at times, but unfaithful? Not a chance! He wouldn’t know where to start. But baiting him had certainly helped her get over her bad mood.

‘Goodnight, Hayd,’ she said. ‘Don’t forget to wash your dirty dishes before you turn in, will you?’

CHAPTER 3

Another of those bad headaches – which had been a curse for so long and were evidently associated with Patient 174's mental illness, according to Larchfield's so-called experts – had returned with a vengeance. Without the sedative medication the hospital had supplied to dumb things down, George Lupin had no choice but to lie on the pile of loose hay which almost filled the barn, eyes closed, listening to the world waking up around the old wooden building until, with the aid of a couple of the strong pain-killing tablets stolen from the dead shrink's medicine cabinet, the pain subsided.

The main A38 Bristol Road was only a stone's throw away and the early morning bank holiday traffic was already thundering by. The noise was not a problem in itself. After all, that was what life was all about, wasn't it? The brash, frenetic life that George had missed out on during all those wasted years locked away in Larchfield. But it was a reminder that people were out and about now, and darkness no longer provided its cloak of invisibility.

Sleep had not come easily the previous night – with every creak of the barn's timbers, every rustle of a bird or a rat a cause for alarm – and it had been well into the early hours before exhaustion had won over. Now though, with daylight stealing into the barn, it was time to make a move before the stolen red car parked at the back of the building was spotted by a visiting farmhand or a police helicopter passing overhead. The murder of the shrink and the audacious escape of one of the hospital's detained patients was bound to have been circulated to all police forces, so, headache or not, George knew that any further delay could be disastrous. Old Bill would almost certainly be looking for the car, so it would need to be dumped at the first opportunity, but for the present it was needed.

Revisiting Talbot Court had been a big mistake, of course. That was obvious now. But seeing the place just one last time had been a compulsion – a desire to lay the ghosts to rest and finally bury the traumatic memories that had haunted every waking hour for all those long years of incarceration. Nevertheless, the visit had almost ended in disaster, with the two heavies turning up to collect whatever it was they had stashed in the old boiler room necessitating a quick dive for cover. But then there had been the police raid and that bitch of a copper materializing just at the wrong moment. It was difficult to comprehend how such a run of bad luck could happen to one person in one place in such a short time. What if the cop had managed to put two and two together about the dosser she had spooked and had sent the balloon up? Even now, half the Avon & Somerset force could be scouring the countryside for their quarry. Time to go …

George quit the barn and stumbled to the stolen VW car. It started first time and within minutes he joined the traffic heading towards Bridgwater.

*

Kate was fully prepared for Roscoe to have another go at her about losing her rough sleeper when she turned up for work in the morning. The crusty DI had warned her when she had first joined the department that he was not a man to forgive or forget misdemeanours, and he had certainly stuck to that philosophy in the years that she had worked with him. So, she fully expected him to resurrect the whole thing the moment he clapped eyes on her. But instead, though he called her into his office before she had even reached her desk, he said nothing about the previous night's operation. Instead, he simply reached across his own desk and slapped a sheet of crumpled paper in front of her.

'Read that,' he growled. 'It's a copy of a letter the Super got this morning – apparently delivered by hand and left under the windscreen wiper of one of our motors parked outside the nick last night. He routed it to the DCI afterwards. Seems our boss is shitting himself over it.'

She grinned mischievously. 'The Super *and* the DCI working on a bank holiday weekend, guv?' she mocked. 'Whatever next.'

'Just read it, will you?' he grated. 'I can do without the funnies.'

Mystified, she picked it up and speed-read the tightly packed, handwritten contents.

Dear Superintendent,

It is an unfortunate fact that I shall always associate sherry with death. As a child, I knew someone had died when I came home from school and detected the sweet, sickly smell of the stuff. It happened when each of my uncles died and finally my mother and father.

I knew that my aunts would be in the house on those scary occasions too, just like the skeletal birds of prey they were. Each one perched on the edge of her chair, with that tiny, over-full glass of sherry in one claw-like hand – a mangy fox fur sneering at me round the collar of her black coat, and red, lipstick-smeared lips twisted into a grim, indulgent smile, ready to imprint their mark on my recoiling cheeks. Looking back now, I realize that at the time they and my uncles must have actually been quite young, but to an impressionable child, they all seemed so old and frightening. To make matters worse, the curtains were always drawn when someone died and I was forced to stay in the front room with them. Forced to sit on the prickly horse-hair sofa, frozen into a statue by the gimlet eyes of my formidable so-called father, and just inches from the open coffin containing the cadaver of the 'dearly departed.'

I used to look at the pale, frozen faces of my aunts and think how like corpses they already were. The only saving grace seemed to be that, over time, their number would decrease as, one by one, they themselves would occupy a sleek, black coffin standing on a gurney in their own front room, just as their husbands – my uncles – had ended up before them. It couldn't have come sooner for me, yet the tragedy was it never did.

The aunts actually made my life a living hell, never losing the opportunity to torment and punish me and encouraging my father to do the same, while my mother looked on, too weak and spineless to intervene.

As a consequence, I used to dream about my aunts and the torments they had put me through. Lie there writhing in my own perspiration as they crowded around me with their red lips and fox furs – prodding me with their long, painted nails – and wake up screaming. I didn't need horror comics as a child. I had my aunts.

Even now, I still think about them all the time, loathing them just as much as I did then, and the scary thing is, they are still there. They probably don't look the same – witches can always change their appearance, can't they? But to me they are there just the same. In fact, aunts are everywhere now, aren't they? In towns, cities, and even in the countryside, with their smeared red lips and pointed red nails, ready to inflict misery on every small child they encounter. As a result, I have finally taken the decision to euthanize some of them – firstly because of the part such loathsome harridans played in ruining my own life and secondly, to satisfy myself that hateful creatures like these are truly gone forever.

Why am I telling you all this? Well, I thought it might help your criminal profiler to understand my reasoning once I get going. Simple really.

Yours faithfully,

George

Kate raised a cynical eyebrow.

'Obviously someone didn't think much of his scary aunts, guv,' she commented drily. 'Any idea who "George" is?'

Roscoe snorted. 'If I knew that, I wouldn't be asking you to read the bloody letter, would I?' he retorted. 'Thing is, what do we do about it?'

She shrugged. 'What *can* we do? Send a note out to everyone who's an aunt? Could be a bit labour intensive.'

He glowered at her. 'Just bin the sarcasm, will you?'

She reread the letter, more carefully this time. 'Probably just a crank,' she said.

'Yeah,' he agreed, 'that's what I reckon, but both the Super and the DCI are worried in case it's a psycho-type crank, so we can't just bury it.'

'Then what *are* you going to do?'

Roscoe stuffed a strip of gum in his mouth and began chewing furiously, his dark eyes darting from side to side as he pondered the problem.

'Dunno right this minute,' he admitted grudgingly. 'We don't want to publicize the damned thing and scare everyone half to death. And if we did go down that route, how far would we need to circulate it – just Highbridge, county-wide, or what?'

She shrugged. 'Since the note was delivered by hand, it's more than likely our George is someone local, so that at least narrows down the area a bit.'

He snorted again. 'Oh, come on, *Sherlock*. Anyone can hand-deliver a letter anywhere. Don't have to be actually living there, do they? Any other bright suggestions?'

'Depending on the quality of the original, we could check it for dabs or do a saliva test on the gummed seal – see if anything comes up on the DNA database. Assuming, of course, that our shit-scared Super hasn't already done that before allowing it to be pawed by half the nick?'

Roscoe stared at her; his mouth frozen in mid-chew with part of the white gum stuck to the underside of his Stalin moustache.

'Tell me you're not serious?' he breathed, sucking the gum back out of sight and apparently choosing to overlook her insubordinate reference to his boss. 'Can you imagine the response from SOCO if every crank letter we received was sent to them with that sort of request? We'd become the laughing stock of the force.'

She sighed. 'Just a suggestion, guv,' she said. 'You asked me for ideas.'

'Yeah,' he agreed, 'but not stupid ones.'

'And what happens if our crank actually carries out his threat?' she queried, a mischievous glint in her eyes as she deliberately wound him up. 'My suggestion wouldn't look so stupid then, would it?'

He blew a bubble with his gum, ignoring the sudden look of disgust on her face.

'It won't come to that,' he said.

'So, we just wait for a murder to be committed first, do we?' she persisted.

'There's not going to *be* a murder,' he retorted. 'As you yourself just implied, this is simply some nutter trying to make us jump, that's all. It's too vague to be legit.'

'So, what are you going to say to the boss when he asks you what we are doing about it?'

He thought for a second, then grinned balefully, making no effort to retrieve the copy letter.

'That one of our best detectives is working on it,' he replied, adding, 'but don't spend too long doing the business. Just go through the motions, eh?'

'Me?'

'Well, you seem to have all the ideas.'

'But … but you know the sort of workload I'm dealing with at the moment?'

He shrugged. 'You know what they say in the job – if you can't stand a joke, you shouldn't have joined.'

Before she could say anything else, he snapped his fingers. 'Oh yeah, and another thing. We've got a new DS joining the department tomorrow – coming straight from the NCS – a bloke called Percival, Des Percival. About time too. We've been travelling light ever since that turd, Sharp, fouled up.'

Kate stiffened, remembering all too well the corrupt, weasel-faced DS, who had almost totally compromised a police murder investigation, and she shivered as mention of his name brought back unpleasant memories of the psychopathic killer known as 'Twister' who had nearly succeeded in killing her.

'Could be an asset to the department,' Roscoe went on, failing to pick up on her reaction, 'and I'll be assigning Jamie Foster and a couple of others to his team.'

'And who do I get to assist me on this inquiry?' she demanded, though she had already guessed the answer from the triumphant gleam in his eyes.

'Can't you guess?' he sneered. 'Danny Ferris, plus that wanker of a husband of yours. That pair should work well together.'

Her mouth tightened. His description of Hayden had really cut into her. She was well aware of his low opinion of the affable man she had married and it was unjust. Hayden was certainly no live wire, was even work-shy at times – as with the previous night's feigned sickness – and he could be totally infuriating, but the ex-public schoolboy had a first-class brain and a number of previous cases had been solved due to his keen analytical mind.

She did not bite this time, however. 'And what about last night's narcotics job?' she said coldly. 'Do I carry on with that as well?'

He shrugged. 'Not our problem anymore. Drug Squad will be taking it over from now on. We've done our bit.'

She waved the letter. 'And how am I supposed to get anywhere with a dead-end inquiry like this?'

'That's for you to work out, Sergeant,' he said, 'but you could always call on that fabled intuition you women are supposed to have.'

*

Elsie Norman loved flowers. In summer, there were blooms everywhere in her garden, cramming nearly every flowerbed with rampant colour. In her eighties now, and alone since the death of her husband so many years before, she got a great deal of pleasure out of tending her shrubs and perennials – just as Tom had done when he was alive – weeding the beds and cutting some of the plants back so that they shot up again in spring. She actually talked to them when they were growing and she firmly believed they ultimately produced better blooms as a result. 'It's the personal touch, dear,' she often told her bosom pal, Agnes Hereford, when she popped over from Wells for afternoon tea. 'They feel wanted and appreciated.'

She could have told her visitor the same thing too when he walked up the garden path of her chalet bungalow at around mid-morning, while she was kneeling on her foam pad with her trowel. But she sensed that someone so smartly dressed as the person standing there wouldn't be interested in her ideas about the benefits of talking to flowers, so she kept her silly thoughts to herself.

The bespectacled caller in the dark overcoat and strange, trilby-type hat might have humoured her, though, for he seemed a nice enough person, greeting her with a pleasant smile. Only the eyes bothered her when he helped her to her feet. They were strange eyes – not smiling at all, but quite cold and expressionless, as if they belonged to someone else living inside him, someone who was hiding behind the smile, looking out at her covertly. The man seemed vaguely familiar too, though she couldn't quite place him, and her poor eyesight didn't help either.

Most peculiar, and her instincts warned her not to let the stranger over her porch. The local police community support officer had told her enough times never to let anyone she didn't know into her home. But this one was so persuasive and chatty that she just couldn't be rude, and, as there was no attempt to sell her anything, where was the harm anyway? In fact, her visitor was apparently from the council, sent to check that her home was properly insulated before the onslaught of winter in a few months. What a nice, kind thought – especially on a bank holiday, when most people would be off work – and, during their little chat in her comfortable sitting room, he explained that the survey was completely free too, even offering to help her sister, Mabel, when she mentioned her to him and asking for her address.

Making them both a nice cup of tea was the least she could do in the circumstances. After all, it had to be very tiring trudging round door-to-door for hours. Leaving her guest sitting there, making notes in his little book, she bustled off to the kitchen to put the kettle on and find some of her special homemade biscuits to go with her best Darjeeling.

But though her new silver-coloured kettle reached its boiling point, then switched off automatically, the nice cup of tea was never forthcoming and the homemade biscuits remained untouched on the fancy rose-patterned plate.

CHAPTER 4

Kate found Hayden in the police canteen – after all, where else would he be? She glared at the lardy cake on his plate, as if she could melt it with her stare.

'Hi, old girl,' he beamed through a mouthful of something that was certainly not the lardy cake.

'Don't—' she began, glancing quickly around her at the other tables, but he cut her off, raising one sticky hand in apology.

'Call you that at work, I know,' he finished for her with a wince. 'I meant *Sergeant*.'

'Don't you think you are carrying enough weight, without adding to it with that crap?' she went on, closing her eyes briefly in resignation as she noticed the stain on his creased green shirt.

He frowned. 'I say, that's a bit strong, isn't it?'

'Guts okay now, are they?' she continued, without answering him.

He nodded, taking a mouthful of the lardy cake. 'Just went,' he said. 'Funny, that.'

'Very,' she agreed sarcastically. 'And they'd better stay like that, as you and I have another job. So, leave the bloody cake and upstairs with you to the office – like now!'

He grabbed his jacket from the back of the chair, gulped some coffee, and followed her to the door, taking bites out of his cake as he went.

The main office was empty. Even Roscoe seemed to have gone out somewhere, which couldn't have been better as far as Kate was concerned. Pulling up a chair for her husband, she dropped into her own behind her desk.

'Read that,' she snapped, adding hastily as he reached out for the letter, '*after* you have cleaned your bloody hands.'

To her horror, he wiped them down his trousers.

'Well?' she said when he had finished reading.

He shrugged, apparently oblivious to the crumbs around his mouth.

'It appears someone has a hang-up about aunts,' he replied.

'I made the same obvious point to Roscoe when he lumbered me with the job of tracing this arsehole,' she said drily.

He tutted. 'I wish you wouldn't use vulgar words like that,' he said. 'It smacks of a lack of breeding.'

'Yeah, yeah, yeah,' she retorted, well used to his aversion to bad language, 'but do you glean anything else from the letter?'

'The handwriting is very cramped,' he commented, 'almost child-like, as if the author is either unused to writing longhand or short-sighted.'

'Anything else?'

He studied the letter again and grunted. 'I am a little intrigued by his description of his childhood.'

'How so?'

'Well, it seems very dated – referring to a period long before you or I were born. His mention of horse-hair sofas pricking his legs – indicating he must have been in short trousers then – drawn curtains at funerals and ladies wearing black coats and fox furs draped around their necks, drinking sherry, conjures up an image of a period my dear old father used to describe. In fact, it all suggests he's talking about the late forties or fifties.'

Kate thought for a second. 'That would mean our crank, or whatever he is, must be elderly, probably in his seventies or even older.' She breathed a sigh of relief. 'Some dangerous psychopath that would be – a geriatric, overdosing on Phyllosan!'

He pursed his lips. 'We shouldn't be dismissive,' he warned. 'After all, historically, there have been a number of cases of elderly people committing serious crimes or trying to rob banks. You only have to remember the Hatton Garden safe deposit job. Some of the villains there were in their sixties and seventies.'

Kate nodded. 'Point taken, but it's beginning to look more and more like we are dealing with a hoaxer, as Roscoe has already suggested. But the thing is, what do we do next?'

'Wait for a murder?' he said, unwittingly echoing Kate's comment to Roscoe.

*

Fred Darby had been the village postman for more years than he could remember. Despite all the modernization that had been imposed on the postal service by the Royal Mail, including the policy of uprooting contented employees from delivery rounds they enjoyed and dumping them on others they didn't, the powers-that-be seemed to have forgotten all about him. As a result, he had been left to carry on driving his little red van around the area he knew so well, without any attempt being made to overrule the local inhabitants' wishes by moving him on. And it was because of this 'lapse' in the corridors of power that Elsie Norman was found much earlier than would otherwise have been the case.

Fred had been paying Elsie a visit for nearly ten years. Her little chalet bungalow had become his personal tea spot and as regular as clockwork, six days a week, he would turn up on her doorstep at around two in the afternoon for his cup of Darjeeling and a couple of special homemade biscuits.

However, when the postie left the sorting office in Burnham-On-Sea on the same sunny day Elsie had received a visit from the nice stranger, he was unaware of the fact that there would be no tea or biscuits awaiting him this day.

To be fair, he did sense something was wrong when he walked up the stone-flagged path through the small cottage garden and found the front door ajar. Elsie usually kept her doors shut, even when she was in the garden – not because she was frightened of burglars but because she didn't want nosy neighbours slipping into her house uninvited.

A very private person was Elsie Norman, Fred had decided that long ago, and though he was uneasy about the open door, he didn't immediately venture over the doorstep, but knocked on the glass panel and called her name several times.

A rook erupted from the ivy above the porch with a harsh cry, making him jump, but otherwise there was no response.

Frowning, Fred peered around the door but saw only an empty hallway. 'Mrs Norman?' he called more loudly, and pushed the door right back against the wall. Still nothing.

All kinds of thoughts were going through his head now. What if Elsie had fallen over and was lying unconscious in the kitchen, or had had a stroke in her bed upstairs? He couldn't just walk away and leave things like this.

Taking a deep breath, he stepped over the threshold and walked slowly along the hall, glancing through the open sitting room door to his left as he went by to satisfy himself that the room was empty. It wasn't until he reached the kitchen and pushed the door open that he found Elsie Norman and knew straightaway that he had drunk his last Darjeeling at this particular tea spot.

*

'Looks like the DI's crank wasn't a crank after all then,' Kate commented. The old woman's corpse was lying on the kitchen floor, the head turned at an unnatural angle towards her.

Hayden stared at the contorted body and then at the crude words, 'Bye, Bye, Auntie Elsie,' scrawled in big red letters on the tiled floor beside it.

The young uniformed police constable, standing in the hallway behind the two detectives, gulped. 'Do you think he wrote that in … in her blood?' he gasped, peering over Kate's shoulder.

Kate shook her head and nodded towards something lying a few feet from the body, something that gleamed in the sunlight streaming through the small window.

'Lipstick holder,' she said. 'I would think he used the lipstick to pen his message and applied the stick to his victim either before or afterwards as a final cruel jest.' She nodded towards the corpse and the heavy red smears over and around the gaping mouth, which gave the face a grotesque, almost clownish look. 'No woman would put on her lipstick in such a messy fashion as that.'

Lydia Summers, the forensic pathologist, nodded in agreement. 'Definitely no blood there,' she said. 'She was manually strangled and, it seems, with excessive force.'

'What do you mean by that?' Kate queried.

Summers made a disagreeable face. 'She was an old woman. It wouldn't have taken much to kill her, but my preliminary examination – which will have to be confirmed or otherwise when I carry out the post-mortem – suggests that the force that was applied ruptured the trachea and may have fractured the hyoid bone in her neck and snapped part of the upper vertebrae, going by the unnatural angle of her head.'

'You mean he broke her neck?' Kate breathed.

Summers nodded. 'I would say that a lot of passion went into this killing. Not that it would be difficult to snap the spine of a lady of her advanced years. Bit like breaking the neck of a pigeon.'

'Hatred, do you think?' Kate persisted.

'Possibly, but that's for you to establish if and when you catch the perpetrator. What I can tell you is that from the position of the body, it's likely that your killer pinned his victim to the floor before strangling her as she lay on her back. Probably applied the lipstick after death.'

'The bastard!' the constable breathed. 'An old lady like that? The filthy rotten bastard!'

Kate threw him a quick, sympathetic glance. 'Don't let it get to you, Dean,' she said. 'Emotion gets in the way of any investigation. Just concentrate on the scene – pick up anything you can from what you can see …' she broke off, sniffing the air, then added, '*and* smell. What the hell *is* that stink?'

'Sherry, if I'm not mistaken,' Hayden replied, making a face. 'Smells like someone spilled most of a bottle in here.'

'Not in *here*,' Summers corrected and nodded towards the corpse. 'On *her*. She reeks of the stuff.'

'What, do you think she was at the bottle prior to the arrival of her killer, or that he plied her with sherry before killing her?'

'Impossible to say, but there does not seem to be any sign of a bottle anywhere and we won't know whether she actually consumed alcohol prior to her death until the PM has been carried out. However, there is evidence of some nasty injuries to the roof of her mouth, together with significant damage to the pallet of her dentures. It is consistent with something being inserted between her teeth with brutal force, either before or after her death.'

'A bottle?'

'Possibly, yes, and it's a moot point as to whether she actually choked to death on the sherry or died from the manual strangulation or the snapped vertebrae – and her demise may even have induced a coronary, due to her age. So, there could be several contributory factors.'

'Going by the broken teapot on the floor in the corner there, she was obviously making a pot at the time,' Hayden commented absently. 'So, it seems pretty unlikely that she was knocking back the sherry.'

'A reasonable deduction, *Dr Watson*,' Summers agreed. 'Also, I would suggest, evidenced by the presence of two cups on the work surface and an open tea caddy beside them.'

The sarcasm in the pathologist's tone brought a faint smile to Kate's lips and she cast a swift sidelong glance at Hayden's flushed face, knowing full well from past crime scenes that Summers liked nothing better than baiting police officers. Before he could say anything in reply to cover his embarrassment, there was the sound of rapid footsteps on the garden path outside and DI Roscoe thumped into the hallway, chewing on some gum.

He slammed to a stop behind them and Kate moved slightly to one side so that he could see the corpse.

'Out!' he snapped at the uniformed constable. 'No one but SOCO comes through that front door from now on, got it?' He turned on Kate. 'And have this crime scene secured – like immediately.'

Kate gave him an old-fashioned look and pointed down at the plastic booties covering the shoes of herself and Hayden.

'We've stayed by the door, guv,' she said. 'Pathologist is the only one who's been in the room, so no problem, and SOCO should be here any minute with crime scene tapes.'

Roscoe grunted, studying the room intently, his gaze roving slowly around the walls. 'Who found her?'

'Postman apparently,' Hayden said brightly. 'She didn't answer the door, so he checked inside and found her like this.'

Roscoe treated the detective to a scathing look, then turned back to Kate as if he wasn't actually there.

'Where is this postie now?'

'Outside in the patrol car,' she said.

Out of the corner of her eye she caught sight of Hayden's face reddening again after what was obviously a deliberate snub. Roscoe had never liked him and he seemed to take pleasure in emphasizing the fact.

'He's twitching a bit about needing to finish his round,' she added.

'Tough. Get a statement off him before you let him go.'

Kate nodded to Hayden and watched him head off down the hallway like a dog with its tail between its legs, then turned back to Roscoe.

'There's a message of sorts on the tiles, apparently made with lipstick,' she said, pointing at the ominous scrawl.

'I'm not blind. I can see it for myself,' he retorted. 'But what's that stink?'

'Sherry, we think, guv. And it seems that someone – no doubt our killer – plastered the lipstick on her lips, making a right mess of it too. I can't see the deceased herself making such a poor job of something like that before she died.'

'So why would the perv apply lipstick to a corpse?'

'No idea, except maybe to make some sort of point, as with the sherry.'

Roscoe began chewing on his gum for a few seconds.

'Seems that that bloody letter could have been legit after all then?' he said.

'Has to have been,' she replied. 'Too much of a coincidence otherwise – which means we've got ourselves another psycho.'

'Boss will love that,' Roscoe retorted. 'Especially as he's up on a chief super's promotion board at the end of the month.'

'No pressure on us then?' Kate breathed. 'At least we would now be justified in getting SOCO to give that letter and envelope the once-over.'

The DI scowled back at her, but without responding to the blatant, 'I told you so' dig, moved aside to allow Summers out into the hallway.

'Time of death, Doc?' he snapped.

The pathologist sighed. 'Impatient as ever, eh, Ted?' she answered. 'From the condition of the body and the presence of developing lividity, I would suggest four to six hours – but that's only a guess.'

'It will do me for starters. Any other thoughts?'

'Well, she was obviously strangled – manually, I would say, going by the bruising injuries which are now beginning to become apparent on her throat, plus the presence of conjunctival petechial haemorrhaging – or blood spots – in the eyes. DS Lewis here can give you my other thoughts.'

'PM?' he went on.

'Bit busy at the mortuary just now – people dying to be there, you know,' Summers replied with a grim smile. 'Probably not until tomorrow at the earliest. I will let you know.'

'Look forward to it.'

Roscoe followed the pathologist with his eyes as she headed for the street, peeling off her surgical gloves as she went, then he focused on Kate again.

'What did you turn up this morning?' he said.

She made a face. 'Not much time to do anything,' she replied. 'I had a long chat with the local intelligence officer to see if he could come up with any ideas, but there's nothing on file about anyone with a hang-up about the elderly. Lots of crank letters, but nothing that would help us with this one. He's been the LIO for around five years and before that a beat officer in Highbridge and Bridgwater. Fifteen years' experience in all, but nothing occurred to him.'

Roscoe blew a bubble with his gum and nodded. 'Okay, so do a bit of legwork. A few initial house-to-house enquiries would be a good start until I can get a full inquiry team together. Someone may have seen or heard something.' He half-turned, then snapped his fingers and wheeled round again. 'And make sure you get all you can out of that bloody postman. He's all we've got at the moment.'

CHAPTER 5

As it transpired, Fred Darby was of little help. He could only repeat what he had already said; that he had found Elsie Norman dead in the kitchen. He had not seen anyone acting suspiciously in the vicinity – in fact, he hadn't seen anyone at all – and he had no idea who could have wanted to kill the gentle, mild-mannered old lady who had regularly supplied him with tea and biscuits. It was obvious that he hadn't recovered from his initial shock and his hands were still shaking as Kate tried to tease more information from him after Hayden had obtained his written statement in the back of the police car, but she quickly realized that he had nothing else to tell.

Finally letting the postie drive away in his van, she got Hayden and a couple of the uniform officers who had turned up at the scene to join her in starting to knock on doors. House-to-house inquiries near a crime scene could sometimes produce useful information, depending on how they were handled, but things did not look very promising as they began the soul-destroying tramp from doorstep to doorstep. Most of the residents they found at home were either elderly, poorly sighted or deaf – or all three – so had not seen or heard a thing, and all, without exception, were more interested in finding out why the enquiries were being made rather than answering pertinent questions.

Kate had almost given up on things when one of the uniformed bobbies called out to her from the other side of the street.

'Skipper, over here.' The middle-aged woman with the peroxide blonde-dyed hair and ample girth was peering round the edge of her front door as if she didn't want to be seen by anyone.

'Tell the detective sergeant what you just told me,' the policeman said to her.

The woman hesitated, then shrugged before replying.

'This feller – I saw him walking down the road from up there,' she pointed to her left. 'I was sweeping me path and I happened to glance up when he appeared—'

'When was this?' Kate interjected.

'Dunno. Maybe two or three hours ago – I hadn't had me morning coffee, so it must have been about ten thirty.'

'Did he get out of a car?'

'No, he seemed to be on foot.'

'Did you see where he went?'

'Can't really say. All I know is when I turned round again, he had disappeared, so he must have gone in somewhere before he got to me. I'd have noticed if he'd walked past my place.'

Kate glanced down the road in the direction she had indicated. The police cars parked outside Elsie Norman's bungalow were only about fifty yards away on the other side of the road.

'Did you see him again later?'

The woman shook her head. 'No, I went in after that to answer the phone. Me sister rang, you see, and—'

Kate cut her off. 'Why did you notice him in particular? Lots of people must use this road all the time, I would think.'

'Nah, not strangers. It's a cul-de-sac, see. Road ends just up there. Becomes just a footpath leading out across the fields to the next village,' and she pointed to her left again. 'You'd have to be calling on someone to be down here and I know all the residents by sight.'

'So, he must have entered the street from the footpath – is that what you're saying?'

'Must've done.'

'What did this man look like?'

'Tall and thin, dressed in a long, dark coat. Oh yeah, and he seemed to be carrying some sort of notebook.'

'You didn't see his face?'

'Nah, he kept his head down under his hat.'

'Hat?'

'Yes, he was wearing one of them Fedora hats – a black one –looked funny on him too.'

'Fedora?'

'It's a bit like a trilby, but with a wide brim – I used to be a milliner, so I recognized what it was straightaway. But it looked too big for him and he was wearing it pulled down low over his eyes.' She gave a low chuckle. 'A bit like a gangster, if you know what I mean.'

Kate's heart was beginning to race as her mind flashed back to the previous night and the rough sleeper she had disturbed in the basement of the derelict mansion.

'Did you see what colour hair he had?'

The woman shook her head again. 'Too far away for that and me eyes ain't what they used to be. I just recognized the hat.'

'Was he wearing glasses?'

'Couldn't say, I'm afraid. Again, too far away and his head was bent down as if he didn't want to be recognized.' The woman leaned forward a little. 'So, what's happened to poor old Elsie? I saw the ambulance there. Did this feller hurt her?'

Kate forced a smile. 'I'm afraid I can't go into that,' she said, turning to make her way back down the path to the road. 'But thanks for your help anyway. The officer here will take down your details in case we need to see you again.'

The footpath the woman had mentioned turned out to be little more than a muddy track. It struck off between the high walls of two bungalows about 200 yards beyond Elsie Norman's home, then meandered across fields, through scrub and isolated trees to a bridge spanning a sluggishly flowing river. Beyond the bridge, waterlogged fields stretched away to a smudge of houses on the horizon. Kate startled a heron as she stepped on to the bridge, the bird rising in an ungainly way from the riverbank with a cry of alarm and flapping over a hedge into the next field.

For a few minutes, she lent on the bridge wall, staring about her with narrowed eyes. Not expecting to see anyone, but feeling her skin crawl in this lonely, exposed place, with just the gurgle of the river for company.

'Where did you go, you bastard?' she murmured. 'Back to your bloody basement, I wonder? Surely not.'

She turned her head quickly at a faint sound behind her, but relaxed as Hayden lumbered on to the bridge.

'Saw you wander off, old girl,' he said with a frown. 'Not a good idea, I thought – not with a vicious thug on the loose.'

'Don't worry, Hayd,' she said tightly. 'I'm not an aunt – not yet anyway – so I'm quite safe.'

He sniffed. 'You really think this job has something to do with that letter then?'

'Don't you?'

He thought for a moment, but didn't answer her question. 'I saw the plod call you over to the house just now. Biddy there give you something useful, did she?'

She told him what the woman had said. 'The description fits the dosser I told you about,' she went on, 'the one I disturbed in the target house – only he had blond hair and was wearing gold-coloured glasses.'

'Any idea what sort of age he was?'

'Unfortunately, no. I only saw his face for an instant and by torchlight. Impossible to say. Why?'

He grunted and tucked into a Mars Bar he had produced from his pocket. 'Just wondered, that's all. You didn't say much about him before – only that he'd got away.'

'I didn't think he was of any relevance to us until now. Roscoe suspected he might have been one of the gang, left at the house to guard the stash, but I don't reckon he was connected with that job. Treated Ferris and me to a clean pair of heels anyway.'

'Ah now, that answers my unspoken question. In short, he doesn't seem like the sort of person who could have written that letter.'

'I don't follow you.'

He pushed the remainder of the Mars Bar into his mouth and pocketed the wrapping, holding a hand up to signify that he couldn't give her an answer until he had finished chewing the wad he was wrestling with. Then abruptly, he swallowed the lot with a loud gulp and wiped his mouth on his sleeve as Kate closed her eyes in resignation.

'Remember what I said to you before? If the fellow who wrote that letter was speaking from personal experience, he wouldn't be an athletic youngster, but someone who was getting on a bit – at least into his seventies, as you yourself said to me after reading the letter. If your dosser managed to outrun a fit little filly like you, he certainly wouldn't be in his twilight years.'

She chose to ignore his reference to her as a filly.

'So maybe he put all that stuff in the letter to make us think he was older than he actually was?'

'Possible. But why would he do that?'

'To throw us off the scent?'

'That doesn't hold water. First, we have no idea who he is, so why would he bother? Second, how come he could provide such a vivid account of his childhood except from personal experience? For me, the letter was totally credible in that respect.'

Kate pushed herself away from the wall with a heavy sigh. 'Logical as ever, Hayd,' she acknowledged wearily. 'My money is still on the dosser, though. The description the neighbour just gave me of the man she saw in the street fits him to a T. There can't be that many men walking about dressed in long, dark coats and Fedora hats.'

He shrugged. 'We can only hope that one of the other neighbours saw your suspect. At least that might give us a bit more info.'

She nodded. 'We'll finish the house-to-house and then I think a trip back to that derelict mansion would be worthwhile.'

'For what purpose? Your man is long gone and he's not likely to return now that there are plods all over the shop.'

She shook her head. 'I gather SOCO have finished there. The brief they had was restricted to gathering evidence in relation to the drugs bust – my man was not in the frame then. Uniform were pulled off to help us here with the door-to-door, so the place is wide open now.'

'But what do you expect to gain from a return trip?'

'In his rush to leave, our man might have left something behind that could help us identify him and anyway, I'd like to take a closer look at where he was dossing. I saw a mattress and a blanket in there and discarded food cartons. Maybe we could get the lot checked out by the lab. There could be prints on the cartons and DNA traces on the mattress and blankets—'

Hayden screwed up his mouth, plainly unconvinced. 'Along with the prints and DNAs of every other wino and itinerant who's dossed there over the past six to nine months, I should think.'

'It's still worth a try.'

'You're the sergeant.'

'It's good of you to notice,' she said with heavy sarcasm. 'It's taken you long enough.'

CHAPTER 6

The small churchyard was deserted – except for the irregular lines of gravestones rising from the tangled, ankle-deep grass like broken teeth in the mist, which was spreading slowly but resolutely through the village from the surrounding marshes. The figure in the long, dark coat and Fedora hat pushed through the iron gate and walked slowly up the path, studying the inscriptions on each of the headstones in passing. Reaching the end of the path, apparently without spotting anything of relevance to the visit, the figure paused a moment by the porch over the front door of the church before stepping off the path and moving among the headstones themselves, crouching at intervals to examine each one in turn.

Within minutes there was a sharp intake of breath and George Lupin stopped in front of a black marble slab, bearing the inscription in faded gold lettering, 'Beatrix James. 1924–2016. Aged 92 years. Now With The Angels.'

'Angels?' George snarled. 'More likely the devil's own, you nasty old bitch. Sorry I couldn't get to you myself before you snuffed it.'

Aunt Elsie had certainly proved to be a mine of information about her elderly sisters, firmly believing that her visitor really was from the council and could help them with the insulation of their homes. She'd claimed that of the other three, Beatrix, the oldest, was dead. Well, here was the proof. She was six feet under, her would-be executioner now almost consumed by an inner rage for being denied the opportunity of being the one to have put her there.

A motorcycle roared past the low wall in front of the churchyard, causing a brief distraction, and at the same moment George caught sight of a man in a grey raincoat threading his way between the headstones towards what he evidently thought was a solitary mourner.

'Can I help you, my son?' the man said from a few feet away, the dog collar around his neck plainly visible through the gap in his coat.

'No one can help me, Father,' came the grim reply and, turning away from him, George walked off briskly between the gravestones, doubling back towards the iron gate and the red VW car parked in the lane beyond.

The clergyman followed the fast-retreating figure with troubled eyes. 'Bless you, my son,' he murmured, half to himself. 'May God be with you.' But Beatrix's last visitor had already started the engine of his car and driven off, vanishing in the mist like a ghost.

*

There was nothing of relevance in the derelict mansion's cellar. The mouldy, evil-smelling mattress and single tattered blanket were soaking wet from the rain, which had obviously found its way into the place down old heating and water pipes from the upper floors, and the detritus Kate had noticed before actually consisted of a few plastic cups, rusted tins and sandwich cartons, which had obviously been there a very long time and were so badly ripped or buckled and covered in so much of the wet filth from the floor, that they were only fit for dumping in the most convenient rubbish bin.

'I don't think your man was sleeping down here,' Hayden observed, holding a handkerchief to his nose, 'not unless he was into leaking, urine-stained "water beds".'

Kate nodded in the gloom, flashing her torch around the damp walls and cracked ceiling.

'From what I could make of him, he certainly didn't look like your usual run-of-the-mill wino, I must admit. But if he wasn't a dosser or a wino, then what was he doing here?'

'Maybe looking for somewhere he *could* doss? Or perhaps he really was the third member of the cocaine gang, as Roscoe suggested?'

'Then how do you explain that the man seen in the vicinity of Elsie Norman's murder matched his description exactly? Bit of a coincidence, wouldn't you say?'

Hayden grunted and walked away from her into the corridor, the beam of his torch stabbing into the gloom ahead of him.

'Come on, old girl,' he said, obviously anxious to be back in the fresh air, 'let's get out of here. I'd prefer a backstreet toilet to this awful pit.'

Feeling both irritated and deflated, Kate followed him back up the stone staircase, through the kitchen on the next level, and up to the ground floor – only to bump into at the top when he stopped suddenly, staring around him.

'What was this palatial old pile anyway?' he asked, crossing the hall diagonally to peer through one of a number of open doorways. 'Some sort of hospital?'

She shook her head, thinking that Ferris had asked the self-same question the night of their surveillance operation.

'An asylum, an approved school, and then an orphanage, I'm told,' she replied, joining him in the doorway. 'It closed after a murder and a major fire in the middle of some sort of investigation into alleged child sexual abuse apparently.'

'*Nice*,' he said drily. 'Sounds a bit like my old public school – well, the sexual abuse bit anyway. And what do you think this room was used for – the headmaster's study? You know, the place for private flagellations and heinous forfeits?'

She peered past him into a small, bare room with an open fireplace in one corner and the remnants of wooden panelling still attached to some of the walls.

'Possibly,' she replied with a chuckle, 'but maybe without the flagellations and forfeits.'

Moving on, they found at least half a dozen other rooms. All were devoid of furniture and some were littered with rubbish, from torn, stained mattresses, almost certainly humped up from the basement, to piles of newspapers, discarded tins and plastic food containers. Clear evidence of multiple vagrancy occupation, though deserted now. One long, galleried room still contained a few broken bench seats. Kate guessed it had once been the dining room, maybe furnished with glittering chandeliers, a rich, wall-to-wall Persian carpet, plus a long mahogany table and tapestried chairs, before the more basic furniture of the Victorian asylum and then the approved school and orphanage had taken its place. A grand old house, which had once echoed to the clink of crystal wine glasses and the hubbub of genteel conversation over dinner before this was replaced by the screams of demented patients and, much later, the sobs of emotionally disturbed children. A grand old house, which was now just an empty shell, weighed down with a heavy, haunted and almost tangible stillness.

'I suppose we ought to take a look upstairs,' Kate said a little reluctantly.

Hayden made a face. 'Do we have to?' he replied. 'Remember that old horror film, *Halloween*? Could be Michael Myers is waiting for us up there? You know, white plastic mask and big knife?'

Kate ignored his attempt at black humour and headed for the upper level, hearing his heavy manufactured sigh as he followed her.

The top floor landing opened on to a long corridor with rooms on both sides and large, gaping voids in the ceiling, which exposed the roof space into which the grey day thrust tentative fingers through holes in the roof tiles. The atmosphere on this level was even creepier than it had been downstairs and Kate found herself darting uneasy glances around her as they followed the corridor along to the end. There, a narrow doorway, now lacking the door, accessed a communal bathroom, complete with rows of vandalized toilet cubicles, wash-hand basins and three shower rooms. Kate shivered as she thought of why Talbot Court had been closed and what might have gone on in the very room in which they were standing.

Retracing their steps and checking each of the other rooms in turn as they went, they found that most were empty, as was the rest of the house, except for a couple which bore evidence in the form of blankets, newspapers and the occasional stained mattress that rough sleepers had been in temporary occupation there too. One room, however, still contained half a dozen bare iron-framed beds with rusted and broken springs and curiosity drew them inside.

'Dormitory,' Hayden declared in a superior, matter-of-fact tone, pinging the springs on one of the bed frames with one hand. He grinned. 'This place is certainly getting to look more and more like my old public school.'

Kate shivered again, noting the bars on the windows. 'I doubt that your public school had barred windows,' she replied.

He waved an arm airily around the room. 'Maybe not, but there are the same sort of testimonials everywhere.'

'Testimonials?'

He crouched down beside one of the beds, studying a patch of wall. She moved over to his side and bent down to peer over his shoulder.

'Oh, the graffiti you mean?' she commented, noting the faded scrawl on the plaster.

'"Hell is empty and all the devils are here",' he read aloud, then turned to stare up at her, still grinning. 'That's rather a good quote, don't you think? William Shakespeare's *The Tempest*, I believe.'

He moved on to the next bed and got down on his hands and knees to study another section of wall. He chuckled.

'"Alistair Scarsfield is a perv",' he said, once more reading aloud. 'That's an indictment in itself. I wonder if poor old Alistair ever saw it? Maybe he sued—?'

Abruptly he broke off and emitted a low whistle, adding, 'Now that really is odd.'

'What is odd?' she said, joining him again. 'Alistair Scarsfield being a perv?'

He shook his head. 'No, look at this other piece. Like the rest of the scrawls, it has faded a bit with time, but it looks as though it has been written with so much pressure that marks have been left in the plaster.'

'Come on, Hayd,' she admonished, glancing quickly around her again. 'We're wasting time on all this bollocks. And the atmosphere in here is starting to get to me. You can actually smell the misery. It's like a sodding miasma all around us.'

He threw a critical frown at her over his shoulder – she guessed it was because of her use of bad language.

'Just listen, will you?' he snapped.

She sighed and crouched down beside him as he read the inscription, trailing his index finger slowly over each of the cramped block capitals.

'"GEORGE WILL SEE THAT THE HARRIDANS PAY".'

She felt an icy shard twist in her gut as he turned his head again to stare at her.

'George?' he breathed. 'Could that be *our* George? Don't forget, he used that same word "harridans" in his letter and it's a pretty unusual term for anyone in this day and age.'

She slowly straightened up. 'And the description of the man seen near Elsie Norman's bungalow just before she was murdered fits the dosser I confronted in the basement. It all ties in.'

Her jaw dropped as another thought occurred to her. 'Hayd, that's why he was here. Don't you see? He must have once been an inmate. He wasn't just a dosser – he was revisiting the place.'

There was an excited gleam in his eyes as he gripped the edge of the bed to haul himself to his feet.

'Bravo, old girl,' he exclaimed. 'Even I have to admit that this time it's all just too *much* of a coincidence.'

Her lips tightened. 'So, let's get SOCO back here,' she said. 'I think we need some pics pdq. After that, I want you to see if you can find out Elsie Norman's maiden name—'

'What on earth for?'

'I thought that that would be obvious to a clever chap like you. Our killer talked in his letter about hating his aunts. If Elsie was *his* aunt, his surname is likely to be the same as hers, which, I think you will agree, would narrow down the field considerably as far as likely suspects are concerned.'

He shook his head. 'Depends which side of the family her nephew might be on and anyway, it might not be any of his own aunts he is after – they could all be dead. From the drift of his letter, it would seem to me that he is targeting any elderly women he can find who remind him of his own aunts. Don't forget, the term "aunt" is also used colloquially to refer to anyone who is a friend or relative of someone with children or who looks after children in an official capacity. They don't have to be old either. Aunts can be any age.'

She sighed. 'You always have to complicate things, don't you, Hayd? Anything to avoid work! But it's still worth a try. At least there's a chance we might turn up something.'

He grunted, unimpressed. 'Anything else, *Sergeant*?' he said sarcastically.

She smiled. 'Yes, there is actually. After you've done that, you can do some digging on the history of Talbot Court.'

'Me again?'

She nodded. 'You again. You see, it's all about RHP – you know, rank has privileges? And I'm afraid you have drawn the short straw in that respect.'

*

Ted Roscoe looked lost in the big club room on the top floor of Highbridge police station, which was still being kitted out with all the necessary furniture and computerized technology for a major incident room. He waved Kate and Hayden towards what had been designated the senior investigator's office at the far end and deposited himself behind the desk with a heavy gasp that sounded a lot like air escaping from a punctured tyre.

'The SIO's been appointed and is on her way,' he growled.

Kate frowned. '*Her* way?'

'Yeah, all I've heard is that our senior investigating officer is to be a woman this time. Probably some bit of skirt no one's ever heard of. Bully for us!'

Kate ignored his sexist comment and smiled faintly. A female boss, eh? A dyed-in-the-wool macho man like poor old Roscoe certainly wouldn't be happy about that, bless him. But he didn't give her time to savour his discomfort. Slipping a wad of chewing gum into his mouth, he sat back in the chair to study his two detectives.

'So, what have Batwoman and Robin got for me now then?' he said. 'I can see you're bursting to tell me.'

And Kate did just that, revealing all that they had discovered before quickly summarizing their conclusions. For once he let her finish without interruption. Then, blowing a bubble with his gum, he sucked it back in again and nodded slowly.

'A possible connection between this investigation and Talbot Court sounds a bit iffy to me, despite the dosser you saw there seeming to resemble the character the witness clocked at the murder scene, but the nephew bit could be promising.'

He treated her to one of his wolfish grins. 'Maybe we'll have this thing sussed and put to bed even before Miss Marple actually arrives.'

'And there again, maybe you won't, Ted,' a voice with a distinct Ulster accent spoke sharply from the doorway.

Kate turned quickly to see a thin, blonde-haired woman of about forty standing there with one hand resting against the upper part of the door frame and the other on her hip. She was dressed in a smart grey trouser suit, which emphasized her trim figure, and her sharp blue eyes were focused on Roscoe's shocked face with evident amusement.

Deidrie Hennessey. Kate recognized her immediately, recalling only too well how Roscoe had crossed swords with the fiery former DI on a previous murder inquiry when he had effectively tried to muscle in on her investigation.

'Sure, it's grand to be seeing you again, Ted,' Hennessey said, moving into the room. 'And it seems we'll be working together from now on too.'

For several seconds Roscoe seemed stuck for words, but then he grinned, though there was no humour in his dark boot-button eyes.

'Heard you'd been promoted to DCI, Deidrie,' he said, standing up. 'Didn't realize they would let you loose as SIO so soon, though.'

Hennessey chuckled, ignoring the barbed comment. 'Aye, Ted,' she replied. 'Well, there's nothing like a baptism of fire now, is there?'

Her expression hardened. 'And if you'd be so good as to get the team together, the incident room briefing will be in half an hour.' She treated Kate to a cold smile. 'Then, Sergeant, you will have the opportunity of telling us *all* what you've just told the DI.'

CHAPTER 7

'Well?' Kate said when Hayden joined her in the police canteen after the main incident room team briefing. 'What have you got for me?'

Her partner had only managed to escape the briefing so he could carry out the background inquiries into Talbot Court and she was keen to find out whether the 'trade-off' had been worthwhile.

'Quigley,' he said.

'Quigley?'

'Elsie Norman's maiden name. Got it from a birth certificate in a drawer at her home.'

'Well, that's something anyway. And Talbot Court?'

Hayden sniffed, looking slightly uncomfortable as he referred to his pocket book.

'Not a lot, I'm afraid. There's a bit about the history on the internet, which I printed off. But it doesn't help us much. Apparently, the place was originally built in the Georgian era, around 1770, by Sir William Makepeace Talbot, a wealthy banker and philanthropist, and it passed to his son, Robert, on his death in 1805. Robert himself died unexpectedly in 1850 and *his* son, Thomas, then inherited the estate. But he was an inveterate gambler and heavy drinker and, basically, he went bankrupt before committing suicide, leaving no heirs. As a result, the house had to be sold to cover his debts and it was subsequently grabbed by the local authority for use as an asylum – or madhouse, as such places were called then. It continued as such until 1935, when it was closed as no longer suitable and turned into one of the first approved schools—'

Kate cut him off with an irritable hiss. 'I wasn't asking for a detailed history lesson, Hayd. Can we get on to this century?'

He looked hurt. 'Okay, okay, give me a chance. I was just being thorough, you know. But I'm coming to the relevant bits, so hang on.'

He took a deep breath.

'In the 1950s, after the approved school system had fallen out of favour, the palatial pile was purchased by a so-called charitable foundation, the Kilburn Trust, a religious group who reopened it as a private orphanage for – and I quote – "challenging juveniles." They ran the place until the late sixties, when there were a series of nasty incidents.

'First, a couple of the inmates tried to commit suicide, then a member of staff was fatally stabbed by one of the kids. The culprit was locked up for murder and in the course of the police investigation, allegations of sexual abuse surfaced. These came to nothing in the end, but for some reason the goings-on at Talbot Court continued to be pursued by a freelance journalist, named Leslie Brookes.

'They seem to have become a sort of cause célèbre for him, before a mysterious fire gutted much of the building and led to the closure of the orphanage and the winding up of the Trust, effectively halting his investigation. Since then, the place has been bought by two different property developers, the first of whom went bankrupt like poor old Thomas Talbot and the second simply left it to rot, due to years of planning objections by the local authority. I hear it's now on the market again with a London property agent.'

'And that's it, is it?'

'Not quite, but you did set me a rather impossible task.'

'How's that?'

'Well, it *is* a bank holiday weekend, which means most corporate and local authority departments, like the district and county council offices, are closed, so not approachable for information. Nevertheless, I did manage to tease out a few more snippets from another source. Ever heard tell of Charlie Dexter?'

She pursed her lips for a second, then shook her head, which seemed to please him and he continued a little more upbeat.

'Well, he happens to be a member of my classic car club. But more importantly, he's an ex-copper and was a DC in Bridgwater about the time of the Talbot Court scandal.'

'Go on.'

'The thing is, after surfing the net, I got in touch with him and it turns out he has a pretty good memory, despite being in his mid-seventies.'

'You do have some useful friends,' she acknowledged, remembering some of his other contacts in past cases.

He grinned, apparently appreciating the compliment. 'Yes, I do, don't I? Fact is, Charlie well remembers the stabbing at Talbot Court and the subsequent fire, which he says was investigated as arson, though it got nowhere. He wasn't actually involved in the murder inquiry as he was on an unconnected rape investigation at the time, but he was aware of the fact that when the Kilburn Trust folded after the fire, it left massive debts and the Principal – one Edward Grace – plus his wife and all the staff simply vanished into thin air.'

'Convenient. And the sexual abuse inquiry?'

'He recalled office chit-chat about some sort of inquiry being set up in that respect, though no specific details of what happened as a result. But he did point out that, prior to the fairly recent Jimmy Saville business and all the child abuse inquiries that that scandal has generated since, complaints of sexual abuse by juveniles in the sixties were unlikely to have been given as much priority – or even as much credence – as they are today. Furthermore, as most of the kids at the orphanage then would probably have been seen as misfits and problem youngsters, with a history of anti-social behaviour, and Grace himself was an eminent psychologist who categorically denied anything untoward had taken place, the authorities were obviously bound to have come down on the side of Grace.'

'You mean he suspects that the alleged sexual assaults were probably cuffed?'

'Precisely – which would not have surprised him as he says the senior police officer who investigated the whole affair was a DCI called Justin Bobbett, who was killed in a car crash a couple of years afterwards. Evidently, Bobbett wasn't that well regarded at the time – a bit slapdash in his methods, it seems, and allegedly rather too well in with the Principal at Talbot Court.'

'You mean bent?'

'Not bent, just a bit too friendly with Grace – maybe overawed by the man's social status – and not someone who would have put too much store on the allegations of a few disturbed children anyway.'

'So, the long and the short of it is that it's unlikely any file record will actually exist in relation to the sexual assault allegations?'

He nodded. 'That was his assessment and since, as I have already said, it's a bank holiday weekend, I've been unable to take things much further in that respect. There's no relevant archival material on our local box – and, to be frank, there is unlikely to have been any after five decades. Similarly, a check on the PNC database proved pointless without the name of an offender, and I understand that all force archived prosecution material was transferred to CPS after they took over prosecution responsibilities in the eighties, and—'

'They're not contactable because of the bank holiday?' Kate finished for him drily.

'Exactly.'

'And I suppose the same would apply in relation to the National Archives' records on Talbot Court?'

''Fraid so – if there are any, of course. But it's worth saying that, after a bit of research on the internet, I was able to establish that they don't keep info on the individual inmates or staff of such institutions anyway. We would need to approach the specific institution itself for that and, since Talbot Court and the Kilburn Trust are no more, that's out the window.'

'But there was a murder. There must be something on record somewhere that would give us the offender's name? Old press reports on the internet, for example?'

He shook his head. 'I haven't been able to turn up anything so far and the press would not have been allowed to publish the name of a convicted juvenile offender anyway, which makes that a total non-starter. In fact, until the bank holiday is over, it's difficult to know where else to look, especially as there were no computers in the sixties, so there is no electronic data trail to follow.'

'Then we're stymied.'

He treated her to a smug grin. 'Not entirely. You see, while the info I got off the internet about Talbot Court was minimal and didn't reveal the name of the kid who was sent down, a brief mention of the stabbing did reveal the name of the victim – an Alistair Scarsfield.'

Kate jumped. 'What? Why didn't you tell me this before?'

'You didn't ask.'

She glared at him angrily, but didn't pursue the point. 'Scarsfield? Wasn't that the name we saw scrawled on the wall at Talbot Court?'

'The very same.'

'Then there has to be a connection between the Talbot Court business and our present investigation. The writer of our letter called himself George, the name George was scratched on the wall at Talbot Court, and another inmate appears to have alleged in that other bit of graffiti that

Scarsfield was a paedophile. The coincidences in this affair seem to be mounting up.'

Hayden compressed his lips. 'There certainly seem to be a whole string of them emerging.'

'But if the two Georges are one and the same person, and he *is* Scarsfield's killer as well as being the killer of Elsie Norman, I don't see how this links into the fixation our man seems to have with so-called aunts.'

'Going by the message he scrawled on the floor with the lipstick at the scene, it's very likely Elsie Norman was one of the aunts or harridans he refers to in his letter and not just some random victim.'

'Okay, okay, but then where do Scarsfield and Talbot Court fit in?'

'Not the faintest idea.'

'Which brings us to Elsie Norman's nephew. Our George could be George Quigley, so he might be known to us.'

'He isn't. I ran the name through the PNC, but it came up negative.'

'And what happened to the rest of the children at the orphanage? Did they all simply vanish into thin air too?'

'Not exactly. They were apparently dispersed among other orphanages around the country. There's no available information on exactly where they went because the fire destroyed all the records and, after all this time, it will take forever to locate their whereabouts – especially as we don't even know who the youngsters were in the first place.'

'Then we will have to try and find the Principal himself, won't we?'

'Already done that.'

'My, you *have* been diligent.'

He grinned again, ignoring the sarcasm. 'According to the press reports on the internet, Grace committed suicide after being traced to an apartment in Malaga, Spain, by our tenacious reporter, Brookes, six months after he'd fled there.'

'What about Grace's wife?'

'No idea. They were both apparently in their fifties then, so unless she has the genes of Methuselah, she is almost certain to be six feet under by now.'

'And the "tenacious reporter"?'

'Retired, obviously. I don't know where yet. He might even be dead. I have yet to follow that one up, but no time so far. Maybe a job for tomorrow.'

'Correction. It has to be *the* job for tomorrow. As it is, we've got bugger all to show for a whole afternoon's work and the guv'nor certainly won't be impressed by it – especially after I persuaded him to excuse you from the briefing in the first place so that you could get on with things.'

He smiled brightly. 'You could always try telling him that the best is yet to come?'

She scowled and glanced at her watch. 'Just for that, my man, you can buy the first round in the bar tonight.'

*

The track was just as George remembered it from all those years ago when he had been taken for a couple of picnics by a mother desperately trying to engage with her own child. It led down a sharp incline to a lake. Normally you needed a permit to fish there, but dumping the shrink's VW Beetle in the still, dark water didn't constitute fishing, did it? It was a relatively easy process too. Stop the car on the slope, engage the handbrake, climb out, then release the handbrake and give the thing a push – sending it rolling down the slope into the water. It needed a couple of extra hefty pushes after that, but then the water seemed to suck it into its cold embrace and within fifteen minutes, there was the immense satisfaction of seeing it disappear beneath the surface. Someone would find it eventually, of course, but by then it would make no difference; everything that he had planned would have been achieved.

The long walk back to the road was a bit of a pain – George was dog-tired – but once there, it was a simple enough matter to thumb a lift into Glastonbury and blend in with the hippies and crack-heads attending an impromptu music festival in a field near the town. Sitting at a table in a small side-street café just before closing time, George sipped a cup of hot coffee and thought about the next move with a sense of anticipation.

CHAPTER 8

Kate awoke, bleary eyed and with a mammoth headache. Sharing a full bottle of red wine with Hayden after returning home around midnight, on top of the couple of pints downed in the police station bar with the rest of the inquiry team, had been a big mistake, but it was too late to regret that now.

She rolled over on to her back, stared at the blinding white ceiling and groaned. Hayden was out for the count and snoring in the big double bed beside her. She nudged him with her elbow.

'Up, you lazy sod,' she exclaimed. 'It's gone eight.'

There was no response and, studying the substantial heap that quivered fitfully under the duvet, she gave a cynical smile, knowing from past experience that, short of the ceiling caving in, nothing would wake her other half until the effects of their heavy night's imbibing had worn off sufficiently. In any event, there was no real rush. He had been assigned to her action team and they had been detailed to work the late shift, so they didn't have to be back on duty until two in the afternoon – which also meant a very late finish. Lucky them.

Forcing herself to sit upright against the headboard, she waited for the room to steady itself. Coffee, that's what she needed – lots of the stuff, strong and black.

The quarry tiles were ice cold on her bare feet when she stumbled down to the galley kitchen to fill the kettle, and she shivered as she waited for it to boil, her mind on the previous afternoon's incident room briefing.

The whole thing had been conducted in an atmosphere so tense that it had been almost tangible. The barely concealed hostility that existed between Roscoe and DCI Deidrie Hennessey had communicated itself to most of the uniformed and plainclothes officers gathered in the room and, although the different action teams had accepted the tasks they had been allocated for the following day with their usual professionalism, there had been something missing – perhaps a lack of obvious enthusiasm – which did not bode well for the future.

But there was nothing Kate could do about the problem. It was down to Roscoe and Hennessey to resolve. All she could do was make sure she did her own job to the best of her ability and manage her own small action team as efficiently as possible. That team had at first consisted of Hayden and Danny Ferris, until Ferris had taken a leaf out of Hayden's book and signed off sick with a so-called stomach bug, leaving her with just her other half as her sole foot soldier. Still, things could have been worse. She could have been taken off the inquiry altogether and lumbered with the mundane job of providing the continuing CID cover that was required for the local area instead – a job which had gone to the new sergeant, Des Percival, and Highbridge's remaining long-serving detective constable, Jamie Foster.

Anyway, whatever. In the few short hours remaining to her before her next shift, she at least had the opportunity of sorting out some domestic chores, which had already been left several days longer than she would have liked. Jerking open the dirty linen basket in the corner, she pulled out a tangle of shirts, socks and underwear, and tossed them on to the floor in front of the washing machine, intending to stuff the coloured garments into its gaping maw and let it run its programme as she enjoyed a mug of strong black coffee. But the coffee was not to be hers for a while.

She discovered the stains on the collar of the shirt as she was extricating it from the bundle. It was one of Hayden's – a fawn, short-sleeved M&S casual she had bought him in a sale maybe three or four months before. She flattened the collar on the draining board and studied the stain. At first she thought it was blood, but closer examination revealed that it was nothing of the sort. It was lipstick – no doubt about it – and it was the sort of vivid red colour that she would never have had the nerve to wear herself. She lifted the shirt to her nose and sniffed, at once detecting a lingering scent above the damp smell of the dirty linen basket. Perfume, and it wasn't hers. She remembered the perfume smell she had noticed in their living room when Hayden had been off sick, and swallowed hard. It seemed like the same brand.

There was a sick feeling in the pit of her stomach as she sat down heavily on one of the breakfast bar stools, and it had nothing to do with her alcohol intake the previous night.

What the hell was going on with Hayden? Perfume, lipstick? Where had that come from? Certainly not from her and if not her, then who and in what circumstances? The thought that he could be over the side with someone else just didn't seem possible – not her Hayd. That big, lovable lump had never shown any interest in any other woman as far as she knew. He was only interested in food, vintage cars, and his beloved football. And her, of course – at least, she hoped so. He was eccentric, lazy, untidy and pompous, but he was also principled and loyal, with moral, old-fashioned values that made him the butt of frequent jokes in the department. Infidelity could never be his bag – or could it? Was there another side to him she knew nothing about? They had been together for over five years now, but with the job taking up so much of their time, they rarely had the opportunity for meaningful, intimate conversation and often passed each other like ships in the night. Maybe Hayden had become frustrated with their lifestyle? Maybe he resented being subordinate to her at work? Maybe he had turned to someone outside the force for some sort of release? Someone younger and less bossy than the woman he had married?

She shook her head fiercely, then winced at the pain that lanced through her temple. All this was nonsense. What the hell was she thinking? There was probably a perfectly rational explanation for it all. *Okay*, a voice snapped inside her head, *so what is it?* But she had no answer for that one and banished the divisive interjection to the back of her mind.

Climbing to her feet, she tossed the shirt back on to the bundle of clothes and bent down to shove the lot into the washing machine. She spilled some of the washing powder on the floor while pouring it from the packet under the sink into the plastic drawer and her hand felt cold and shaky as she closed the drawer again with more force than was needed before slamming the washing machine door shut and switching on the programme.

She stood there for a moment, staring unseeing at the circular window as the machine throbbed into life. She realized that she was in the process of washing away evidence she could have used in a confrontation with Hayden, yet she made no effort to halt the programme to retrieve the shirt. It was ironic. She had always prided herself on being the tough, no-nonsense cop, prepared to face up to any situation in order to get to the truth, and yet here she was, unable or unwilling to tackle her own husband over a festering suspicion of infidelity. Maybe deep down she didn't want to know the truth anyway, and believed that by destroying the evidence she could avoid having to face up to reality and the potential risk this posed to her marriage. If so, then she was not only a coward, but based on the persona she had always projected, a hypocrite too.

She grimaced. But no, it wasn't as simple as that, was it? After all, what real evidence had she uncovered anyway? A smell of unfamiliar perfume and a couple of red streaks on a shirt collar? That was hardly enough to point the finger, was it? And she would look bloody stupid if it all turned out to be perfectly innocent. Not only that, but it would cause immense hurt and indicate a lack of trust that could be just as damaging to a marriage as a proven infidelity.

So, common sense dictated caution. Say nothing, do nothing. That was the wisest course for the present, while at the same time keep a watchful eye open, just in case.

Her decision made, she re-boiled the kettle and poured herself the strong black coffee she had been gasping for, but it made little difference to her mood and she was still brooding over things half an hour later when the telephone rang.

It was the control room. '*There's been another incident*,' the operator said tersely. '*Guv'nor wants you over at Street pdq.*'

Kate banished her worries about Hayden to the back of her mind. 'Street?' she echoed, thinking of the large village close to Glastonbury, once famous for its shoe-making industry and now for its factory outlet shopping site. 'That's way off our patch. What sort of incident is it – another stiff?'

'*Mr Roscoe didn't say. He just said to call you out.*'

'But Hayden and I are on lates.'

'*Yeah, I know that, but those were his instructions. And it was just you. He said your other half can report for late duty as per normal.*'

'So, I'll be on a double shift then?'

There was a chuckle. '*Think of the money, skip,*' *the operator retorted.* '*And anyway, you can't do enough for a good boss, can you?*'

'Yeah, right,' Kate replied drily. 'Now unless you've got any more funnies, you'd better give me the address, hadn't you?'

She headed upstairs to get washed and dressed before undertaking the mammoth task of waking Hayden to tell him the change of plan.

*

The bungalow was on the outskirts of the town, in a small development, and it couldn't have been easier to find. Two marked police cars had been parked illegally in the narrow road outside – half on, half off the pavement –

and what she recognized as Roscoe's battered Honda Civic appeared to have been abandoned at an angle a few feet away from them, its rear wing projecting at least two feet out from the kerb. She smiled grimly. Her boss was not known for his driving skills and that was a fact.

Leaving her own Mazda MX5 in a layby several yards away, she walked quickly towards the knot of casually dressed figures, some with cameras, who were standing by a rickety looking garden gate. Press, without a doubt.

The group surged towards her as she approached, firing questions, as cameras clicked and bulbs flashed. She ignored the babble of voices and pushed through them to the gate, which was opened by a burly uniformed constable.

'Mr Roscoe's inside, skipper,' he advised in a low voice and stepped aside to let her through before adding, 'with the doc.'

She frowned. 'The pathologist, you mean?'

He shook his head soberly. 'No, skip, not this time. Local GP. But it was a close call, I can tell you that.'

'SIO not here then?'

The constable grinned. 'On her way apparently, though I think Mr Roscoe wishes she wasn't.'

Kate threw him a critical glance after the insubordinate remark. 'Just make sure you keep the press out,' she said coldly and pushed past him.

She found the DI in a small, comfortably furnished sitting room. He was talking to an elderly, white-haired man with horn-rimmed glasses and he turned quickly as she entered the room, his eyes narrowing.

'Dr Fuller,' Roscoe said by way of introduction, waving a hand towards her as the other man also turned to face her. 'This is DS Lewis, one of my team.'

The doctor nodded gravely. 'This is a bad business, Sergeant,' he said. 'Mrs Strong is very lucky to have survived, but she is in a bad way.'

Kate frowned in puzzlement and Roscoe coughed and started to fill in the blanks.

'Mabel Strong. Another widow. Lives here alone. Apparently, she got a visitor this morning who waylaid her in her kitchen and tried to give her neck a terminal massage.'

It was the doctor's turn to frown at Roscoe's insensitive terminology, but he said nothing.

'The perp was interrupted by the arrival of her carer, who had her own key,' Roscoe continued. 'Belted the woman, then fled.'

Kate grimaced. 'A tall man dressed in a dark coat and Fedora hat?' she suggested.

Roscoe gave her an old-fashioned look and pushed a roll of chewing gum into his mouth. 'Something like that,' he growled reluctantly. 'And that's why you're here. You claim to have some personal experience of an arsehole dressed like that, so I want you to talk to the carer and see what she can add to your description of that dosser. Maybe she can remember something significant, eh?'

'What about Mrs Strong?'

'That will have to wait, Sergeant,' the doctor put in before Roscoe could respond. 'She is well over eighty and apart from nasty bruising to her neck, she is severely traumatized. I have dispatched her to hospital in an ambulance. Fortunately, the carer's injuries are superficial, but she is still very shocked and should be handled with care.'

In fact, the carer had a fast-developing black eye and noticeable heavy bruising to the right side of her face. She was a slight woman in her early twenties and she was still trembling in the carver chair at one end of a highly polished table when Kate walked into the dining room.

'You should have gone to hospital, Miss … er—' Kate began with a smile.

'Dawn Frobisher,' the young woman replied in a soft, shaky voice and shook her head. 'And I don't need to go to hospital. I'm not badly hurt and this,' she pointed to her eye, 'will soon heal.'

Kate raised her eyebrows. 'Well, that's very brave of you,' she said, pulling out a chair and sitting down next to her. 'And it seems you saved Mrs Strong's life.'

Dawn shrugged and smiled briefly, though there were tears in her eyes.

'I just happened to turn up at the right moment,' she replied. 'Poor Mabel, she didn't deserve this at her age. That … that brute, picking on an old woman like that. I mean, why her? She'd hurt no one.'

'Which is why we have to catch the swine before he strikes again,' Kate said with feeling. 'Any idea how he got in?'

Dawn sighed and wiped her eyes with a handkerchief.

'I've warned Mabel a million times about locking her front door,' she replied. 'She lives in the past – still thinks it's the nineteen fifties, when people were more trusting. He … he must have slipped in without her noticing. She's an early riser and was probably making herself a cup of tea when he attacked her.'

Kate nodded slowly. 'And you walked in on him?'

Dawn took a deep breath. 'I heard her cry out as I opened the front door and thought she was having a heart attack. I … I ran down the hall and saw … and saw—'

She broke off and began to cry again. Kate waited patiently, reaching out to touch her wrist in a gesture of reassurance.

Frobisher cleared her throat and straightened in her chair, wiping her eyes again with her handkerchief.

'He was standing behind her, with his hands around her neck. She is a tough old lady – a former Wren – and she was putting up quite a struggle, despite her age. The man heard me come in behind him and let her go. As she fell on the floor, he hit me hard across the face with the back of one hand, knocking me flying. Then … then he just ran off.'

'You were very lucky,' Kate commented soberly. 'He could have killed you both.'

Dawn nodded. 'I think he just panicked,' she said.

'Good for you that he did.' Kate paused, then asked, 'Can you describe the man? What he looked like, what he was wearing, anything strange about him?'

Dawn frowned, evidently trying to marshal her thoughts.

'Well, he was very tall, but did not seem particularly muscular. He was wearing a long, dark coat and a wide-brimmed hat – like the sort you see men wearing in the films about the forties—'

'Like a trilby?'

'I … I don't know what that is, but it had a very wide brim.'

'What colour was it?'

'Dark – black, I think.'

'And his face, what did he look like?'

Dawn frowned again. 'He had glasses, gold-coloured glasses, and was wearing brown leather gloves. Oh yes, and he had blond hair, I think. I could see it sticking out in places under the hat.'

'Did he say anything?'

The carer shook her head. 'He just hissed as he hit me, as if irritated, then promptly ran off.'

'Nothing else you can remember about him?'

Dawn shook her head, then hesitated. 'Well, now I think of it, there *is* one thing.'

'Go on.'

'It was his eyes.'

'His eyes?'

Dawn shivered. 'Yes, they were really strange, cold, lifeless. I can't explain what I mean, but it was almost as if—'

She broke off, staring at the floor, then she raised her head and stared directly at Kate. 'As if they belonged to a fish or … or a corpse. Empty of any expression, any emotion, just … just dead.'

Kate shivered inwardly. 'You saw all this in that split second?' she queried doubtfully.

Dawn nodded. 'His face was just a couple of feet from my own and those eyes will haunt my sleep for a very long time, I can tell you.'

CHAPTER 9

Ted Roscoe was incredulous. 'Funny eyes? What the hell does that mean? First our suspect is a tall, blond-haired bloke with gold-coloured glasses, dressed in a Fedora hat and a long, dark coat – a cross between John Lennon and Doctor Who. Now we're told he also has funny eyes. Unbelievable! Next, someone will be telling me that he has horns instead of ears.'

Kate glanced quickly at Deidrie Hennessey, who was leaning back in her swivel chair behind the battered wooden desk, and risked a small smile at the DI's frustrated outburst, guessing what was behind it.

Hennessey had insisted on this pre-briefing in the SIO's office shortly after Kate had got back from the crime scene, and it was evident that it rankled with their truculent, misogynistic boss. Roscoe obviously resented having to submit to the demands of a senior female colleague who had been the same rank as himself just days before. To his mind, it relegated him to a position of unforgivable subservience and the fact that on this inquiry she had also laid claim to the chair and desk that were usually his, only served to rub salt into the wound.

Hennessey, on the other hand, seemed either unaware of his barely supressed animosity or was simply indifferent to it and she ignored his facetious comments, instead staring directly at Kate as if she was the only other person in the room.

'So, we have a vague description from a witness of a man she saw at the murder scene, who may or may not be connected with the murder and whom you say resembles your dosser. But what else do we have, Sergeant Lewis?' she said.

She began counting the points off on the fingers of her left hand with the index finger of her right as she summarized the facts.

'One, he seems to have a particular hatred for certain unnamed elderly women whom he refers to as "aunts" – first murdering Elsie Norman and then attempting to murder Mabel Strong. Two, he sent us a letter with an advance warning of his intention to commit murder, though why he would make a point of giving us the heads-up is unclear.'

She frowned and cast Roscoe a scathing glance as he slipped some gum into his mouth and began chewing noisily.

'Three, considering his MO, it seems he strangles his victims manually after gaining access to their homes on some sort of fraudulent pretext. In the case of his first victim, he applied a thick layer of lipstick to her mouth, scrawled a message on the floor – also with lipstick – and either forced sherry down her throat or drenched her clothes in the stuff. Hopefully, the PM will provide some clarity on this aspect in due course. And four, if the assumptions you put forward at yesterday's pre-briefing turn out to be correct, it is possible that he was an inmate of Talbot Court at an early stage in his life and that the elderly women he has attacked were aunts of his.'

Kate nodded. 'Or maybe even female employees at the orphanage who acted as surrogate mothers to the kids and were each accorded the title of "aunt",' she replied, referring to the DCI's last point. 'In any event, I firmly believe that there is a Talbot Court connection. As I said at the briefing, the man I confronted in the basement of the derelict mansion definitely matches the description of the suspect spotted close to the scene of Elsie Norman's murder, and the graffiti we found on the wall of the upstairs dormitory seems to have been written by someone called George and carries a threat to punish "the aunts". This effectively ties the author of the graffiti, and therefore Talbot Court itself, into the letter we received.'

'So, what would George's motive be for multiple murder then?'

'Maybe he was an orphan and was put into care at Talbot Court because of behavioural problems, which would explain his return there on what could have been just a nostalgic visit—'

Hennessey cut her off with an irritable wave of her hand. 'That doesn't answer my question. Why would being an inmate of Talbot Court lead to a hang-up about aunts? After all, going by his letter, all his aunts ever did was disgust and torment him. There's no mention in the letter of them doing him any physical harm or putting him away in Talbot Court, yet he says they ruined his life – so, how did they do that?'

Kate made a face. 'Not sure, ma'am,' she replied, unable to think of a suitable answer, but anxious to give the DCI something to bite on. 'But as you know, we've been doing a bit of digging into the background of Talbot Court itself and some interesting facts have emerged.'

'Which are?'

Conscious of the fact that what she had to give did not amount to much as far as the inquiry was concerned, Kate provided a summary of what Hayden had discovered, omitting only the less relevant facts about the history of the building, but including the new information that had come to light regarding the murder of Alistair Scarsfield and its possible connection with their suspect.

'Unfortunately, we've very little else to go on at the moment,' she finished almost apologetically, fully aware of Roscoe's malicious grin as he sensed that she was waffling. 'It seems that just after the place was closed down, following the murder and allegations of sexual abuse, the fire in the admin wing destroyed everything, including all records held there, and, as I've explained, the case file on the murder seems to have completely vanished, together with any reference to the name of the kid responsible. We even checked National Archives, but they don't hold the specific information we require.'

Hennessey grimaced. 'This all sounds mighty convenient for someone and I hate to think what it could suggest, knowing some of the high-profile figures who have been exposed in recent sex abuse scandals. But that inquiry is for another day and not for the here and now. I have to say, though, that the suggested connection between the decades-old murder of an alleged pervert like Alistair Scarsfield and the current targeting of two elderly women seems to me to be less than conclusive, and I wouldn't want us to get so hung up on this that we exclude other avenues of inquiry. Despite the tenuous links you have come up with, including your run-in with the dosser, it is still entirely possible in my view that George the letter writer is a totally different person to George the killer, and that we could be putting two and two together to make five.'

She flicked the fingers of one hand with apparent impatience.

'Nevertheless, staying with your hypothesis for a moment, what about this journalist – Brookes – who you say was carrying out an investigation into the sexual abuse allegations at Talbot Court? Any luck with him?'

Kate hesitated, conscious of the fact that Hayden was supposed to be following that one up that afternoon.

'We … er … haven't managed to trace him yet, ma'am,' she said, clearing her throat to hide her embarrassment. 'The problem is, we don't know who he was working for or whether he was freelance – and it was a long time ago, of course, so it's possible he is no longer with us.'

'Your digging expedition so far seems to have been a total waste of time then?' Roscoe interjected, his malicious smirk broadening.

After feeling humiliated himself, he was obviously keen for someone else to suffer the same fate.

Kate glared at him defiantly. 'Not at all, guv. I am still convinced that there is only the one George, that he was a victim of sexual abuse while at Talbot Court, that he stiffed Alistair Scarsfield and that he is now targeting these elderly women.'

Hennessey sighed heavily. 'But I come back to my earlier query, Sergeant. Why would being abused at Talbot Court cause this George to target these women? I can't see them being part of some nasty paedophile ring, even when they were younger.'

'Perhaps they failed to protect him, turned a blind eye or, as I suggested before, were themselves female staff at the orphanage who were somehow involved in the shenanigans—?'

'But why strike now, after a lapse of what must be almost fifty years, and where could George, or whatever his real name is, have been all this time anyway – in suspended animation?'

Kate bit back the angry reply that had formed on the tip of her tongue. 'There could be any number of reasons for that,' she replied coldly. 'He could have been in prison or in a secure mental hospital, but without a name it is obviously impossible to carry out any realistic search. However, it did occur to me that he might be a relative – a nephew perhaps – who is targeting his own aunts rather than elderly women at random, as first appeared likely. So, I got Hayden to make some inquiries into Elsie Norman's maiden name, working on the assumption that the nephew is likely to have the same surname as her and could be known to us.'

'Good move. And?'

Kate shrugged. 'Her maiden name turned out to be Quigley, but a search on the PNC produced a negative result, so we're back to square one.'

Roscoe's grin faded, to be replaced by a resentful scowl on the realization that his number two had exonerated herself after his earlier criticism and had actually out-thought him.

Hennessey, on the other hand, nodded approvingly. 'Nice work anyway, Sergeant,' she acknowledged. 'That closes one avenue of inquiry. But as a next step, perhaps we should try and establish for certain what family ties Elsie Norman may have had. In view of the fact that Mabel Strong also seems to have been attacked by the same individual, there's a chance she could be a relative of the deceased – maybe even her sister – and would be able to help us with a bit more info when she is well enough to be interviewed.'

Roscoe cleared his throat. 'I'll see to it,' he muttered, glowering at Kate.

Hennessey nodded. 'Excellent. But back to what we were just discussing before we got side-tracked and staying with the possibility that there is a link between the Talbot Court business and the present case, we still have no rational explanation for the fifty-year gap we were talking about.'

'Our killer might have been living abroad or in the services and just returned home,' Kate said. 'But I still think the most likely answer is that he was in prison or in a secure mental hospital and has only just been released – though, as I've already said, we would need a name to check that out.'

Roscoe, clearly still smarting over the fact that he had been upstaged by Kate, gave a disparaging snort. 'Released after nearly fifty years?' he sneered. 'That would have been one hell of a sentence. What could he have done to deserve that? Wiped out half the population of Manchester or Liverpool with nerve gas?'

Kate's lips tightened. 'You forget people like Ian Brady and Myra Hindley, guv,' she retorted. 'They were put away in the mid-sixties for the Moors Murders and both were still inside when Hindley died in 2002, while Brady himself has only just pegged it.'

Hennessey stood up, reaching for her coat, which she had draped over the back of her chair. 'Whatever,' she snapped, seemingly tiring of the hypothesizing. 'We need to concentrate our minds on catching this creature before he kills again. At least we have something of a description to put out to the media – if indeed that is our man.'

Roscoe's eyes narrowed. 'Do you think that's a good idea?' he growled. 'If the scumbag sees it in the press, it's likely to panic him into changing his appearance.'

Hennessey nodded, unsurprised by his interjection as his hostility towards the media was well known. 'A valid point, Ted, but at the same time, it might produce some useful public sightings and it will also serve to put our elderly residents on their guard before he pays someone else a visit. We can't afford to miss this opportunity.'

Roscoe scowled. 'I don't like it.'

She smiled without humour. 'I'm not asking you to, Ted, but in the meantime, I want you to get hold of Mabel Strong's carer again and see if we can try for an E-FIT of the old lady's attacker. If we move quickly enough, we might be able to get a good likeness of our man out to the media in the next twenty-four hours.' She glanced at her watch. 'Before that, however, there is another incident room briefing requiring our presence. Then I have what I expect to be a very lively press conference to attend. Wish me luck!'

Kate stood up quickly as Hennessy marched smartly from the room, but Roscoe remained seated in his chair, blowing a bubble with his chewing gum as he glowered after her.

Happy families, Kate mused grimly, then felt a stab of acid in her stomach as that thought prompted other disquieting thoughts about Hayden and the suspicions still festering inside her.

*

Patient 174 sat for a long time in the allotment shed, every now and then peering through the side window for any sign of pursuit. But there was none and the allotment appeared deserted.

Taking a deep, trembling breath, George leaned back against the wall of the shed – fists tightly clenched, head swimming, heart hammering out a rapid erratic beat in a barely suppressed fit of angry frustration. How could things have gone so terribly wrong? Wasting Mabel Strong should have been a piece of cake – just like the murder of Elsie Norman – but instead, it had turned into a complete and utter disaster, which had the potential to ruin everything.

True, no one could have anticipated the carer putting in an appearance at exactly the wrong moment, but aborting the whole job and simply running away had been plain stupid. Wasting that slip of a girl in addition to the old woman herself could have been accomplished with relative ease, and at least that would have ensured there were no witnesses. Now the police were bound to have a description to circulate, which meant finishing all that had been planned was going to be a lot riskier.

Okay, so it was highly likely that Larchfield Security had hit the panic button themselves by now and, if so, Old Bill would already have the description of their dangerous absconder anyway. But there was a chance that the break-out had still not been detected or if it had, that the psychiatrist's body had not yet been discovered – allowing a few more hours' grace at least.

Either way, the situation called for a strategic rethink and the number one priority was to get rid of the Fedora hat and coat. The psychiatrist's gold-coloured driving glasses, which had been in the glovebox of his car, would have to go too – and maybe it would be wise for a change of hair colour. It shouldn't be difficult getting hold of some sort of hair dye, but a change of clothes could be problematic. It would be the height of folly to walk into a shop to buy new gear dressed in clothes that might already have been described in a police press release. On the other hand, simply dumping them and trying to do the same thing in just an open-necked shirt and trousers on such a cold day would attract just as much attention.

It was then that George spotted the scarecrow, the long, shabby raincoat draped over its skeletal frame stirring faintly in the breeze, the grey cloth cap tilted at a jaunty angle on its misshapen turnip head. At once a slow smile of satisfaction spread over Patient 174's pale face, but the blue eyes exhibited no expression whatsoever, remaining as cold and lifeless as those of a corpse on an undertaker's gurney.

CHAPTER 10

The second incident room briefing lasted just three-quarters of an hour. There was little new information of any consequence, apart from that which Kate and Hayden had to impart, and they ended up having the floor for much of the time, with questions and suggestions toing and froing across the room until Deidrie Hennessey called a halt to it all and hurried to her press conference with Roscoe.

Kate's head was buzzing as she made her way down to the canteen. So much had happened since the sinister letter had been delivered to the police station and all sorts of fragmented thoughts were rolling around her brain – so many ifs, buts and maybes that she needed some peace and quiet to consolidate them. But she was interrupted en route.

The young uniformed sergeant stopped her on the stairs before she was even halfway down. He was on the way up and had a wad of paper under his arm.

'Sergeant Bradley,' he announced with a cheery grin. 'Jacob Bradley. I've been designated Incident Room Admin Officer.'

He counted out three of the sheets and handed them to her. 'Month's shift duties for your team,' he said. 'I've just been photocopying the lot – bloody bind, I can tell you, but there you are.'

She studied the topmost sheet for a second. 'Lates all week, is it?' she said ruefully.

He nodded. 'Rest days Friday and Saturday – everyone has to have a day off, you know. Regulations and all that.' He grinned again. 'Hayden could take you out to dinner somewhere.'

She treated him to an old-fashioned look. 'Yeah, right,' she retorted drily. 'I can see that happening.'

The canteen was empty and just closing when she walked in. One of the staff in a stained white apron was disappearing back into the kitchen, having apparently just finished swabbing down the tables. After six, the teams on late duty would have to rely on local takeaways for meals. No wonder there were so many fat police officers about with that sort of calorie intake, she mused. And Hayden was one of them.

Grabbing a coffee from the urn that had been set up in one corner, she helped herself to a currant bun that had been left with a couple of others on a plate, deposited some change on the counter, and drew up a chair at one of the recently swabbed tables, wrinkling her nose at the strong smell of disinfectant that came off the gleaming plastic top.

So where *was* Hayden, she asked herself, automatically staring about the empty room. She had left him with the job of trying to trace the journalist, Leslie Brookes, who had made the sexual abuse allegations about Talbot Court, but it was unlike him not to have made a bee-line for the canteen before it closed – all those sticky buns and lardy cakes normally proved irresistible to him.

She frowned, thoughts of her other half immediately reawakening her sense of unease now that the pressures of the murder investigation had eased for a few moments. She just could not forget the smell of perfume on the shirt in the dirty linen basket and the trace of lipstick she had found on the collar. However much she tried to dismiss the suspicions from her mind, they refused to go away. She shouldn't have simply put the shirt in the wash, but tackled Hayden about it first. She realized that now, but at the time she had been scared – scared of hearing something she didn't want to hear and scared of what that could mean for their future together.

Unwittingly dropping some sugar lumps from the dish on the table into her mug, she stirred the coffee with her biro, then made a face when she took a sip. Bugger it! She didn't take sugar. What the hell was the matter with her?

Abandoning the coffee and her bun, she climbed to her feet and headed back out into the corridor, intending to return to the incident room to find Hayden. As it turned out, however, she found him before she had gone more than a few yards.

She heard his voice coming from one of the witness interview rooms as she was passing the half-closed door and stopped in mid-stride, reaching for the door handle. Then abruptly she froze, her eyes narrowing. It was apparent from the one-sided conversation that he was on the telephone, and that the conversation had nothing to do with police work.

'I can't risk it, old thing,' she heard him say. 'She might suspect something.'

Kate's senses reeled and she clutched at the door post for support, feeling sick.

'Of course I want to see you,' she heard him add, 'but it will have to wait until I can slip away.'

He gave a loud, exasperated sigh. 'I know that, but I'm on a murder investigation and I can't just disappear for a couple of hours—'

There was a pause, then he said quickly, 'Look, I have to go. I've got your mobile number. I will ring you when I see an opportunity.'

Gritting her teeth, Kate pushed the door open. Hayden was leaning against the windowsill with the receiver of the wall telephone still in one hand, and his eyes widened as he slapped the phone back on its cradle.

'What are you doing in here, Hayden?' she rasped. 'And who were you talking to?'

He swallowed hard and she could almost see his brain working in the restless movement of his eyes. 'Oh that,' he replied. 'I was … er … ringing the secretary of the classic car club about the … um … next meeting.'

'Oh, who was that?'

'Josh Tomlinson. I was telling him I might not be able to make it because I was on a murder inquiry.'

She nodded slowly, a tight set to her mouth. 'Always refer to him as "old thing", do you?'

He swallowed again and treated her to a weak grin. 'Call everyone old thing, you know that – like I call you old girl. Sort of hang-up from my public school days.'

She hesitated. It was on the tip of her tongue to grill him further about the things she had overheard him saying – why he was evidently so keen to see the mystery person he had been talking to, exactly what it was he couldn't risk, and whether the 'she' he had referred to was actually his own wife. But for some reason she once again copped out on a confrontation.

'So what about that journalist you were supposed to be trying to trace?' she asked instead. 'Ringing the classic car secretary more important than that, is it?'

''Course not,' he retorted, his face reddening at the rebuke. 'I'm already on to that, but it was a long time ago and will take time.'

Before she could take him up on that, she was rudely interrupted by the station's tannoy system.

'*Detective Sergeant Lewis,*' the metallic voice blasted, '*contact Detective Inspector Roscoe urgently.*'

Pushing past Hayden, Kate grabbed the telephone and dialled the internal number of the SIO's office.

'*Get your arse up here pronto,*' Roscoe rasped down the phone. '*There's been a development.*'

'A development?'

The DI swore. '*You a bleedin' parrot now, Lewis?*' he snarled. '*Just get up here, will you? Our psycho's been sighted.*'

Slamming the telephone back on its cradle, as Hayden had done a few moments before, she turned back through the door. 'Get on with what you're paid to do,' she snapped over her shoulder. 'But this isn't over, believe me.'

Unbeknown to Hayden, she meant that in more ways than one.

*

Travelling in the front seat of Roscoe's battered Honda Civic was not for the faint-hearted. It was hard to imagine that the DI had ever been on the obligatory police training course all officers were required to pass before they were authorized to drive in their official capacity, or that he had even managed to get through the basic MOT driving test. In fact, his reckless, ham-fisted method of car control was almost legendary. He demonstrated that now as he negotiated the narrow lanes across the Somerset Levels through a newly arisen mist with Kate clinging desperately to the front passenger seat, an expired filter-tip cigarette clinging just as desperately to his bottom lip as he growled an explanation for their haste.

'Bastard was spotted stripping a scarecrow in an allotment this side of Street,' he said.

Kate raised an eyebrow. 'Stripping a scarecrow?' she echoed, wincing as the offside wheel of the old car found a deep pothole in the road, then bounced out of it again. 'That's a new kind of perversion anyway.'

He threw her a sideways glance. 'Very funny, Lewis,' he retorted, finally losing his cigarette somewhere in the gloom of the footwell. 'Thing is, he's a bit of a joker, this one, as you'll see.'

There were a couple of marked police units and what Kate recognized as a local CID car drawn up in the lane beside the allotment. She caught sight of torches probing the patches of rotting vegetables beyond the perimeter hedge as they climbed out of the Civic.

A dark-haired young woman, dressed in an anorak and slacks, approached them from a gap in the hedge.

'DC Mandy Herbert, guv,' she said to Roscoe by way of introduction, then turned slightly. 'This is Mr Harold Grey. He reported the incident.'

A short, tubby man in a sweater and jeans stepped through the gap after her and nodded to Roscoe.

'Bloody queer, what he done,' he commented. 'And in broad daylight too.'

Roscoe sniffed, staring around him in the gathering murk.

'Nicked the clothes off your scarecrow, did he?' he said.

'Yeah,' Grey replied, turning back through the gap so that they could follow him. 'But what he did after that was even dafter.'

There was a wooden shed to the right of the track they were following and just beyond it, Kate spotted the scarecrow. It was leaning over at a sixty-degree angle, maybe three or four yards behind the shed.

'Used to be vegetables in here,' Grey explained when they reached the patch of ground into which the scarecrow's supporting pole had been driven. 'Haven't bothered to take the thing down yet, but look at that.'

Kate was already looking, however. The scarecrow may have been stripped of its original garments, but it was fully clothed now – in a long black coat and a matching Fedora hat.

*

'So, no idea where he went?' DCI Hennessey asked a couple of hours later from behind her requisitioned desk in the SIO's office.

Roscoe shook his head, chewing on another wad of gum. 'The witness – Grey – couldn't help us with a more detailed description either,' he said. 'Just a tall, slim figure making off across the allotment towards the fields bordering the Glastonbury road.'

'Dressed in a blue raincoat and grey cloth cap?'

'Nicked from the scarecrow, ma'am,' Kate confirmed.

'And a full search of the area was carried out?'

'Just before the mist really came down, yes. There was no point continuing it after that. We could hardly see a thing.'

'We have the clothing he left behind?'

'With SOCO as we speak. They'll arrange for a full examination of it by the lab tomorrow to see if they can capture any DNA traces that will achieve a match with what's held on our database. SOCO have also given the shed a thorough going over, but they haven't reported back yet on that or the Mabel Strong crime scene.'

Hennessey's expression was noticeably gloomy. 'Waste of time anyway. Same as the scenes of crime search of Elsie Norman's bungalow will turn out to be.'

Kate shrugged. 'Well, according to Mabel Strong's carer, the assailant *was* wearing gloves, but everything's worth a try and we have to go through the motions regardless.'

Hennessey nodded. 'I accept that,' she said, 'but a possible future sighting of our man is all we seem to be left with, and after going to all the trouble of putting out a description of a suspect wearing a long, dark coat and Fedora hat, we're now looking for someone dressed in a blue raincoat and grey cloth cap.'

'For the moment, it seems like that, yes.'

Roscoe shook his head. 'I don't reckon the arsehole will be wearing that gear for long anyway. He'll be looking for another change of clothes from somewhere – maybe a charity shop or an unattended washing-line.'

'More than likely, Ted,' Hennessey agreed. 'So what about that E-FIT you were to arrange? Maybe we will be able to produce a good enough facial of our man after speaking to Mrs Strong or her carer.'

'All in hand,' Roscoe replied with a self-satisfied smirk. 'It's set up for tomorrow morning with the carer.'

The DCI frowned. 'Can't it be done any earlier than that? Time is of the essence here.'

Roscoe's smirk faded and he shook his head. 'Earliest we can do it is tomorrow,' he said brusquely. 'But neither Mrs Strong nor the carer are going anywhere in the meantime, so it won't hurt to wait a few hours.'

As it turned out, however, Roscoe was horribly wrong about that.

CHAPTER 11

Kate was not looking forward to going home after the last episode with Hayden. She was deeply hurt and she didn't really want to see her husband while she was feeling this way. She hadn't made any effort to find or speak to him since overhearing that devastating phone conversation. For his part, he had secreted himself in another office somewhere else in the building, deliberately avoiding any contact with her while he ostensibly carried out his trace inquiries on the journalist, Leslie Brookes. He'd obviously realized he was under suspicion and did not relish the prospect of a further grilling, which meant that it was unlikely he was looking forward to going home either.

But it had been a long, tiring day and as far as Kate was concerned, bed had become an essential requirement if she wasn't to fall asleep at her desk. Even so, she didn't leave Highbridge police station until well after eleven, having wasted another couple of hours fruitlessly surfing the net for any new scrap of information she could find on Talbot Court.

Then, following the rear lights of Hayden's Jaguar as he left the station just ahead of her, she drove slowly back across the moor. Her mind was in partial limbo, but it was alert enough to make sure she didn't follow him too closely. She wanted to allow him ample time to get indoors and find somewhere as much out of her way as was possible in their small cottage before she put her own key in the door. When she finally did pull into the gravel drive behind his Jaguar, the lights were already on in the upstairs bedroom and she was not surprised to find him curled up in the big double bed with his head buried beneath the sheets.

She felt him tense slightly when she climbed in beside him, but she said nothing and he seemed to relax when she turned away from him on to her right side, feigning sleep as she tried to stem the flow of tears that welled up in her eyes the moment her head touched the pillow.

She had no recollection of drifting off, but she must have done so and when she awoke at just after eight in the morning, she was surprised to find the bed empty beside her – Hayden had broken the habit of a lifetime and got up before her. He was not downstairs either and a glance out of the window confirmed that his Jaguar was gone. There was a brief note on the kitchen table, telling her that he had had to go out, but no explanation as to why or where.

Sitting down heavily on the breakfast bar stool with a mug of coffee once more cupped in her hands, she tried to marshal her thoughts. She knew she would have to have it out with him sooner or later, but that opportunity had now been taken out of her hands by his early departure to heaven alone knew where and she guessed he would not be in a hurry to return home, but would only reappear when he had to report for duty at Highbridge police station later in the day. That way, he knew that the presence of other colleagues would prevent her buttonholing him with embarrassing questions.

How long would he be able to keep up this avoidance strategy, however? Sooner or later they would both find themselves together again at home. What then? How would Hayden be able to avoid facing those awkward questions in a small, five-roomed cottage? And there was an even bigger problem. How would she herself be able to find the courage to tackle him face-to-face about her suspicions if that meant learning the unpalatable truth and precipitating the end of their marriage?

The mug was shaking in her hands now and in trying to set it down, she spilled some of the contents on the work surface. She was in the process of mopping up the mess with a cloth when the telephone rang.

She snatched the phone from its cradle, but before she could say anything, a hesitant female voice blurted her own query.

'*Hayden? Is that you?*'

She had the good sense to say nothing and the voice became even more agitated.

'*Hayden, why aren't you here yet? You promised.*'

Kate took a deep breath and gritted her teeth to force herself to keep control.

'Who is this?' she said softly.

The phone went dead.

For a few moments she just stood there, the telephone receiver gripped tightly in one trembling hand as the full implication of the call sank in. This was the evidence she had been seeking and yet had most dreaded – the final proof of what she had already suspected. Hayden was having an affair. He was knocking off another woman. *Her* Hayden!

Forcing down her shock, she dialled the BT 1471 number and wrote down the details the automated voice gave her on the pad beside the telephone. Then, with hardly a pause she dialled the number herself, waiting for a response with bated breath.

At first it seemed that she was going to be disappointed. The telephone rang for several seconds without being answered. But then, just as she was about to give up on the call, there was a 'click' and a bored male voice responded.

'*Yes? The Loft?*'

Kate was taken aback for a moment. 'The what?' she said.

'*The Loft Private Hotel,*' the man replied impatiently. '*What can I do for you?*'

'That depends. Where are you?'

'Well, I'm here and you're there.'

Kate felt her anger rise and she controlled herself with an effort. 'Look, I've … er … been given your number, but I need to know exactly where the hotel is situated first—'

'Uphill, Weston-super-Mare, love. Any good to you?'

'Oh no, sorry, a bit too far from where I want.'

'Where do you want?'

Kate quickly put the phone down without answering the question.

A private hotel in Weston? Was Hayden's bit of stuff staying in a hotel or was she just staff?

There was only one way to find out. Abandoning her coffee and going back upstairs to quickly shower, dress, and run a comb through her hair, she grabbed her car keys and left the house.

Half an hour later she was in Weston-super-Mare. She found the dingy-looking redbrick hotel tucked away in a side street behind high hedges. Even without the wooden sign screwed to an entrance pillar she would have known it was the right place. Hayden's red Mk II Jaguar was parked directly outside.

*

Patient 174 was glad to be rid of the smelly raincoat and cap that had previously adorned the scarecrow's angular frame, even though the coat's long pockets had been ideal for accommodating the bottle of sherry Larchfield's former resident had selected as an appropriate 'calling card'. Those garments now lay in the bottom of a plastic wheelie bin at the back of the isolated farmhouse George had stumbled upon after fleeing the allotment.

The elderly farmer had not expected someone like George Lupin to come a-calling, nor had his middle-aged daughter. Neither of them had expected to be dead by the evening either, but George couldn't afford to leave witnesses behind for the police to interrogate and be provided with a description of the green wax coat (similarly equipped with a convenient long pocket) and black woollen hat the psychopath had taken from the clothes peg in the hall.

George had throttled the farmer while he was dozing in his armchair in the sitting room – the old man should have locked the front door, shouldn't he? And that had been a lot easier than killing the buxom daughter. She had walked in at precisely the wrong moment and had turned out to be imbued with the sort of raw strength that comes from the constant physical effort of managing a mixed pig and sheep farm. In the end, after an exhausting struggle on the floor of the stone-flagged kitchen, George had had to resort to using a carving knife snatched from a plate of cold beef on the kitchen table to slit her throat from ear to ear.

The double killing had had the effect of stimulating the old appetite, and the escapee had polished off the whole plate of beef, together with the remains of a bottle of local cider standing beside it, even before the woman's blood had begun to congeal on the quarry tiles.

Then had come the onerous task of disposing of the bodies and cleaning up the blood-spattered kitchen. Discovering the slurry pit in the farmyard had been a stroke of luck – obviating the need to dig holes in the ground – but though George was able to carry the old man out to the yard draped over one shoulder and tip him over the low concrete wall into the pit's yawning maw, the woman had been a different proposition, requiring the use of a rickety wooden bin trolley from an adjacent barn. In the end, however, she went the same way as her father, gurgling obscenely as she disappeared below the surface.

On the return to the house, George was smiling with satisfaction, secure in the knowledge that it was likely to be quite a while before the corpses were found – if they were ever found at all – and after using a mop and bucket borrowed from the rear porch to thoroughly clean the kitchen floor and cupboards, which had been sprayed with blood from the woman's severed carotid artery, there was even time to sit down in front of the television to watch the local news.

George treated the screen to a contemptuous sneer when the description of the murder suspect was broadcast. Apart from the long, dark coat and Fedora hat, and the gold-coloured spectacles and blond hair, it was obvious that the police had very little to go on, while the anticipated E-FIT of 'the man they wanted to interview' was, as yet, conspicuous by its absence. There was, however, a reference to the suspect as having dead, soulless eyes. George had not been personally aware of this characteristic before, and found the observation quite intriguing, until a check in the nearest mirror confirmed the fact and prompted a frantic search of the house for sunglasses. Luckily, a nice silver-framed pair turned up in a drawer in one of the bedrooms, resolving that particular problem, but another identifying feature – the escapee's striking blond hair – called for more drastic action.

In the absence of any trace of hair dye, George had to resort to using a pair of scissors and a cutthroat razor from the bathroom instead. Two hours and many oaths later Patient 174 was appraising a perfectly shaved head in the bathroom mirror, the lean, pallid face wearing a satisfied smile, despite the number of very visible and very sore-looking abrasions that the razor had left behind.

'All done,' Larchfield's AWOL patient murmured, returning to the television in the sitting room with a mug of coffee and a slice of fruitcake from the pantry and dropping into the armchair previously occupied by the old farmer.

No one would think of looking for a wanted murderer in a place like this, would they? And it sure as hell beat the pants off the damp, draughty barns that had provided temporary shelter since breaking out of Larchfield. George took a sip from the mug and stared through the window at the Land Rover Defender parked outside and the patchwork of fields beyond, stretching away to the misty horizon. Yes, the place would make an excellent hideaway from which to pursue the business that still had to be completed, and the police were unlikely to show any interest in a farmer dressed in a green wax coat and cap, innocently chugging across the Levels in a beaten-up old Land Rover, were they?

*

Kate had parked her car in a small entranceway, a few yards from the parking spot Hayden had chosen for his Jaguar, well out of sight of the hotel where he was evidently meeting up with the other woman. She had intended breaking in on their little tête-à-tête, once she had found which room he was in, but with the driver's door half open and her right foot already feeling for the tarmac driveway, she was stopped in her tracks by a sharp voice.

'I hope you don't intend parking here?'

The rotund, balding man in the short-sleeved pullover and flannels was bristling with indignation as he emerged from behind the car.

Kate automatically reached for her warrant card, but then stopped herself in time. She wasn't on police business and identifying herself in that way would have caused her nothing but grief if a complaint were to be made.

'Sorry, but I will only be five minutes—' she began.

'You'll be nothing of the sort,' the man cut in. 'This is private property. Move the car or I'm calling the police.'

It was useless trying to argue. Kate knew she was on a hiding to nothing. With a grimace, she slipped back behind the wheel and slammed her door shut, scowling at the man as she started the engine and pulled back out on to the road. She was looking for somewhere else to park when she saw Hayden's Jaguar pull out of his parking spot and head off in the opposite direction.

'Damn it!' she breathed, and swung on to double yellow lines behind a parked van, staying low in the seat in case her husband saw her in his rear-view mirror. But there was no tell-tale flash from his brake lights, which might have indicated his reaction to a glimpse of her car, and then he was gone.

For a while Kate just sat there, her heart pounding. Hayden had appeared to be alone in the Jag, which meant his 'bit on the side' had to be still in the hotel. She chewed her lip, thinking about what to do next.

The safest option was to drive away and tackle Hayden when he got home that night, but what if he simply denied it all and made up some cock-and-bull story about the phone call and why he was parked outside the hotel? The other option was to approach the hotel reception desk to try and find out who he had been visiting, then confront the woman concerned in her room. But that meant concocting some plausible story of her own to justify her interest and being prepared for the ugly scene that might result.

She continued to sit there weighing things up for several minutes, but in the end her innate curiosity, heightened this time by a desperate emotional need for answers, won the day, blinding her to the possible consequences. Climbing out of the car, she locked up and walked quickly towards the hotel entrance, a determined set to her jaw, but with her plan of action still only half-formed in her mind. Whether she would have managed to persuade the reception clerk to divulge the information she was seeking remained unknown, for she was denied the opportunity. Within feet of the hotel entrance the shrill voice of her mobile phone stopped her in her tracks.

Scowling angrily, she jerked the offending device from her pocket and peered at the tiny screen. It was Ted Roscoe. For a second, she thought of ignoring the call – after all, she was off until the afternoon – but her sense of duty won the day.

'Guv?' she answered sharply.

Roscoe cleared his throat. '*Where are you?*' he rasped. '*Tried your home phone, but no reply.*'

'Er … Weston,' she replied.

'Weston? What are you doing there?

'Shopping,' she lied, adding sarcastically, 'Presumably I am allowed to go shopping in my own time? I'm not on until this afternoon.'

There was a grunt. *'Cheeky cow! Well, you're on now. I want you to get yourself over to the hospital to see Mabel Strong. It seems she is well enough to be interviewed and it would be better for her to be seen by a female officer. While you're there, don't forget to go into this family background thing the DCI mentioned.'*

Kate glanced at the hotel entrance and muttered an oath under her breath, away from the phone. She was so close to getting to the bottom of things regarding Hayden's infidelity and to be pipped at the post like this was just too much.

'There are other female officers on the inquiry, guv,' she reminded him tartly.

'All tied up,' he said. *'Anyway, I want an experienced detective on this one. The old biddy could have valuable info for us and it might have to be teased out of her. I don't want her being discharged or pegging out on us before she can give us the necessary SP. Report back as soon as you've seen her, understood? I should be back from Elsie Norman's PM by the time you finish there.'*

Before Kate could think of anything else to say, he cut off.

'Shit!' she said aloud, glaring at the phone as if it was directly responsible for frustrating her plan to confront Hayden's secret lover. 'Shit! Shit! Shit!'

It occurred to her that she could still do what she had set out to do and head to the hospital afterwards, but even as the thought was born, she discarded it. If her plan went wrong – for example, if the desk clerk took exception to her questions or there was a hysterical reaction by 'the other woman' – the whole thing could end badly, resulting in an unforeseen delay as she tried to smooth things over or, at worst, some of her uniformed colleagues being called. That might prevent her getting to the hospital at all, plunging her into some very deep water indeed, and it could even cost her the stripes she had not long earned. That didn't bear thinking about.

With another rueful glance at the hotel entrance, she turned and marched angrily back to her car, but as she drove away, she promised herself one thing – this business was definitely not over.

*

Mabel Strong had had enough of the hospital. She was an independent soul and hated all the fuss that the assault on her had generated; smiling nurses trolleying her to the X-ray suite, then plumping up the pillows on her bed and asking how she was feeling after her return to the private room she had been allocated. The thin, grey-haired doctor in his white coat in and out seemingly every hour to check her over and assess her suitability for release, and the young police officer stationed outside the room regularly poking her head round the door with an even bigger smile – maybe to make sure she hadn't escaped out of the single window, she mused drily.

'You've had a terrible experience,' her doctor had told her. 'You have a badly bruised throat, and some nasty cuts and abrasions to your face and arms. You're also suffering from shock, and at your age that could cause serious complications.'

'Bum!' she'd retorted. 'I am fine and I want to go home.'

But deep down she knew that he was right and she succumbed to the light sedative he gave her without a murmur, and almost immediately drifted off to sleep.

She awoke much later, feeling very thirsty and conscious of someone moving about close to her bed. Through a haze she glimpsed the white coat and smiled slightly. The doctor was back, making sure she was all right. He really was a nice man. Then her vision cleared and the smile froze on her lips, her eyes widening as she shrank back against her pillow under the gaze of the figure standing there.

‘You’re not the doctor,’ she gasped.

‘No, I’m not,’ her visitor replied, treating her to a thin, humourless smile and producing a bottle from under his coat. ‘But let’s keep that to ourselves, shall we?’

CHAPTER 12

The receptionist seated behind the imposing wooden desk in the hospital foyer had the bored look of someone who could hardly wait for her shift to finish, and she gave Kate's warrant card just a cursory glance when it was thrust under her nose. Then, checking her computer screen with a long yawn, she gave directions to Mabel Strong's private room before turning back to the newspaper crossword she had been trying to complete, as if this was the most important task of the afternoon.

The lift to the first floor was a long time coming and, in the end, Kate lost patience and went for the stairs instead, mounting them with the weariness of someone twice her age as her thoughts once more centred on Hayden and what he had done to her.

It was probably because of her preoccupation with her domestic situation that she failed to notice the door swinging open at the top of the stairs and the white-coated figure on his way through. The collision was inevitable and as she slammed into him, the clipboard holding the statement forms she would need for her interview with Mabel Strong flew out of her hand and skated across the landing.

'Oh, I'm so sorry,' she exclaimed. 'I wasn't looking where I was going.'

She received a thin smile in return and the doctor bent down to pick up her clipboard and papers, and handed them to her.

'No problem,' he muttered. 'My fault too.'

Then he was on his way again, no doubt late for an appointment as he took the stairs two at a time.

Feeling angry with herself for allowing her personal problems to intrude on her official duties, Kate pushed through the double doors and marched smartly along the corridor to where a uniformed police officer was sitting on a plastic chair outside a room at the other end.

The constable stood up quickly when he saw her approaching.

'Everything okay?' she snapped, flashing her warrant card.

'All quiet here,' he replied. 'Doctor's just been in to see her, but he's the only one.'

She nodded. 'Good. I expect she will be discharged shortly anyway.'

He grunted. 'Can't happen soon enough as far as I'm concerned. I didn't join this job to be a bloody nursemaid.'

Kate gave him an old-fashioned look, but made no comment on the insensitive remark.

'I might be a while in here,' she said, jerking open the door. 'Depends on what Mrs Strong has to tell me.'

As it turned out, however, she was no more than a matter of seconds, for it was apparent the moment she entered the small room, smelled the strong distinctive odour of sherry, and saw the elderly woman in the hospital gown hanging over the side of the bed that Mabel Strong would not be telling anyone anything ever again. Someone had strangled the life out of her.

*

'I must have actually bumped into the bastard on the stairs,' Kate breathed half an hour later. 'He was dressed as a doctor – white coat, stethoscope sticking out of his top pocket.'

Roscoe chewed rhythmically, his boot-button eyes fixed on the corpse in the bed through the open door with an intensity that might have suggested he was trying to will the life back into the tiny wasted frame.

'Yeah,' he replied, a note of resignation in his tone, and for once making no effort to lambast anyone for the murder of the old woman. 'He slugged a casualty doctor downstairs and stuck him in the laundry cupboard before borrowing his stuff. Cool customer, this one. Plod on the door never had any doubts that he was a doctor when he let him go in.'

'If I had got here just five minutes earlier,' Kate went on miserably, 'I might have caught him in the act.'

The DI seemed not to have heard her. 'Lipstick plastered all over her mouth and this time with "Bye, Bye, Auntie Mabel" scrawled on the wall above her bed,' he summarized tonelessly. 'And that stink of sherry – how the hell did he get *that* in here?'

But Kate was too committed to wallowing in her own self-recriminations to comment on his observations or answer his question.

'I should have suspected something when he bumped into me,' she said bitterly. 'He was wearing dark glasses – you couldn't see his eyes – and he smiled, he actually had the audacity to smile at me after … after doing … doing this.'

Roscoe surfaced from wherever his own musings had taken him.

'Dark glasses, you say? That means he must have changed his appearance again. The swine is a bloody chameleon. Anything else you noticed about him?'

Kate frowned and the next second snapped her fingers, her blue eyes widening.

'Yes, there was. He was totally bald, I remember that now, with a gold earring in his left ear, and he had a number of abrasions to his scalp. It was as if he had shaved his head himself.'

'Clothing?'

She shook her head. 'I couldn't see what he was wearing under his white coat, but maybe hospital security cameras picked him up walking in?'

'Good point. We'll have that checked out pdq.'

He spat his chewing gum into a large tissue and dropped it into a nearby wastepaper bin.

'Meantime, pathologist and SOCO are on their way, plus' he added, 'our better-late-than-never boss, so you should make yourself scarce.'

Kate looked puzzled. 'But the DCI will probably want me to brief her about this.'

Roscoe shook his head firmly. 'I'll do that. I've got another job for you.'

'What job?'

He pulled a piece of paper from his pocket, studied it for a second, then handed it to her.

'Vicar at a church out on the Levels apparently clocked a character answering our man's original description loitering in the church graveyard, following Elsie Norman's murder. Rang us after the news story on TV. Get over there and see if you can find out what he may have been up to. Name and address of the vicar is on the note. Bloke called Glover.'

She frowned again. 'But why me? What's wrong with someone from one of the other teams doing this?'

He scowled. 'Because I've told you to do it, that's why.'

She met his hard gaze without flinching. 'I'm not trying to duck out of the job, guv,' she persisted, 'but officially I'm on lates this week and it's going to look pretty funny to our colleagues if you keep calling me in to do jobs that those already on duty should be doing.'

'So?'

She hesitated. 'It's just that they might begin to think you don't trust them and that I've become your personal gofer.'

There was a glint in his boot-button eyes now. 'Well, haven't you?'

Kate took a deep breath. 'Guv, why do I get this feeling that you are hell-bent on running your own inquiry, outside the official one?'

His scowl broke into a humourless grin. 'And why on earth would I do that?'

'Maybe to steal a march on the DCI?'

He emitted a throaty chuckle. 'What a thing to suggest!' he retorted, refusing to confirm or deny the fact.

Then abruptly he returned to the job he had just delegated. 'Incidentally, while you're closeted with the vicar, you might ask him for some sort of divine guidance to help us catch this killer before he adds someone else to his list.'

*

The church was over 400 years old – or so it said on a plaque attached to the wall in the porch – and the heavy, creaking door certainly looked as if it was old enough to have been witness to the very first parish service.

Kate had always experienced a sense of unease on the few occasions in her life that she had had to visit a church. Awe perhaps? Or maybe guilt as a non-practising Catholic who had not taken Communion or uttered so much as a prayer within the sacred portals of any church since she was confirmed as a child? Whatever it was, she felt that unease now as she stood in the nave, inhaling its musty gloom.

Her leather boots rang on the flagstones as she approached the white-frocked priest crouched in apparent supplication before the altar, but he didn't stir until she was standing behind the raised bar of the communion rail and had given a less than discreet cough, which raised a multitude of mocking echoes.

'Yes, my child?' he said, climbing slowly to his feet and turning to face her. 'Can I help you?'

She forced a smile and produced her warrant card. 'DS Kate Lewis, Reverend Glover,' she said. 'Highbridge CID.'

‘How can I help you?’ he said, returning her smile. ‘Is it to do with our visitor in the churchyard?’

Kate nodded. ‘Yes, sir. Did you get a good look at him?’

He shook his head and produced a pair of spectacles from his vestments. ‘Sadly, no. I didn’t have these on at the time and my sight is not so good these days. But I did see that he was dressed in some sort of long, dark coat – black, I think – and he had a hat on. I believe they call it a Fedora. But I didn’t see his face clearly enough to describe him. I did catch a glimpse of his car, though.’

Kate pricked up her ears. ‘His car? What sort of car?’

‘It was difficult to see clearly as it was quite misty at the time and the vehicle was parked in the lane, mostly hidden by the wall of the churchyard, but I am sure it was a VW Beetle – an old one by the sound of the engine – and it was red.’

‘No number?’

‘’Fraid not, sorry.’

Kate thought about that for a moment. ‘Any idea what he was doing in the graveyard?’ she said.

‘Well, he appeared to be looking at the headstones. When I approached him, he was studying a particular grave and muttering something I couldn’t catch. He seemed to be very agitated.’ He sighed. ‘I had no idea that he was a police murder suspect until I saw the news.’

‘Could you take me to the spot where you saw him looking at the headstone?’

‘Of course.’

A few minutes later Kate was standing beside him in front of what appeared to be a recently erected headstone, bearing the name ‘Beatrix James.’

‘The lady was a dedicated member of my congregation,’ the clergyman explained. ‘Never missed the Eucharist or evensong services, you know, and so generous to our church too.’

‘Beatrix James,’ Kate murmured. ‘Why on earth would he be interested in her?’

'I have no idea. But at least she died in peace and from natural causes, unlike her poor sister.'

Kate raised an eyebrow. 'Why, what happened to her sister?'

He gave a sad smile. 'You would know that better than me.'

Kate looked puzzled. 'I don't follow you.'

It was his turn to look puzzled. 'Elsie Norman – your department is currently investigating her murder, aren't they?'

Kate's jaw dropped and her mind flashed back to the DCI's comment at the last briefing about possible family ties.

'Beatrix James was her sister?'

'One of four actually. I understand that they were all born in this diocese to Hector and Elizabeth Quigley – a very religious couple who lived not far from here, out on the Levels. Long since dead now, of course.'

'What do you know about them?'

'Well, all their girls were staunch Christians – their late parents saw to that – and all were married in this church by my predecessor many years before I came here. There was a son too – John, I believe he was called. Didn't worship here and I don't know a lot about him, except that he was also apparently a very committed Christian and quite rigid in his beliefs. Inherited the old Quigley house too, and continued to live there after his sisters got married and moved out. Got married himself to a nurse from down south somewhere before settling up here, I heard – Margaret or Margery somebody? Can't quite remember. Anyway, tragically, he and his wife were killed in a road accident on the A39 some years afterwards. Bad business.'

Kate's mind was working fast. 'So, who were the other two sisters?'

'Well, there was Iris Naylor and Mabel Strong, and I gather poor Mabel is now in hospital after also suffering a nasty assault, like Elsie.'

'How do you know that?'

He shrugged. 'Local radio, following the police press conference yesterday.'

'The identity of the victim would not have been revealed at that stage.'

'Ah, but news travels fast on the local grapevine, Sergeant, you should know that. I only hope poor Mabel recovers from such a dreadful ordeal. I had it in mind to visit her in hospital this evening.'

Kate grimaced. 'I'm afraid the lady died earlier today, Reverend Glover,' she said with brutal candour. 'So, your visit would have been a waste of time.'

Glover was visibly shocked. 'Mabel dead too? How absolutely awful. And she was so looking forward to her eighty-ninth birthday. Elsie told me that just a week or so ago.'

'And how come you know so much about the sisters?'

'Beatrix, as I have said, was a loyal member of our congregation, and she often brought Elsie and Mabel with her when they were visiting. I got to know the ladies very well, particularly Elsie, who became a regular here, just like Beatrix, after her sister died.'

'Can you remember whether John Quigley or any of his sisters had children – a boy perhaps?'

He shook his head.

'Two of the sisters, Elsie and Beatrix, had daughters – they were both christened at this church – and I believe John and his wife had a daughter too. Well, so one of the sisters told me. But there were no boys as far as I know.'

'And where will I find the fourth sister, Iris Naylor?'

He frowned. 'Not a clue, I'm afraid. She apparently moved out of the area after she was married – some sort of family disagreement, I believe – and I have no idea where she went. Is it important?'

Kate released her breath in a pent-up burst. 'It is, if we are to save her life,' she replied tightly.

CHAPTER 13

'So, they *were* sisters then?' Roscoe growled, following Kate's return to the incident room and her report on her interview of the Reverend Glover. 'Which means we now know the connection between the killer's two victims, and we also know he could be driving a red VW.'

He snatched the desk telephone from its cradle. 'At least that's something for the troops to be looking for.'

She held up one hand to check his move. 'I've already circulated the info, guv, so there's no need.'

He grunted. 'You *are* on the ball today,' he replied with heavy sarcasm, replacing the phone. 'I hope you're going to start making a habit of that.'

Kate ignored him and turned instead to the DCI sitting behind Roscoe's treasured desk, unable to conceal her agitation. 'It now seems obvious that our man is killing his victims one by one,' she said. 'First Elsie Norman, then Mabel Strong and, as the Grim Reaper got to Beatrix James first, Iris Naylor will be next.'

Deidrie Hennessey nodded grimly. 'And we have no idea where this Iris Naylor is right now?'

Kate shook her head. 'I checked the church records with Reverend Glover and discovered she was married to a man by the name of James Edward Naylor, but according to the vicar, who knew the other three sisters well, it seems that after living in Cheddar for a while, there was a big family row and she left the area for heaven knows where.'

'What about this man, Naylor? If he has surviving family, they might know where the couple went.'

Kate shook her head. 'Checked that too. Naylor was an only child and both his parents are long since dead.'

'John Quigley or any of the sisters have kids?'

'Only daughters, according to the Reverend Glover.'

'Brilliant,' Roscoe growled. 'So, apart from this VW and the family link between our two victims, all we've been able to establish for definite is what the pathologist told me at the PM today – in short, that Elsie Norman died from a combination of manual strangulation and a broken neck. The doc was also able to say that she had ingested a substantial amount of sherry before death, so the bastard obviously did force it down her throat. Apparently, she was probably dead before the killer finished choking her.'

'Any luck on the CCTV at the hospital regarding Mabel Strong?' Kate put in.

He shook his head. 'We've got a hazy pic of some tall bloke, walking through the hospital's main doors. He might or might not be our man, but his face is obscured by a folded newspaper he's holding up in front of him as he's passing through. All we know is that he's wearing a dark, thigh-length coat of some sort, and it's possible he is bald. Pic is of very poor quality – about time the hospital got some better kit.'

'So, nothing for us to go on?' Hennessey said.

Roscoe shrugged. 'All we can hope for is that Naylor picks up the murder of her sisters in the press and contacts us on the number we've already put out.'

Hennessey shook her head. 'Even if she sees the story, she's unlikely to appreciate the murdered women are her sisters. We cannot confirm the identities of our victims until formal identification has been made, but I've already got one of the other inquiry teams working on the job of trying to trace relatives as we speak.'

'Everyone knows who the old biddies are anyway,' Roscoe commented sourly.

The DCI frowned. 'Maybe they do, Ted, but it's a matter of procedure, as you are well aware. We need official ID first before we can officially release the names, and we have an agreement with the media that they will not publish the names of victims until that confirmation is given.'

'And meanwhile we've got another potential victim due for the chop, while we just sit here on our bleedin' arses?'

Hennessey's eyes hardened. 'We follow procedure, Inspector, is that clear?'

'Crystal,' Roscoe muttered. 'But it stinks.'

Hennessey overlooked the remark and studied Kate fixedly. 'Keep at it anyway, Sergeant. See if you can find a way of tracing her. But on another matter, how are we getting on with the journalist who reported on the Talbot Court sex abuse case?'

Kate felt her stomach muscles tighten. *Bloody Hayden*, she thought. *Still nothing from him. Too busy chasing skirt.*

'DC Lewis has been working on that, ma'am,' she said blithely. 'I am seeing him later for a full progress report.'

Hennessey continued to stare at her for a moment, as if trying to make up her mind about something. But as Kate inwardly squirmed under her gaze, sensing that the DCI suspected she was feeding her a line and was about to follow up with further embarrassing questions she couldn't answer, the telephone shrilled urgently.

'Yeah,' Roscoe barked into the mouthpiece, then noticeably stiffened, adding, 'Got it. On my way.'

He slammed the phone back on its cradle. 'Control room,' he snapped, grabbing his pork-pie hat from the corner of the desk. 'Plods have found a car dumped in a lake on the Levels.' His eyes gleamed. 'A red VW Beetle.'

*

The Volkswagen was already out of the water and being loaded on to a low-loader when Roscoe and Kate arrived on the scene. A couple of uniformed Traffic officers were standing by their patrol car, watching the operation with mild interest and one, a woman inspector, extricated her once shiny shoes from the mud of the lake shore and met them halfway up the steep slope leading to the main road.

'Couple of walkers saw part of the roof just below the surface,' she explained, 'and reported it on one of their mobile phones.'

She glanced back at the car and grinned. 'Don't know why anyone would want to nick a heap like that anyway.'

'Maybe just a psychopathic killer,' Roscoe retorted drily.

The inspector was obviously taken aback by his comment. 'Control never said,' she responded apologetically. 'They just told us to wait here when we called it in.'

Roscoe stuffed some chewing gum into his mouth and began chewing, his eyes darting quickly over the scene, missing nothing. 'RO check?' he continued.

The inspector nodded and produced her pocket book, flicking to the back page. 'A Dr Emrys Jones,' she said. 'Address up north. But no report of it being stolen.'

Kate quickly took down the information in her own pocket book. 'Thanks,' she said. 'We'll have the address checked out.'

'No need,' the inspector replied. 'I've already asked the control room to contact the relevant force and get someone round to see the owner—'

'Walkers see anything or anyone?' Roscoe cut in.

The other shook her head. 'No, just the bit of roof sticking out of the water. The car was probably dumped there a while ago.'

'Anything interesting in it?' Kate asked.

The inspector grinned again. 'Well, no stiffs, if that's what you were thinking, but we haven't gone over it thoroughly yet. We'll do that when we get it back to the garage.'

Kate nodded. 'I'll take a quick look now,' she said, seeing that the car had been fully loaded on to the truck.

'Your prerogative, but you'll find it a bit wet.'

Wet was not the word for it. The car was still streaming with water when Kate climbed up on to the trailer, and a glance through a window told her that a search, even a cursory one, was out of the question until it had had a chance of drying out.

'Satisfied?' the inspector asked with another grin when Kate returned to where she and Roscoe were still standing.

'Well, we have the car,' Kate replied grimly, her gaze roving around the lake and the sparse woodland on the far side. 'But that's a long way from finding its former driver.'

*

George had a problem and it was Iris Naylor. So far everything had gone more or less according to plan. Two of the lesser harridans had been dispatched – although the premature demise of Beatrix James had been a big disappointment – and there was just one more to go. The most important of the odious quartet. The trouble was, that particular one was Iris Naylor and she had long since vanished into the blue, apparently leaving no forwarding address. Even Elsie had claimed she'd no idea where her sister could have gone. Big family bust-up apparently many years before. Maybe Iris was already dead, just like Beatrix, or had gone to live abroad – bloody hell, hopefully not! But wherever it was she had disappeared to, finding her looked like being a real challenge and George was only too painfully aware that there wasn't much time left to finish things before the Grim Reaper came for the very person who had been helping him increase his quota of departed souls.

Sitting at the kitchen table of the farmhouse that had now been so permanently 'vacated' by the previous owners, Patient 174 tried to work out how Iris Naylor could be traced. Making even discreet inquiries at such places as the local church or county rating office was out of the question, as that would almost certainly arouse unwanted curiosity and could ultimately lead to police interest. No, there had to be another way of doing things that could be achieved quietly and unobtrusively – but what? That was the point.

Think, think, think. There had to be a way. Father always used to say that there was a solution to every problem. It just needed to be teased out of the old grey matter. George's face twisted into a malevolent sneer at the thought of the cold-hearted religious freak who had made one innocent child's life such a total misery. All well and good for *Daddy* to come out with one of his pearls of wisdom, but there again, that evil bastard had had a lot to say about everything, and most of it had been pure crap anyway.

George poured another glass of whisky from the bottle that had been left on the Welsh dresser by the late farmer and sipped from it thoughtfully, trying hard to shut out the sound of the dog in one of the sheds outside, barking its head off. In the absence of any brilliant ideas, there was only one course of action that could be taken – a bit of old-fashioned burglary. Maybe somewhere in either Elsie Norman or Mabel Strong's bungalow there was an address or telephone number of the estranged sister. It was risky returning to either of the crime scenes and certainly very much of a long shot that it would turn anything up, but what other option was there?

Downing the whisky, George glanced out of the window and then at the watch on his wrist. It would be a few hours before it was dark, which was the best time for nefarious operations like this. But there was no rush, and in the meantime, that dratted barking dog could be dealt with once and for all. The psychopath smiled mercilessly at the thought and threw a glance at the double-barrelled 12-bore shotgun on the hooks above the range cooker before pouring yet another whisky in the lead crystal glass.

*

Kate tracked down Hayden to the office of the Local Intelligence Officer. The LIO was out and she cornered her husband before he could leave, determined to have it out with him.

'I want a word with you, Hayd,' she said.

To her surprise he simply shrugged. 'I know you do,' he said, 'but not now.'

'What do you mean not now?'

He thrust an A4 sheet of paper under her nose. 'I've traced Leslie Brookes, the reporter, but it's a fair distance from here.'

Thrown by this new development, Kate hesitated for a second, then snatched the piece of paper and glanced at the hastily scribbled notes.

'Minehead?' she said.

He nodded. 'I said it was a fair distance from here – around an hour from Highbridge by my reckoning.'

'Byways?'

'I gather it's a residential home.'

'He's in a *home*?'

'Apparently so. Alzheimer's, it seems.'

'Damn! Then he'll be no good to us.'

'I'm told it's in the early stages.'

'Who told you that?'

'It's a long story. I've been through so many people, but I finally managed to get hold of an ex-colleague of his, who gave me the SP.'

'That will get the noses of half of Fleet Street twitching.'

He shook his head. 'It won't. I was very discreet. Said I was an independent hack following up on an old story he did about the floods on the Somerset Levels. Pretty boring stuff.'

'Good work.'

'Thanks.'

Kate took a deep breath, all thoughts of tackling Hayden about his 'other woman' temporarily dismissed from her mind.

'I'll drive,' she said, 'but we'd better let the guv'nor know where we're going first.'

CHAPTER 14

Byways was a big, white building, sitting grandly among neat landscaped gardens in a side street not far from Minehead's railway station. Kate pulled up in the car park, tense and irritable.

Forced to use her own car to get to the hospital, then claim back the mileage costs later as no CID pool car had been available, she had found the tight squeeze sitting alongside Hayden in the limited confines of the Mazda MX5 particularly awkward, to say the least, and for the first half hour not a word was spoken by either of them. Then quite suddenly both Kate and Hayden tried to break through the tense atmosphere at the same time with blurted comments that they failed to finish, putting paid to any further conversation for a while longer.

Kate finally managed to open things up again as they were passing Dunster Castle.

'I wanted to talk to you about us,' she said as she braked for a slow-moving car in front, which suddenly chose to turn left towards the town at the last minute, without a signal.

'There's nothing to talk about,' Hayden replied.

She cast him a sideways glance as she accelerated away. 'We have to,' she said. 'I want to know what's going on.'

'Nothing is going on – nothing for you to worry about anyway.'

'That's not good enough.'

'It's going to have to do until I can sort things out.'

'What *things*?'

'I'm not able to say.'

Kate lost her cool completely. 'Not able to—?' she ejaculated without finishing the sentence and swerving as she glared across at him. 'I'm your bloody wife!'

'Would you mind keeping your eyes on the road, old girl?' he said, tensing in his seat. 'I'd like to get to Minehead in one piece.'

'I want to know who you are shagging, Hayd,' she persisted in a tone pent-up with emotion and once more swerved slightly in the road.

A car coming the other way blasted them and Hayden gripped the edges of his seat with both hands.

'I wish you weren't so crude,' he said. 'It's totally unnecessary.'

'Don't change the subject, Hayd. You're seeing someone behind my back and I want to know who it is.'

'It's not what you think.'

'Then what is it?'

'I can't go into it just now.'

'Then you can find somewhere else to sleep tonight until you decide *to* go into it. I don't want you anywhere near me.'

'It's my cottage.'

'Okay, then *I'll* find somewhere else to sleep, you moron. Maybe I'll pick up some guy with a nice flat.'

'Now you're being stupid. You've simply put two and two together and made five.'

She swung into a layby and hauled on the handbrake.

'Have I? Then correct my arithmetic by telling me the truth.'

He stared straight ahead through the windscreen, avoiding her gaze. 'I can't tell you anything just now, but you've got it all wrong.'

It was on the tip of her tongue to tell him she had found out about the girl in the Loft Hotel, but she thought better of it.

'I found lipstick on your shirt collar and the thing reeked of perfume,' she accused. 'I also got a phone call from some little bitch asking for you – what am I expected to think?'

He took a deep breath. 'You have to trust me, that's all.'

She gave a shaky, humourless laugh. 'Oh, that's what I've got to do, is it, just trust you?'

'Why wouldn't you?'

'You mean why the bloody hell would I?'

She slammed the car into gear and pulled away with a shriek of tyres, but Hayden made no further comment. He was too terrified by her driving to say anything.

A smiling carer in a neat blue uniform met them in the foyer of Byways with the usual 'Can I help you?' approach and five minutes later they were in the expansive lounge, being guided to a winged armchair by the window with the warning that 'Poor old Les' was in the early stages of Alzheimer's and 'apt to wander mentally'.

The elderly man in the slightly rumpled cardigan and grey flannels put down his cup of tea on the chair arm to peer up at them as they approached and frowned when the carer swung two smaller chairs round to face him.

'Couple of police officers to see you, Les,' she said and, nodding to the two detectives, walked briskly away as they sat down.

Kate found herself studying a pale, lined face with watery blue eyes that met her gaze curiously from under a mop of thinning grey hair.

'Police?' Brookes asked in a soft voice, smoothing his small moustache with the index finger of one hand. 'Well, you've finally got me.' He held out his thin wrists in front of them. 'Just put the bracelets on.'

Kate smiled back. 'We'll let you off this time, Mr Brookes,' she said, humouring him. 'But don't do it again.'

'Don't do it ag … don't do it again?' he chortled as he reached for his cup with one trembling hand and took a noisy sip. 'That's classic.'

Then he set his cup back on the chair arm, suddenly curious. 'So, how can I help you, Miss … er—.'

'DS Kate Lewis and DC Hayden Lewis, Mr Brookes,' she replied.

He raised his eyebrows. 'The Lewis duo, eh?' he said. 'Keeping it in the family, are you?'

Kate smiled. 'We are here to tap your memory, Mr Brookes.'

He seemed to deflate. 'Memory?' he muttered. 'What memory? Most of it's gone now.'

She paused a moment. 'You were a reporter once, remember that?' she went on. 'You carried out a sexual abuse inquiry at a place called Talbot Court.'

He thought for a moment and then his eyes gleamed. 'Now there's a blast from the past,' he replied. 'Can of worms, that one was. You reinvestigating it?'

'Not exactly, but it's very relevant to a current murder inquiry we are conducting. What can you tell us about it?'

He shook his head, his expression sombre. 'Never really managed to get to the bottom of that business. Just scratched the surface. Not allowed to, you see. Too many people in high places involved. Buggers shut down everything.'

Then abruptly the light seemed to go out of his eyes and his face changed, exhibiting confusion.

'Who are you?' he asked suddenly. 'What are you doing here?'

Kate started, thrown by the unexpected question and the sudden change in his demeanour.

'We're police officers,' Hayden said gently, immediately cottoning on to the problem. 'You were telling us about Talbot Court.'

Brookes shook his head. 'Don't know what you're talking about. Why are you asking me?'

Kate followed Hayden's example. 'It happened many years ago,' she encouraged. 'You were a reporter and you investigated a child sex abuse inquiry at an orphanage called Talbot Court.'

The old man's face twisted into a heavy frown and he pressed the bridge of his nose between his finger and thumb.

'Talbot Court,' he said slowly. 'Yes, I did, didn't I? There was a fire, I think, and the place burned down. Principal took off. I found him somewhere. Can't remember where—'

He brightened. 'There was a stabbing, that was it. Some kid got sent down for killing a teacher. Can't recall the poor little bugger's name either.' He shook his head irritably. 'The kid, not the teacher, I mean. Teacher wasn't a poor little bugger at all. He was touching the kids up, wasn't he? Dirty—'

He broke off. 'Have they offered you tea?'

Kate took a deep breath. 'Yes, Mr Brookes, they've offered us tea, but we didn't want any. Now, can you remember the name of the child who was sent down?'

His face went blank again. 'Down? Who was sent down – where?'

'Talbot Court?' she encouraged. 'The stabbing? You investigated it—'

'Bad business, you know,' he cut in, suddenly back on track. 'I reckon that the Principal or one of the others started the fire to get rid of all the evidence. Nothing left, you see,' and he tapped his forehead with the index finger of one hand, 'but it's all up here, you know. Filed away.'

Yet another frown. 'They're a long time with your tea. You might get a cake if you're lucky.' He straightened up and stared around the room. 'Nurse, where's that tea?' he shouted.

Kate clenched her fists tightly in her lap. So near and yet so far. She mentally forced herself to count to ten.

'Do you remember George?' Hayden said quietly. 'You must remember George?'

'George?' Brookes echoed, his eyes sharpening again. 'Mad, you know. Only a kid, but mad nevertheless. Someone said the father and his sisters – the aunts – made the kid like that too. Religion at the back of it. Bible-bashers, the lot of 'em – just like their father had been before them. Turned the youngster into a maladjusted freak.'

Kate felt the hair on the back of her neck stand up.

'Who were these aunts, Les?' Hayden asked. 'Can you remember their names? Was one of them called Elsie?'

Brookes nodded. 'Think that was her, but she was the weak one – just went along with what the others said. Iris, though, she was something else. Hard case, that one. Bloody solicitor too.'

He leaned forward. 'She persuaded the other sisters to have George put into the orphanage when the parents were killed in that car crash, you know. Said the youngster was too unruly and had to be put away. I reckon money was at the back of it – some sort of inheritance.'

He shook his head sadly. 'Once in Talbot Court, George became cannon fodder, see? Grace – yes, that was his name – offered the poor mite up to his bigwig friends on party nights. Politicians, judges, councillors, all the bent ones got invites to Talbot to sample one of Grace's treats. Couldn't prove it, though. Too many powerful people implicated. Got shut down.'

He yawned. 'Bit tired. Need my nap.'

Kate tried to tease more out of him, conscious of the fact that she was running out of time.

'Do you remember George's surname, Les?' she asked. 'It's very important.'

He frowned again. 'George? I don't know any George. There's good old George Formby, of course. Liked his old songs. Good entertainer, he was. Before my time, though.'

The carer materialized at Kate's elbow.

'Sorry, Sergeant, but I must call a halt to the questioning now. Les needs his medication and some sleep.'

Kate nodded. 'Just a couple more minutes, then we'll be gone.'

She leaned forward towards Brookes. 'Les, do you remember where George went after the murder trial?'

Brookes squeezed his nose again with finger and thumb. 'George?' he repeated slowly. 'Put away, wasn't he? Can't quite recall why …'

'Where did George go, Les, can you remember that?'

Brookes looked up at her. Suddenly his eyes were alert and focused as the clouds briefly cleared from his brain.

'One of them juvenile detention places, I was told – youth units or something—'

'You mean a young offenders' institution?'

'Yes, that sounds about right. Didn't last long there, though. Crazy kid attacked another person and got sent to some hospital or other. Call them secure units now, you know, or special hospitals. Still nuthouses in my book, though. That's where George went – some special hospital.'

He sighed. 'Mad, you know,' he went on, repeating what he had said earlier. 'Stabbed someone – a teacher, I think – after being abused. I investigated the case. I was a journalist, you see. Got shut down, though.'

'I'm afraid that will have to do,' the carer interjected again. 'Come on, Les, time for your sleep. I'll give you a hand up.'

'The name of the hospital, Les?' Kate persisted desperately. 'Surely you can remember that?'

'That's quite enough for one day,' the carer said sternly, as she assisted the old man to his feet. 'He's confused as it is.'

Kate and Hayden had to watch helplessly as Brookes was led away, muttering about not having had his tea.

'Bugger it!' Kate breathed. 'Back to square one.'

'And we haven't even been offered a cup of tea,' Hayden added, mimicking Brookes.

Kate glared at him. 'Shut it, Hayden,' she said. 'Or I'll leave you here and you can walk back.'

CHAPTER 15

Roscoe was finishing off a chicken madras from a silver foil takeaway dish when Kate and Hayden walked back into the SIO's office. Unsurprisingly, there was no sign of DCI Hennessey amid the 'fumes.'

Kate sniffed disapprovingly as she was hit by the powerful odour of the curry when she pushed the door open.

Roscoe had a pint of beer beside the dish containing the remains of his curry, and he took a swig from the bottle before picking up the foil dish and dropping it into the wastepaper bin beside his desk.

'So, the prodigals return,' he growled, sitting back in the swivel chair behind the desk usually occupied by Hennessey, trying to pick his teeth with the thin handle of the plastic spoon supplied with his dinner. 'About time. So, what have you got?'

'Not a lot,' Kate replied. 'Brookes has Alzheimer's, which means his memory is patchy.'

'How patchy?'

Kate told him all that the reporter had said and the DI scowled his disapproval. 'Sod all then really?' he commented.

Hayden frowned. 'Not entirely, guv'nor,' he retorted. 'We know a lot more about the background to this business than we did.'

Roscoe studied him for a moment, his boot-button eyes registering nothing.

'Which still amounts to sweet FA,' he said. 'We're already pretty sure this arsehole is named George and that he's a nutter, and we've already surmised that he was probably an inmate at Talbot Court, who was sexually abused and stiffed his abuser.'

'We didn't know until now that he was committed to one of the old YOIs after the stabbing and then ended up in a mental hospital,' Kate threw back at him.

Roscoe leaned forward across the desk, his gaze hard and uncompromising.

'But we still don't know the bastard's name, do we?' he grated. 'And if you had tried just a little bit harder with Brookes, we might have managed to get it.'

He slumped back in his chair and waved Kate to silence as the angry protest started to form on her lips.

'Okay, okay, I'm out of order,' he said in an unusually contrite tone. 'You did your best, I know, but we seem to keep heading into one blind alley after another. It turns out that inquiries to trace the RO of the VW Beetle dumped in the lake – an Emrys David Jones apparently, from some village up north – have also drawn a blank. The car has never been reported stolen, but Jones is apparently on holiday, believed to be fishing somewhere in Scotland. None of his neighbours seem to know where he has gone, so we can't confirm anything. I've now called out an underwater search unit team to check that his body is not lying at the bottom of the lake where his car was found.'

Kate made a grimace at the thought. 'It's possible that his car has nothing to do with our case, though,' she said. 'Maybe the vicar I interviewed about the intruder in the church cemetery got it wrong and the car he saw was not a Beetle at all. Could be the VW we recovered was simply stolen from Jones' home while he was away and that the culprit was just some dipstick who nicked it to get back to Somerset.'

'So why would the RO go on his hols and leave his car behind?'

'Perhaps he went to Scotland with a friend in their car or he travelled up by train? Anything's possible.'

Roscoe thought about that for a few seconds and gave a curt nod. 'True, anything *is* possible,' he agreed, his usual pugnacious attitude reasserting itself. 'It's also possible that Lord Lucan is still alive and living in a house in Bath.'

Before Kate or Hayden could think of a suitable retort, he stood up and disentangled his jacket from the back of his chair.

'Anyway, I've had enough for today, so I'm off for a pint down the road. Either of you feel like joining me?'

Kate hesitated, her thoughts once more returning to Hayden's infidelity and regurgitating the acid that had been swirling around in her stomach all day at the prospect of having to go home again.

'Only if you're buying, guv,' she replied.

'What about you, Fangio?' Roscoe barked.

Hayden flushed. 'I … I think I'll have an early night, if you don't mind,' he replied lamely.

Roscoe nodded. 'As you wish,' he said, 'and there's me thinking you two were joined at the hip.'

Not anymore, Kate mused bitterly, *not anymore*.

*

The dark figure had remained motionless behind the wheel of the old Land Rover ever since parking up in the alleyway, which ran along the backs of the bungalows forming the cul-de-sac. The strange, dead eyes that had so unnerved Mabel Strong's carer, Dawn Frobisher, had been fixed rigidly on Elsie Norman's bungalow for at least half an hour – watching for the slightest movement or sign of life. Finally, satisfied that the police had not left anyone there to guard the place, George climbed out of the vehicle and headed through the moonlit shadows to the rear gate.

The pane in the kitchen door of the bungalow shattered with a single blow from one gloved fist, and it took only a moment to reach inside and turn the key that had been conveniently left in the lock.

George well remembered the kitchen. Well remembered creeping up behind Elsie Norman when she went to make her visitor a cup of tea after their little chat in the sitting room about her sisters. Well remembered seizing the old woman by the hair and forcing her to her creaking knees before spinning her over on to her back and pinning her down. Well remembered staring into her face as the bottle of sherry was forced into her mouth, reading the terror in her eyes and hearing the delicious sound of her choking on the stuff. Well remembered finally gripping her by the throat and finishing her off with the thumbs of both hands pressed with extreme force against her windpipe, and the ecstatic moment when those hands felt the feeble struggles cease as the life went out of her.

Disappointing that the old girl hadn't realized who her caller really was until it was too late, but age, failing eyesight, and the passage of time had no doubt made that inevitable. Anyway, George had made sure she'd known the identity of her executioner just before she'd choked her last, made sure she'd gone to her Maker knowing that her sins had finally caught up with her – which for Patient 174 was the most satisfying part of it all.

Now, however, the priority was to find out where Iris Naylor had gone and that meant a thorough search of the bungalow for any note, address book or scrap of paper that might provide the necessary information. The search would have to be meticulous, of course, but there was plenty of time for that, wasn't there? The whole night if necessary. After all, who would ever suspect that Elsie Norman's killer would be brazen enough to return to the scene of the crime – and so soon afterwards?

That was probably true, but Fate can be notoriously fickle and, unbeknown to George, time was already running out. An inquisitive pair of eyes had witnessed the arrival of the intruder and for a while they continued to watch from behind part-closed curtains as the narrow beam of George's torch went slowly from room to room. Then finally, a hand picked up a telephone handset from its cradle and dialled 999.

*

'Okay, so what gives?' Roscoe growled, turning to Kate sitting beside him on the stool in one of the DI's local hostelries.

Kate took a sip from the glass of red wine he had bought her and cast him a puzzled glance.

'What gives?' she echoed. 'I don't know what you're talking about.'

He stared into his frothy pint, then studied her critically for a moment. 'You and that husband of yours,' he said. 'What's going on?'

She started, her stomach lurching. Damn! Was their problem that obvious?

'Nothing's "going on", as you put it,' she lied.

He took a long pull on his pint, then set it down and wiped off the residue clinging to his moustache with the back of one muscular hand.

'Do you think I'm stupid?' he said, staring at her intently.

She forced a grin. 'Not stupid, guv,' she replied, 'but a pain in the arse sometimes – with respect, of course.'

His expression didn't change. 'I haven't been a copper for nearly thirty years not to notice when things are out of sync,' he persisted. 'You two having problems?'

She flared suddenly. 'That's my business,' she snapped back.

He was undeterred. 'No, it bloody well isn't,' he retorted, 'not when it affects your job.'

'My personal life has never affected my job.'

'Maybe not yet, but I can see trouble brewing on the horizon.'

'Like what?'

'Like your mind isn't fully focused on what you are supposed to be doing and sooner or later you're going to cock up. You're not with us half the time, woman – I can read it in your eyes – and what was that crap Hayden came out with just now about having an early night? When have you ever known him to turn down the offer of a pint? The body language said it all. You two were behaving like a pair of stiff-legged dogs, circling each other before taking a bite.'

Her hand was noticeably trembling as she gulped some more wine and she was conscious of tears welling up in her eyes. She turned her head away from him.

'It's … it's nothing, guv, honestly,' she said. 'Just a spat, that's all.'

'Bollocks!' he snarled. 'Don't try that one on me. It's a lot more than that. But if you two *are* having a problem, I need to know about it.'

The tears were trickling down her cheeks now and, left with no alternative, she jerked a handkerchief from her pocket and dried her eyes, aware of the barman at the end of the counter casting curious glances in her direction.

Roscoe leaned towards her and she felt his hand on her arm as his tone suddenly became uncharacteristically sympathetic.

'Another woman, is it?' he asked. 'Been playing away, has he?'

She gave a quick shake of her head. 'I don't know,' she replied huskily. 'Please, just … just leave it, will you?'

'I know you see me as an insensitive prick who's always on your back,' he went on, 'but I'm not the person you think I am and if I can help in any way, you only have to ask.'

She swallowed hard and dabbed her cheeks again with her handkerchief, then turned her face briefly in his direction, once more forcing a smile.

'Thanks, guv, but there's nothing anyone else can do. It's between the two of us.'

'Would you like me to have a word in his shell-like?'

She froze, her eyes widening.

'No, please – definitely not. That would only make things worse.'

'What about a few days off then to give you some time to sort it all out? I'm sure I can persuade the DCI to agree to—'

'No!' she cut in, more sharply than she had intended, then added more evenly, 'Look, no, thank you. I want to see this inquiry through to the end.'

He grunted and straightened up, draining the rest of his beer in the manner of a man dying of thirst.

'As you wish,' he said in a heavier tone. 'But if the pair of you *are* to continue, I need a hundred percent commitment. No distractions from what we're here to do. Understand?'

She gulped the rest of her wine and nodded. 'Totally, guv. You have my word on it.'

His familiar wolfish grin was back. 'Good. Now, having got that out of the way, you can buy *me* a drink this time – and it's a double Scotch.'

CHAPTER 16

The female cleaner wrinkled her nose in disgust at the sweet, nauseating smell hanging in the air like a poisonous miasma. Rose Nicholls had been at the Larchfield Secure Psychiatric Hospital for five years now and looking after Dr Emrys Jones' small consulting room – cleaning the place and emptying the wastepaper bin in the evening twice a week – had always been part of her duties. On this occasion, she'd been told that the good doctor had gone on holiday, leaving the flat assigned to him when he was on cover duty locked up, so she hadn't expected to have much to do when she dragged her vacuum into the consulting room, but the smell in the place really bothered her. It was almost as if something – a rat maybe – had died and was rotting away somewhere behind the skirting boards. Yet the strange thing was, the smell seemed to be emanating from the flat itself, which she had no access to. Most peculiar.

In the end, unable to stand it any longer, she went to find one of the security officers and left him with the problem. 'You might need to call out a pest control officer,' she advised him, 'unless it's the drains again.'

But Terry Bradley didn't need to do any such thing. When he finally managed to open the door of the flat with his skeleton key, it immediately became apparent that the smell had nothing to do with a dead rat or a blocked drain, and at the same time it also became apparent that Dr Jones was not away on a fishing trip, as the hospital had been led to believe. In fact, the psychiatrist was still there, in his private quarters, but his corpse was showing definite signs of degeneration and the pencil projecting from his right eye-socket indicated that he had certainly not died from natural causes.

*

Kate was reluctant to leave the bar she had gone to with Roscoe, since that meant having to return home to Hayden, and she did her best to try to delay the inevitable for as long as possible. As a result, she consumed more red wine than was advisable and by the time the DI dropped her back at the police station she was developing a nasty headache. To make matters worse, it was only after she had climbed into her car – blatantly ignoring the fact that she had to be well over the alcohol limit – and was a couple of miles down the main road, that the disembodied voice which suddenly joined her in the car reminded her that the TETRA police radio she should have returned to the station at the end of her tour of duty was still in the long pocket of the leather coat she had dumped on the front passenger seat beside her.

But the lapse paled into insignificance with the message being broadcast by the control room operator.

'*Burglary in progress. Any mobile able to attend …*'

She didn't wait to hear the full address. She already knew it. She had been there before, following the murder of Elsie Norman. Disentangling the radio from the lining of her pocket and clutching it in her left hand and the steering wheel in her right as she gunned the little car to well over 70mph, she acknowledged with her call-sign and confirmed that she was on her way. But there was a sting in the tail.

'Single crewed,' she added breathlessly. 'Request back-up.'

'*Negative at present,*' the operator replied after a brief pause. '*All other units committed.*'

'Great!' she muttered cynically to herself, remembering having to respond to similar 'shouts' on her own in the recent past and wondering why this sort of thing always seemed to happen to her.

But there was nothing she could do about it – it was just sod's law – and she could only hope that another unit would be freed up by the time she got to Elsie Norman's home.

She was out of luck, though, and when she finally pulled in on the opposite side of the road to the former crime scene, extinguishing the lights of her car as she did so, she saw just an empty, moonlit street in front of her.

For a moment she sat there, studying the chalet bungalow through narrowed eyes, but the place was in darkness – not even the faintest glimmer of a torch showing in either of the front windows. The driver's window was partially open and she listened intently. A dog barked from one of the bungalows further down the street, but otherwise there wasn't a sound, save for the ticking of the Mazda's hot engine.

Then, quite suddenly, her radio barked, shattering the silence, and with an oath she snatched it from the front seat and switched it off. Damn it! She should have thought about that and silenced the thing before her arrival, but the damage was done now. She could only hope that the sound of it had not been picked up outside the car or if it had, it had not been recognized as a police radio.

Very carefully she opened the car door and stepped out, her torch in her hand. Then, closing the door with equal care, she walked quickly across the street to the opposite pavement. The dog was barking again and she heard the faint sound of music coming from one of the other adjacent properties. The gate to the chalet bungalow stood wide open and, slipping through, she resisted the temptation to run for the cover of the porch. Instead, she walked slowly and as quietly as possible up the concrete path to the bay window, which jutted out to her left.

The curtains had been pulled across, so she was unable to see into the room that lay beyond. She pressed her ear against the window, closing her eyes to concentrate on her sense of hearing – a trick she had learned from an old sweat during her probationary constable days – but she could detect no sound of movement inside.

She had seen on her approach that the bay window on the other side of the porch was also curtained, so made no effort to check it out, but instead headed down the side of the house along the narrow passage that led to the back door. She found the smashed window in the door immediately, her feet crunching on the broken glass before she picked out the shards glittering in the moonlight.

She tried the door and felt it give. Gritting her teeth, she pushed it open, waiting for the creak of hinges, which never came. She forced herself to stand still for a few seconds. Silence, but her sixth-sense told her that she was not alone. Her straining eyes failed to pick out any sinister figures lurking among the shadows, but something told her that someone else was there, in the bungalow, maybe someone who had detected her arrival and was standing motionless somewhere in the gloom.

Common sense dictated a quick withdrawal. Perhaps the intruder was just some opportunist tearaway, capitalizing on Elsie Norman's death and simply breaking in to steal whatever he could find? A no-account tea leaf, who was likely to make off as soon as he realized he had been sussed? On the other hand, this could be an entirely different kind of villain. A nasty thug or deranged junkie perhaps, who had no intention of taking to his heels, but would stand his ground, come what may. If that were the case, she could be running the risk of a violent confrontation that could end very badly for her. But she had never been a quitter and her inherent stubbornness, coupled with an adrenalin-fuelled determination to 'feel someone's collar', overruled any fears she might otherwise have had for her own safety.

Gripping her heavy torch in one hand – and cursing her negligence in leaving her police issue CS gas spray in her drawer in the CID office – she advanced a few cautious steps across the kitchen to the inner door and paused again, her heart thumping and her eyes searching the gloomy hallway.

Then, satisfied that there was no one hiding there, she stepped through the doorway and turned to check the half-closed door on her left, directing the beam of the torch into the room on the other side. It proved to be a bathroom and toilet, and was too small for anyone to use as a hiding place.

Next to this room was another much smaller door and she found it accessed an airing cupboard, complete with slatted shelves over a copper hot-water tank. Nowhere to hide in there either, she mused grimly, pushing the door to.

On the same side of the hallway, just beyond the staircase, she found a dining room, furnished with a long table and chairs, an old-fashioned sideboard, and some sort of glass-fronted cabinet containing porcelain figurines. Again, there was no sign of anyone inside.

Conscious of the fact that she was trembling, she crossed to the opposite side of the hallway, pausing for a second to pluck up courage before pushing another door open with the butt of her torch. She glimpsed the settee and two armchairs of a neat sitting room, but only briefly, for the next instant she heard the sound of footsteps overhead. The intruder was in one of the bedrooms under the eaves.

Quickly switching off her torch, she shrank back into the shadows as a beam of light illuminated the stairway from above and she heard the creak of the risers. Whoever had broken into the bungalow was now on his way down from the upper floor, but his unhurried, clomping steps suggested he was, as yet, unaware of her presence and saw no need for speed or stealth.

She tensed as a tall, thin figure dressed in a dark coat stepped into view. But on the point of springing from the shadows to challenge him, she froze as the figure suddenly turned towards the kitchen. There was a mirror on the wall beside the kitchen door, facing down the hall towards the front of the bungalow, which briefly reflected not only the beam of his torch but also the face of the person holding it. In its glare the completely bald head and single glittering earring were unmistakable. This was no opportunist tea leaf or spaced-out junkie, but none other than the ruthless psychotic murderer half the force was currently looking for.

Taken aback by the killer's sheer audacity in returning to Elsie Norman's home, Kate stared after the retreating figure with a sense of shock. What the hell had drawn him back to the scene of his brutal crime? Curiosity? To gloat? Or was there a more sinister reason? Like maybe to search for an address or any other information that might reveal the whereabouts of Iris Naylor?

Whatever the reason, Kate was now presented with a terrible dilemma and, as she finally managed to shake herself out of her shocked reverie and stumble after her quarry, the question was burning in her brain; what could she possibly do on her own? As a police officer, she had a duty to try to make an arrest, but knowing she was up against someone who had already killed twice and from her own experience had shown himself to be a powerful antagonist, the likelihood of her being able to overpower him was virtually zero – and George was unlikely to throw his hands up in the air and say 'It's a fair cop.'

There was no sign of the killer when she got to the end of the short garden and stopped to peer out of the open gateway into the lane that lay beyond. At first, she thought her dilemma had been resolved for her and she had lost him. But in the act of reaching for her radio, she saw an old Land Rover Defender with a light-coloured canvas hood parked a few yards away and caught a glimpse of the tall figure climbing in behind the wheel.

Without thinking, she lurched forwards at a trot and managed to reach the rear of the vehicle just as the Land Rover's lights came on. As the gears were noisily engaged and it began to pull away, she sprang for the tailboard and hauled herself up over it. Only when she had landed among the pile of hessian sacks that the back of the vehicle contained did the thought suddenly occur to her – what if the killer had spotted her climbing aboard in his rear-view mirror? She studied the back of the cab in the gloom and made a grimace. Well, it was too late to worry about that now and whether she liked it or not, she was going wherever George chose to take her. It was then that she checked her pocket and found she must have dropped her police radio in the lane and, not for the first time, had also left her personal mobile in her car.

*

Ted Roscoe was about to climb into bed in his small flat when the telephone rang. Muttering curses under his breath, he lifted the handset and snarled an answer.

'What?'

'*Highbridge control room, guv,*' the caller replied. '*We have an incident in progress.*'

Roscoe shook his head quickly to try and clear the fug that had developed after the two double whiskies he had downed following his visit to the bar with Kate Lewis.

'What sort of incident?' he retorted.

'*DS Lewis, guv,*' the operator continued. '*She's gone missing.*'

'Missing? What the hell do you mean by that?'

'*She attended an "intruders-on-premises" shout an hour ago and didn't call in afterwards.*'

Roscoe's anger almost boiled over. 'I dropped her off at the nick earlier tonight and she was to go home. What the hell was she doing attending anything?'

The operator remained calm. '*She responded to an intruders-on-premises call, but failed to report back afterwards. We sent back-up to the address, but though the team found her sports car parked in the street outside, she was nowhere to be seen, and her radio was later found lying in a lane at the rear of the place. There's an intensive search underway as we speak.*'

Roscoe was fully compos mentis now. 'But surely you didn't send her there on her own?' he exclaimed, reaching for his trousers and shirt which he had draped over a chair beside the bed.

'*All other units were committed at the time,*' came the slightly defensive reply.

The DI practically exploded. 'Bloody hell, then she could have walked into almost anything,' he fumed. 'Give me the address.'

And it was when the operator passed on those details that Roscoe started to feel really sick.

CHAPTER 17

Kate was a lot more than uncomfortable in the back of the Land Rover. George's standard of driving was about as accomplished as a teenage novice on their first lesson, with noisy lurching gear changes and sudden heavy braking that could have rivalled Ted Roscoe's worst efforts. As a result, she was forced to cling to the tailboard of the vehicle to avoid being tossed about from one side to the other like a straw bale.

So far it did not seem likely that her unintentional abductor was aware she was on board and it was at first unclear where they were actually heading. But their destination did not remain a mystery for long. When the Land Rover slowed right down to turn into a suburban side street twenty minutes later, she was at last able to let go of the tailboard, slide across to one side of the vehicle and lift up part of the canvas soft top for a quick look. At once recognition dawned and she knew exactly where they were going – to Mabel Strong's home address.

She guessed George was aiming to break into the dead woman's bungalow in much the same way as Elsie Norman's place. She had already suspected that; he *had* to be after Iris Naylor's address and now, having drawn a blank at the first crime scene, he had obviously decided to try the second. Why else would he risk capture by returning to both scenes so soon after the murders? But whatever his motives actually were, this time they were thwarted by circumstances he obviously had not foreseen. As they drove past the bungalow, Kate glimpsed a police area car parked outside the property and a uniformed figure standing at the lighted sitting room window, staring out into the street.

She smiled grimly in the gloom, remembering that Roscoe had insisted on the latest crime scene being kept secure until the SOCO team had had the opportunity of carrying out a further forensic sweep in daylight. *You're out of luck, this time, George. So, what will your next move be? Slink back to your grubby bolt-hole to try and work out what to do next?*

As it turned out, she had hit the nail right on the head. Speeding away from the bungalow, the Land Rover headed deeper into the Levels, finally turning into a narrow, rutted track off a back road a few miles from Glastonbury. About a quarter of a mile further on, the vehicle came to an abrupt halt on a concrete hardstanding.

Kate quickly burrowed into the sacks, pulling some of them over herself, just in case George decided to take a look in the back for some reason. But it didn't happen and moments later she heard the killer climb out of the vehicle and slam the door shut. Heavy footsteps receded and shortly afterwards there was the faint sound of another door slamming shut a lot further away.

Carefully removing the sacks, she crept to the tailboard and peered out into a moonlit farmyard flanked by open fields on her right and a line of wooden barns and other ramshackle buildings on her left.

Craning her neck to peer round the edge of the soft top, she saw that the Land Rover had been halted by a fence and five-barred gate, which separated the farm outbuildings from a wide area of broken tarmac with a two-storey, stone-built house at the far end. Pale yellow light flickered in one of the downstairs windows.

The tailboard quivered uneasily as she climbed over and dropped to the ground, and she flinched as it then slammed back into the body of the vehicle with a loud metallic 'crack', which she felt sure would have been carried to the farmhouse on the still air.

Darting across the yard to a gap between a wooden barn and what appeared to be some sort of low-walled enclosure, she crouched down in the gloom and stayed perfectly still as a door was thrown open and heavy footsteps marched quickly towards her hiding place. George obviously had very sharp ears despite the distance of the house from the Land Rover.

The footsteps stopped just feet from where she was crouching and she shrank back against a large cattle trough, screwing up her nose as a nasty chemical-like smell, apparently issuing from the walled enclosure, enveloped her.

There was silence for several anxious minutes and she visualized the killer standing there, motionless, eyes searching the moonlight while listening for a repeat of the sound that had alerted him – and the night was certainly alive. She became aware of faint rustlings in the stubby grass at her feet and something, probably a mouse, scurried from under the cattle trough and over her foot before vanishing into the shadows. Then a bat whirred past her face, barely missing her, and somewhere out in the fields the blood-curdling scream of a vixen cut through the air like a knife. Nocturnal country sounds that at any other time she would have found intriguing, but at that precise moment she had more important things on her mind than nature's wonders.

For a start, her left knee had begun to develop an unwelcome wobble and she could also feel the muscles in the calf knotting up with the onslaught of cramp. Gritting her teeth against the pain, she willed herself to remain perfectly still, determined that her patience would outlast George's, despite the cramp and the awful stink rising from the enclosure. But it was touch and go, and she had actually got to the point where the desire to stretch her legs and relieve the agonizing pain in her calf could no longer be ignored when she heard a muttered curse and the scrape of feet as George blinked first. There followed the sound of his receding footsteps, then a door slammed once more and she was left alone with just the silence for company.

She forced herself to wait several more minutes before making a move, conscious of the fact that George's departure may have actually been a ruse. But hearing nothing and sensing he had returned to the house, she climbed gingerly to her feet, bending down again almost immediately to massage her left calf with both hands and wincing as the returning circulation sent the muscles into erratic spasms. Even after the spasms had lessened sufficiently for her to be able to straighten up, her leg continued to feel weak and unresponsive, and she remained standing there for a while longer, stretching it out in front of her to flex the muscles and holding on to the low wall of the enclosure for support as she did so.

It was while she was doing this that she happened to glance over the wall into what she now saw to be an old-fashioned slurry pit and abruptly stiffened. Whether a trick of the moonlight or not, it seemed to her that something bulky was floating in the midst of the glistening sludge – something, her brain told her, that should not have been there. At first, she couldn't make out what it was and craned her neck to get a better view. But then, as she narrowed her gaze and focused more directly on the object, it suddenly dawned on her with a sense of horror exactly what it was; the body of a woman, with only the upturned face and part of the torso visible and an arm projecting just above the slurry, as if trying to affect a grotesque wave.

*

Ted Roscoe stood in the lane at the rear of Elsie Norman's bungalow with an even bigger scowl than usual on his slab-like face. The young uniformed constable who had earlier been in his direct line of fire fidgeted uneasily with the radio clipped to the webbing of his tunic as he stood in the background behind the elderly black man who had just approached him as a witness.

'So,' the DI queried sharply, 'you're saying you saw this intruder breaking into the house, Mr … er—.'

The witness nodded. 'Patton,' he replied. 'Dr Gabriel Patton.'

Roscoe raised an eyebrow. 'Doctor?' he echoed. 'You are a medical man?'

Patton smiled faintly. 'No, Inspector,' he replied. 'I am a senior university lecturer – in Philosophy.'

'And you rang the control room?'

'I certainly did. Twice actually.' Patton shook his head. 'Breaking into that poor deceased woman's home – absolutely disgraceful.'

Roscoe nodded. 'And I believe you told the officer here that you got a good look at the intruder?'

'Yes, I live over there, you see.'

Patton waved a hand towards a cottage a few yards further along the lane on the opposite side to Elsie Norman's rear garden.

'I happened to get up for a drink of water when I heard a vehicle pull up in the lane, then saw this character sneaking into the back garden of Mrs Norman's bungalow. Shortly afterwards I heard the sound of breaking glass and realized he had to be burgling the place, so I rang the police. After about twenty minutes – when none of your lot had turned up incidentally – I saw him leaving again and rang the police a second time.'

Roscoe winced at the implied criticism and quickly ploughed on.

'So, can you describe him?'

Patton shrugged. 'Tall, thin, about six feet or more in height, I would say, wearing a dark coat and a woollen hat.'

'What about his face?'

'Too much in shadow to see, I'm afraid.'

'And our officer – you saw her too, I understand?'

'I didn't know she was a police officer then, but I saw her shoulder-length, auburn hair in the street light over there and wondered why a woman would be following this man out of the house.'

'Did you see her arrive?'

'No, she must have entered the house originally from the front.'

'Where did she go afterwards? Did you see that?'

Another nod. 'She stopped for a second in the rear gateway – evidently to see where the man had gone – then hurried after him. Unfortunately, at that point I was distracted by my wife calling me to ask what I was doing, and when I looked back in the lane, the Land Rover was pulling away again and the woman had disappeared, so I don't know where she went.'

Roscoe gaped. 'He was driving *a Land Rover*?' he exclaimed incredulously.

'Yes, an old one with a canvas top. Green, I think. Not much of a driver either by the sound of his gear changes.'

'Why the hell didn't you mention this before?'

'You didn't ask me about a vehicle.'

Roscoe glared at him, his bullet head thrust forward belligerently.

'I don't suppose you got the number?' he grated.

Patton chuckled. 'Of course I did,' he said and produced a crumpled piece of paper from his trouser pocket. 'Shouldn't take you long to trace him.'

For a moment Roscoe seemed taken aback, but then recovered.

'And you're sure the woman police officer wasn't still in the lane after the Land Rover had gone.'

'Positive. There was that street lamp over there and quite bright moonlight, so I would have seen her.'

'Do you reckon she might have climbed into the Land Rover voluntarily and driven off with the man?'

'I wouldn't have thought so. After all, why creep after him in the first place, if she was going to go with him anyway?'

'So, you think she may have been abducted?'

Patton sighed heavily, as if in frustration. 'Well, you're the detective, Inspector,' he retorted. 'But the fact that one of your colleagues seems to have found her police radio lying in the lane near where the Land Rover was parked is rather significant, don't you think?'

Arrogant bastard, Roscoe thought, but the alarm bells jangling in his head were almost deafening.

*

Kate had been violently sick and she was ashamed of herself for it – especially since she had criticized others in the past for letting such things get to them. After all, it wasn't as if she hadn't seen a dead body before. There had been plenty of those in the course of her police career and in some pretty gruesome circumstances too. But this was different and there wasn't just *a* corpse either. She had spotted another one shortly afterwards, jammed face down in a corner of the slurry pit. A man, it seemed, with a balding head and part of his back clearly recognizable in the blaze of moonlight. There was the corpse of a dog too – some sort of collie by the look of it – draped over the wall at the far end of the pit like a bit of old carpet. It was like a scene from some gory horror film except for the fact that it was real, and even after throwing up Kate found it almost impossible to tear her gaze away from the sight.

It was apparent now how George had managed to secure such a convenient bolt-hole – by simply removing the 'opposition' and callously dumping their remains in the pit, as if disposing of nothing more than farmyard waste and adding a new dimension to the term 'cuckooing.' Even after the particularly brutal murders of both Elsie Norman and Mabel Strong, this double killing had to come close to the top of the infamy list for its sheer barbarity, and Kate shuddered at the thought of where she herself was likely to end up if she was unfortunate enough to fall into the hands of this depraved creature.

Caution was the watchword then – extreme caution. But at the same time, now she had succeeded in tracking the creature down, she had to do something to prevent him once more vanishing back into the mists of the Somerset Levels until he finally managed to locate Iris Naylor and add her and anyone else who got in his way to his list of victims.

Her decision made, she tore herself away from the grisly scene and returned to the front of the barn, peering around the corner of the building to study the farmhouse a good hundred yards away. A single ghostly light still flickered in one of the downstairs windows, but otherwise there was no sign of life and after a moment's hesitation, she darted diagonally across the hardstanding into the comforting shadow cast by the Land Rover.

The window of the room from which the flickering light issued was wide open on its metal stay and she heard a chair scrape on what sounded like a tiled floor, followed by the clink of a glass. So, George was helping himself to a drink, was he? Well, that suited her just fine.

Glancing through the front passenger door window of the vehicle, she saw that the keys had been left in the ignition. It would have been a simple enough matter to have climbed aboard and high-tailed it to the main road, but she had other ideas. If she had done that, George would have legged it again, defeating the whole object, while simply purloining the keys wouldn't be guaranteed to prevent his escape as there was possibly a spare key in the house anyway. No, what she needed to do was to maroon him at the farm by immobilizing the Land Rover and trusting in fate that he wouldn't tumble to the fact until she'd had time to get to a phone to summon help.

Decision made, she crouched down beside the front wheel with the ignition key of her own car in her hand. Then, removing the dust cap from the tyre valve, she used the key to deflate the tyre completely before moving to the back wheel and repeating the process.

She had just finished the job and returned to the other side of the vehicle when she heard the door of the farmhouse open again and from a crouched position by the front nearside wing, saw George re-emerge and stand for a moment staring about the farmyard. At first, she thought some sixth sense must have alerted him to her presence and she shut her eyes tightly in an involuntary spasm as she visualized him studying the Land Rover. If he came closer, he couldn't fail to spot the deflated tyres in the bright moonlight and she gripped the top of the wheel beside which she crouched, the muscles in her legs now tensing for flight as she anticipated the thud of heavy feet rushing towards her.

But it didn't happen and, after a tense few moments, she heard the door slam shut yet again as he went back inside the house. Relieved that she had managed temporarily to immobilize his only means of transport without being detected, she leaned against the wing for a few moments to give her pounding heart time to return to its normal rhythm. Then, straightening, she left the cover of the Land Rover to head off back along the track towards the main road. But it was then that her luck ran out.

'Going somewhere, bitch?' George sneered from a few feet away. 'I don't think so – not after what you've done to my tyres!'

The lisping voice had a strangely effeminate quality and in normal circumstances would have commanded little authority, but there was an almost tangible air of menace about the tall, thin figure blocking her way, while the twin barrels of the 12-bore shotgun aimed at her chest conveyed an authority all of their own.

CHAPTER 18

Roscoe wasted no time acting on the information the witness, Patton, had given him. Following an immediate registered owner check on the Land Rover, he pulled in every available unit via the control room and within half an hour a convoy of police vehicles was converging on the isolated farm near Glastonbury, just as the moon was beginning to wane and first light make its presence known on the far horizon.

It may have been more in accordance with official police procedure to have set up a fully briefed operation, complete with a search warrant and back-up from one of the highly trained and properly equipped tactical police support unit teams, but with his DS likely to be in the gravest danger the crusty DI had reasoned that now was not the time for observing bureaucratic protocols. He was in no mood for softly-softly tactics either and while the police vehicles crept into the farmyard in a low-key silent approach with all lights extinguished, there was nothing low key about their entry to the farmhouse.

There had not been time to obtain one of the steel enforcers – or battering rams – the police normally used in raids, and it would have involved too much red tape anyway. Instead, the boot of a burly constable directed at the weakest point of the front door served the same purpose and two hefty kicks sent it crashing back against the wall, enabling four or five of his uniformed colleagues to precede him into the hallway. Roscoe knew something was not quite right when the short, middle-aged man in boxer shorts staggered on to the landing of the ornate staircase in a blaze of light, clutching what looked like a cavalry sword.

*

Kate had faced shotguns in the hands of criminals before, but it didn't make the experience any the less traumatic on this occasion and she felt her mouth suddenly dry up and a familiar little worm begin to crawl around her insides.

Where George had got the gun from was unclear – probably somewhere in the farmhouse itself – but with only a few feet separating them she was acutely aware of the fact that however poor a shot he was, at that range there was no possibility of a miss.

'Inside, ahead of me,' he ordered and she sensed the anxiety in the lisping voice. 'Any funny business and I'll blow a hole in you big enough for someone to climb through.'

She relaxed slightly and did as she was told, relieved that, for the moment at least, she was still breathing.

She was conscious of her captor following very closely behind her as she walked slowly to the front door of the farmhouse. Obviously, George had somehow sussed her presence crouched beside the nearside wing of the Land Rover. He had then slammed the door to convince her that he had gone inside again, but had no doubt left the house by another door, doubled back behind the barns and crept up on her from the other side of the vehicle. A clever cookie, this one, it seemed.

Pushing through the doorway, she found herself in a large, shabby kitchen, equipped with an Aga cooker and an old-fashioned Belfast sink, and illuminated by an intermittently flickering strip-light, which left deep shadows beyond its reach. She felt the shotgun dig her none too gently in the back, prodding her forward towards a pine table in the centre of the room. She saw that the table was bare except for a bottle of Talisker single malt whisky and a bottle of Harvey's Bristol Cream sherry standing on a metal tray at one end. George was obviously making himself at home, she mused grimly, but the presence of the sherry took on more sinister connotations.

'Sit there,' her captor directed and, as she sat down, he backed away from her to the sink. Then, jerking the net curtain back from the window and with the shotgun still pointing in her direction, he peered out into the moonlight.

'You're that meddling cop, aren't you?' he accused. 'I should have fixed you when we first bumped into each other in that bloody basement.'

She didn't answer. Her attention was on the shotgun instead.

'Where's your mates?' he went on, still searching the night, and she could read the tension in his tone.

'Nearer than you think,' she lied.

He pulled the curtain back into place and, reaching towards the door, turned the key in the lock and faced her again.

'Bollocks!' he retorted, suddenly a lot more confident. 'So, where are they?'

'On their way,' she replied.

'Yeah, right,' he said with a sneer, adding: 'They'd be here by now if that was true and there's no sign of anyone else out there. You're on your tod, aren't you? A bloody lone wolf. So how did you get here? Sneak into the back of the Drover when it was parked behind the old girl's bungalow, did you?'

She said nothing and he joined her at the table, pulling out another chair and sitting down opposite with the shotgun resting on the table top, pointing at her chest.

Plainly in the sixty-plus age group, he had gaunt, pallid features and was completely bald with inflamed abrasions on both sides of his head – suggesting the heavy-handed use of a razor – and a drop-style gold earring in his left ear. Unblinking eyes (now minus the gold-coloured spectacles he had been wearing in the basement at Talbot Court) appraised her from dark hollows and the thin lips were slightly parted in the semblance of a sardonic smile, as if he were actually enjoying her scrutiny. Like the timbre of his voice, it was a face with an indefinable effeminate quality, despite the shaved head, hinting at a deep and protracted biological challenge to the gender identity which had been assigned him at birth, and this impression was further enhanced by the long, delicate fingers which held the shotgun in what was now a deceptively casual grasp.

'So how did you find me?' he went on, his tone much harsher than before. 'Someone see me break in and ring Old Bill, did they?' The sneer returned. 'You all they had to send?'

She said nothing and his eyes narrowed briefly in the flickering light.

'Cat got your tongue, Occifer?' he taunted. When she still made no reply, he added, 'So what do you suggest I do with you now, eh?'

'That's your decision,' she replied in a strangled voice, her gaze still locked on to the shotgun. 'Nothing I can do about it.'

'Scared then?'

'Who wouldn't be?'

He nodded slowly, considering her reply. 'I could blow your head off now.'

'You could, yes.'

'But if I'd wanted to waste you, I would have pulled the trigger when I caught you doing the tyres on the Drover.'

'So, what stopped you then?'

There was a short, humourless laugh. 'Curiosity, I suppose. You see, you've become such a meddling nuisance that I thought we'd have a little chat first – besides which, it occurred to me that you might be just the person to tell me where I can find Iris Naylor. I think it's high time she and I got reacquainted.'

Realizing that she would only remain alive as long as George thought she had the information he wanted, Kate quickly turned the conversation on to another tack.

'What, so that you can brutally murder her like you murdered Elsie Norman and Mabel Strong?'

He shrugged. 'What other reason could there be? And if it's a confession you want, you can have it.'

He smirked and placed the palm of his free hand on his chest and stared up at the ceiling, as if addressing a higher authority.

'It's me what done them two old bitches, Lord, and I enjoyed it.' His grin broadened as he turned his gaze on her again. 'Satisfied now, Occifer?'

Kate swallowed hard, but persisted with her distraction strategy. 'So, why do you hate your aunts so much?'

There was a brief pause and when the reply came, it was in a tone that was suddenly laced with menace.

'Wouldn't you hate them if you were in my shoes? Sadistic harridans, all of them. Taunted and humiliated me all through my childhood. Said I had the devil's mark and that my soul needed to be purified.' He gave a derisory snort. 'Purified? Tortured would be a more appropriate word. I used to dread it when they dropped in to see my parents at our home because I knew that they would wind up that shit of a stepfather to inflict more misery on me.'

'Quigley was your stepfather?' Kate said.

He studied her with contempt, seemingly unsurprised by the fact that she already knew something of his background

'You didn't think that arsehole could ever be my real father, did you? Not a chance, and he wouldn't let me have his own family name anyway. He only took me in because I came as a package with my mother. I didn't want the name Quigley either and I have stuck to my birth name, Lupin, ever since.' Another smirk. 'Confuse you all, did it, when you were trying to find out who I was?'

Kate started as realization dawned. No wonder there had been no trace of Quigley on the PNC database. They had been searching under the wrong name.

'But what about the authorities – schools, doctors and so forth? You couldn't have just disappeared in this day and age.'

'It wasn't in this day and age, and anyway, I was only four then. No one really knew – or cared – if I existed. Furthermore, Quigley apparently met my mother when we were living in Essex and we simply upped sticks and disappeared to Somerset – no one being any the wiser. As far as the authorities were concerned, I didn't exist. I was a non-person.'

'And what happened to your real father?'

He scowled. 'He died when I was about three, I'm told,' he replied, 'and my mother was stupid enough to shack up with that religious freak, Quigley, before she knew what she was getting into.'

His eyes became strangely hooded, as if his mind was reliving the past.

'Any idea what it was like being a little child raised by a family of religious maniacs?' he went on, without waiting for a reply. 'No childhood fun or laughter, no love, no nothing. Imprisoned in that bloody awful house as if I were a leper. Kept away from school and educated in my cell of a room by my Aunt Beatrix, who was a teacher, with prayers before breakfast, prayers before lunch and prayers before tea – and, of course, Bible readings in between. Constant beatings, and deprivations – like being stripped naked, caned or shut in the cellar for forgetting some meaningless drivel from the scriptures or for failing to do well enough in my studies.' He paused a second, his gaze fastening on her again. 'Beatings and deprivations that drove me to self-harm with any sharp object I could find.'

He leaned forward, his grip tightening on the shotgun, so that she flinched in horrible anticipation of an accidental blast.

'And do you know what they did when I caused the injuries to myself? Nothing, that's what. No tears, no sense of guilt, no self-recriminations, no trip to the hospital or even to see a doctor. Instead, my mother – an ex-nurse – just patched me up, and the whole coven condemned me as a sinner for what I had done and inflicted further punishment on me, while my mother just looked on, too weak to intervene.'

He relaxed slightly and to Kate's relief, slumped back in his chair, releasing his grip on the weapon completely, so that it slewed round on the table top away from her to point at the Aga cooker in the corner.

'And there was worse to follow,' he went on. 'When I was orphaned, as a result of both my parents dying in a road accident, did my aunts rally around in support? Not a bit of it. They simply washed their hands of me. Said they wouldn't be able to cope with a child who was so mentally disturbed. Was it any wonder I was mentally disturbed after what they and my arsehole parents had put me through?'

'What about your uncles?' Kate cut in hastily, anxious to calm him down before he lost it completely and used the shotgun on her. 'Didn't they do anything to stop what was going on?'

He snorted. 'They'd all died, one by one before I'd even reached my teens. Two copped it from cancer, another committed suicide – a blessed relief for him, I would think – and the fourth died in a railway accident at work. I had no friends, never allowed any, so there was no one I could turn to, no one to stop Iris Naylor and her bitch sisters shunting me off to that hell-hole at Talbot Court—'

'Where you were sexually abused?' Kate finished for him, without meaning to say anything.

She was treated to a thoughtful nod. 'You are very well informed, Detective. But you are exactly right. And that abuse was carried out on numerous occasions over a pretty long period. Not only by the so-called Principal, Edward Grace, and his *darling* wife either, but by other members of staff, as well as the well-heeled friends he regularly invited to the orphanage for a night's fun and games.'

'Until you lost it and stabbed one of them to death?'

'Right again. An odious character called Alistair Scarsfield. Pity it wasn't Grace too, but by then it was too late and I was carted away by the police, eventually ending up in what at that time was called borstal. I wasn't there long, though. After so-called behavioural problems, I was labelled psychotic by the trick cyclists and soon shunted off to the funny farm – or rather, a succession of them, as I proved to be a continuing embarrassment to the shrinks and unresponsive to their imaginative treatment regimes.'

A lengthy pause before the reminiscences resumed and Kate made no effort to interrupt this time.

'It wasn't until I was much older that it dawned on me that the best way of handling my situation was to play the good doctors at their own game and pretend to cooperate. It worked too. That's how I ended up in Larchfield Secure Psychiatric Hospital, where the privileges I earned as a trusted inmate eventually provided me with the freedoms I needed to achieve my escape.'

'So why didn't you just run and keep on running? You could have got clean away – to Ireland or the Continent maybe. Started a new life. Why take the risk of coming back here after all this time, just to waste a few harmless old ladies—'

'Harmless?' he cut in with a new vehemence. 'Harmless? Haven't you listened to a word I've said? Those old crones were never harmless and Iris Naylor was the worst of them. As my guardian, she had all the power to do what she liked with me. Furthermore, as she was well in with Edward Grace, who professed the same fanatical Christian beliefs as her – which was a real joke when you think what a perverted scumbag he actually was – my incarceration in Talbot Court was inevitable once my parents were out of the way. Grace and Aunt Iris cooked up everything between them and the other old bitches just fell in behind the plan – and do you know why? Money, that's why. What do you think happened to my inheritance when my mother and father died, eh? Well, I'll tell you – it disappeared.'

'Disappeared? But surely there must have been legal safeguards to protect your interests as a minor?'

'Legal safeguards?' he sneered. 'You have to be joking. Iris Naylor was not only my guardian, she was also the family solicitor. She had all the expert know-how to get around such legal niceties and, in those days, official scrutiny was pretty lamentable.'

'But why would she bother to do that? When your parents died, she could just as easily have cut you out of any inheritance there and then and claimed it for herself and the other sisters. After all, from what you say, I can't imagine your stepfather leaving it to you.'

He treated her to a cold, sardonic smile. 'Iris had no choice in the matter. John Quigley was killed outright in the accident, but my mother lived on for another three months and, as the sole beneficiary in the old man's will, before she died of thrombosis, she forced Iris to bequeath it all to me as her heir. Obviously, Iris had to comply with her wishes as her legal representative, but she managed to persuade my mother to name her as my official guardian.

'As a result, after my mother had passed on, some dodgy trust fund was set up for me – ironically in the name of Lupin, as per my birth certificate, so all would appear above board and nothing would rebound on Grace. But while on paper the money was used to pay for my keep and so-called education at Talbot Court, in reality, through some imaginative accounting, most of it eventually found its way into the coffers of Grace and my dear old aunts.'

He lurched forward in his chair and thrust his face to within a couple of feet of Kate's.

'Those wicked bitches stole what was due to me and helped to make my childhood a living hell. Turned the family home into a place where nightmares were born. A place that still haunts me like a living thing after all this time. A place that, in my mind, has come to symbolize the beginning of my mental and physical degeneration. It was because of those witches that I ended up in Talbot Court, because of them that I was abused, because of them that I have spent over fifty years incarcerated in bloody institutions.'

Kate froze, reading the madness in his twisted features and unsure what to do to defuse the situation. She had encountered psychopaths in her career before, but this one was plainly so unhinged that it was almost impossible to predict how he would react to anything.

'So … so why pre-warn the police about what you were going to do in advance?' she stammered, in an effort to quieten him down and once again change the direction of his thoughts. 'What was the sense in that?'

For a moment it was touch and go, but then it seemed that her words had struck a chord and he relaxed again, back in control.

'Vanity, I suppose. I didn't want to go down as just another psycho, killing for the fun of it. I wanted to establish my credentials right at the start – to set the record straight, so to speak.'

'But wasn't that taking a big risk?' she blurted, trying to prolong the conversation for as long as possible. 'You could have been caught before you'd had the opportunity of doing anything.'

He shook his head. 'Not a chance. That's why I was less than specific about my identity or my intentions. "George" could be the name of anyone and I was careful not to say anything in the letter that would point to the actual identities of my intended victims before I had dealt with them. But by sowing the seed, I had ensured that after I had finished what I'd set out to do, my celebrity status would be assured and the justification for my actions established.'

'But what was the point of the sherry and the lipstick?'

'You obviously didn't pay enough attention to the letter I sent, Detective. It was all in there about my nightmare experiences as a child and it seemed to tie in admirably with the message I wanted to send out.'

Without taking his eyes off her, he dug a hand in his pocket and produced a plastic lipstick holder, placing it on the table beside the bottle of sherry.

'Easy enough to obtain too, courtesy of my dear old shrink's wallet. I got the sherry,' and he tapped the bottle with the fingers of the same hand, 'from a motorway services, so I could share it with my precious aunts before I sent them off to the next world. As for the lipstick, nicked, I'm afraid – from a local chemist. There were two sticks originally, but I accidentally left one behind at Aunt Elsie's, so I had to make do with just this little fellow when I popped in to see poor old Mabel. Slightly different shade of red, but there you are, you can't have everything, can you?'

Abruptly his expression hardened. 'Right, Detective, you have prevaricated long enough. Do you think I haven't already realized what you've been up to with all your stupid questions? Playing for time and hoping for a miracle rescue, were you?'

He leaned forward across the table again. 'Well, there's not going to be one and now it's the moment of truth. So, tell me, where can I find Iris Naylor?'

'I don't know,' she replied simply.

'Rubbish,' he retorted. 'You don't expect me to believe that, do you? With all your resources, you're saying you can't find one decrepit old woman?'

'I can't help you. I have no idea where she is.'

He sighed, leaned back in his chair and raised the shotgun again. 'In which case, Detective,' he said grimly, 'what further use are you to me?'

And he smiled as he once more slid his index finger back inside the trigger guard.

CHAPTER 19

The man with the sword was quivering with rage.

'What the hell is this?' he yelled. 'Get out of my house!'

Conscious of his colleagues fidgeting uneasily at the foot of the staircase where they had come to an abrupt halt, the DI pushed his way through them to the front.

'Put the weapon down, sir,' he ordered sharply, 'before someone gets hurt.'

The man in the shorts squealed his anger. 'Someone gets hurt?' he exclaimed. 'You burst into my house in the middle of the night, breaking down my door, and have the audacity to—' He broke off in a semi-choking fit. 'Do you have a warrant?'

A tall, younger-looking blonde-haired woman in a very short nightdress that revealed more than it concealed had now joined him on the landing and was staring down at them with wide-eyed astonishment.

'What on earth do you want?' she said nervously before Roscoe could respond to her partner's question, and she pushed the hand holding the sword down so that it was pointing at the floor.

Roscoe grimaced. 'You own a Land Rover Defender,' he said, producing a crumpled piece of paper and quoting the registration number.

'So?' she said. 'Is that a crime?'

'No, ma'am,' Roscoe continued impatiently. 'But we have reason to believe that the vehicle was involved in a burglary and the possible abduction of a police officer tonight.'

'A *what*?' the man blazed. 'That's bloody ridiculous.'

Roscoe's eyes narrowed. 'Do you own this vehicle or not?' he snapped.

The woman frowned. 'That old thing?' she exclaimed. 'Yes, we own it. But it's only used as a farm vehicle. It's not reliable enough for anything else.'

'So where is it now?'

She glanced quickly at her partner. 'Not here. My dad has borrowed it.'

'Your father?' Roscoe exclaimed.

'Yes, he owns the farm just down the road ...' Her voice trailed off and she quickly raised a hand to her mouth. 'If ... if it's been stolen,' she exclaimed tremulously, 'then what about my dad and my sister?'

But Roscoe was already ahead of her there and he didn't like the direction in which his thoughts were taking him.

*

Kate was relieved to still be alive, though she guessed it wouldn't be for too much longer. Instead of blasting her from the other side of the table, George had ordered her to stand up and move towards the door. Then he unlocked it and prodded her through, out into the yard.

'There are some people I want you to meet,' he said with the by now familiar sneer. 'So, walk.'

She didn't need to be told where they were going, for he turned left outside the door and was pushing her towards the barns that had afforded her shelter earlier. He was going to shoot her and dump her body in the slurry pit – that fact was pretty obvious – saving him the trouble of doing the job at the house and carting her body the hundred yards he would otherwise have had to cover with her corpse draped over one shoulder. And the awful thing was, she could do nothing about it. She was totally helpless, incapable of doing anything to save herself, and he knew it.

She thought of Hayden then, suddenly realizing that she hadn't thought about him and his infidelity for some time now. She couldn't help wondering what his reaction would be when her body was dragged out of the slurry pit. Would he be horrified, upset, or just relieved? No doubt horrified – who wouldn't be in such circumstances? But she guessed that he would be more relieved than upset. After all, her death would leave him a free man, wouldn't it? Free to shag whoever he wanted. Oh, there would probably be a few tears, just to show willing, and maybe even a convincing period of mourning for the benefit of colleagues and relatives. But then it would be a case of 'Ah well, life has to go on, doesn't it?' and back to bed with his bit of spare.

In the midst of her bitter reflections, she was hardly aware of the gun barrel prodding her on and only surfaced from her shock-induced reverie when George suddenly rapped, 'Stop here!'

She could smell the gas from the slurry pit already and she clenched her fists tightly by her sides as she turned slowly to face him.

'You don't have to do this,' she said hoarsely, wondering why she had bothered to say something as pointless as that.

He studied her for a moment, then sighed. 'It's nothing personal,' he said, 'but I'm afraid you've brought it on yourself and I have no option.'

The shotgun was held out in front of him now, pointing at her stomach, and his eyes were strangely hooded in the moonlight.

'What is it the villain asks at this point in all the good films?' he continued. 'Oh yes, I know – any last requests?'

But she never got the opportunity to reply. At precisely that moment they were caught in a blaze of headlights, which had suddenly appeared around the bend of the approach road, and she glimpsed a convoy of vehicles hurtling towards them.

The effect on her would-be killer was instantaneous. The shotgun in his hands exploded with a deadly roar, but Kate was already on him, grabbing the weapon with both hands so that the double blast erupted into the night sky as she wrenched it from his grasp. Then the first police vehicle had skidded to a halt in front of them, discharging several uniformed figures – including the for once welcome shape of Ted Roscoe – even before the wheels had stopped turning and sending George into panic-stricken flight.

Kate saw the killer vault a five-barred gate on the far side of the road and vanish into the scrub on the other side, a lean, loping figure merging with the moonlit shadows as effectively as a ghost.

*

Dawn was breaking when Kate got home from the murder scene and, even from the bottom of the stairs, she could hear Hayden's snores. Unbelievable. He had actually gone to bed after leaving her at the nick the previous evening and had slept through the whole night's drama in complete ignorance of what had happened to her.

Despite her angry resentment, she didn't seek to enlighten him by waking him up. From past experience she knew that trying to rouse Hayden once he had fallen into a deep sleep was next to impossible – besides which, she was exhausted and in no mood to submit herself to what would be certain to develop into a protracted interrogation regarding her whereabouts over the past five or six hours. Instead, she knocked back the half bottle of red wine he had left on the living room coffee table and, grabbing a blanket and a pillow from the airing cupboard upstairs, she dossed down on the settee to try and capture a few hours' much-needed rest.

But sleep did not come easily after her lucky escape and she was unable to get George out of her mind. The ruthless killer had completely vanished again and despite a thorough sweep of the fields by the search teams, not a trace of him had been found. Even the police dog-handler, who had arrived fifteen minutes later, had met with little success, his wolfish-looking Alsatian managing to raise nothing more than a marauding fox.

Characteristically, Roscoe had shown no obvious concern over Kate's traumatic experience. To be fair, he had to be well used to her getting herself into tight corners in the years he had worked with her, but his apparent lack of interest in her welfare this time was in stark contrast to the sympathy he had shown towards her marital problems a few hours before. That seemed to indicate that the crusty DI had something of a Jekyll and Hyde personality, but on the other hand, maybe in the one-to-one at the pub he had been motivated by nothing more than self-interest in relation to the efficient operation of his department and his sympathy had only been skin deep.

On balance Kate suspected that there was no room for either sympathy or empathy in his old-school mentality. Now his focus was concentrated entirely on the hunt for the ruthless killer – driven perhaps by the knowledge that embarrassing questions were bound to be asked by both the media and the top hierarchy as to why the fugitive had been allowed not only to kill again, but to escape arrest with apparent impunity despite such a heavy police contingent at the scene.

In fact, Kate had gained the distinct impression from the demeanour of her scowling gum-chewing boss that, deep down, he blamed her personally for what had happened. It was all her fault that George had killed again and had managed to escape arrest afterwards. Her fault that she had been abducted and subjected to such a terrifying ordeal. Her fault that he had raided the wrong house, was about to be pilloried by the press, and maybe done for illegal entry and breach of police procedure on top of it all. *Situation normal*, she thought cynically as she plumped up the pillow and tried unsuccessfully to will herself to sleep. But then if he didn't have her to blame, who would he have?

Sleep did eventually come, but when she finally awoke – to find to her horror that it was past eleven in the morning – a surprise awaited her. The double bed upstairs was empty. Hayden had gone, without so much as a goodbye, and, as her small team were still officially on late turn, she guessed immediately where he was off to; his other woman.

She didn't bother to try and verify the fact by heading back to Uphill. She was fast losing interest in his extra-marital affair. If that was what he wanted, then sod him and let him get on with it. She was past caring. At least that was what she told herself repeatedly in the shower and, more as proof to herself of her new ambivalence towards his infidelity than anything else, she grabbed a slice of toast and a cup of coffee before heading into work ahead of her designated shift time.

Pushing through the double doors of the incident room twenty minutes later, however, she soon had a lot more to think about than Hayden Lewis.

Both Roscoe and the DCI were in the SIO's office, closeted with a lean, balding man in a rumpled blue suit, and the DI beckoned her to join them as soon as he clapped eyes on her. The visitor was introduced to her as a Dr Jeremy Falls; at first, she was puzzled as to why she had been invited into the office.

But then the DI provided the doctor's credentials.

'Dr Falls is senior consultant at Larchfield Secure Psychiatric Hospital, up north,' he said, studying her face intently to see her reaction.

'Larchfield?' she echoed, remembering the killer's account of his incarceration. 'That's where George said he escaped from.'

Falls nodded gravely. 'Chief Inspector Hennessey and Inspector Roscoe have told me all about your abduction by one of my patients,' he replied, 'and I'm relieved that you came to no harm. Sadly, the same cannot be said of one of my senior psychiatrists. We found his body locked away in his private apartment at the hospital several days after Georgina Lupin's escape.'

Kate stiffened. '*Georgina?*'

The DCI nodded. 'Apparently we've had it wrong from the start,' she said grimly. 'Our man, George, is actually a bloody woman!'

CHAPTER 20

For a few seconds Kate said nothing in response to the bombshell that had just been dropped and Roscoe studied her intently for a moment.

'Bit of a shock, eh?' he suggested.

She frowned and slowly shook her head, angry with herself for not tumbling to the truth when she had faced George across the table in the old farmhouse. The indicators had all been there, right in front of her – the timbre of her captor's voice and the tell-tale facial characteristics and demeanour. It had been so obvious, yet she had simply assumed she was dealing with some effeminate male psychopath. It hadn't occurred to her that George was displaying feminine characteristics because he – or rather she – *was* in fact female.

Now she knew the truth, however, she was surprised that she did not feel a lot more shocked than she would have expected. Maybe at the back of her mind she had actually suspected what had now been revealed without realizing it. Maybe the trauma of her situation at the time had skewed her focus and temporarily buried her suspicions as her emotions tried to cope with the perilous position in which she had found herself. Who could say? Except perhaps the shrink now sitting on the edge of the desk in front of her, she mused wryly.

'Thought you'd have sussed this nutter out when you were with her, though?' Roscoe went on, his tone hard and critical. 'Can't understand how you could have overlooked the obvious fact that she was a woman.'

Kate felt the anger boil up inside her, but before she could round on him, Falls coughed discreetly.

'That's not really surprising under the circumstances, Inspector,' he said. 'The problem is, Georgina is not a woman in the true sense of the word. Her gender is a lot more complicated than that.'

Roscoe snorted. 'Well, if she's not a man or a woman, what the hell is she?' he snapped. 'A bloody android?'

Falls treated him to a humourless smile. 'No, Inspector,' he said with heavy sarcasm, 'we can be confident that she is not an android. But although she was born and christened female, in her own psyche she is a man, a man trapped in a woman's body – someone society would label transgender or more accurately in her case, transsexual – and this has led to a serious emotional problem or what, in medical terms, we would call gender dysphoria—'

'Yeah, yeah, yeah,' the DI cut in. 'And I suppose the next thing you'll be saying is that this dysphoria – whatever that actually is – turned this "poor mixed-up cow" into a psychopath?'

Falls' expression tightened in a brief show of irritation at the DI's choice of language, but he controlled himself with an effort.

'No, Inspector,' he said patiently. 'I'm not about to say anything of the sort. For your information, in basic terms, gender dysphoria relates to feelings of distress or anxiety caused by a mismatch between a person's biological sex and their perceived gender identity. It is not in itself a mental condition and it has absolutely nothing to do with personality disorders, such as psychopathy, which is a definite psychological condition on its own. The fact that Lupin was diagnosed as suffering from a psychopathic disorder is not in any way linked to the gender identity issue or to her dysphoria.'

Deidrie Hennessey threw Roscoe an angry glance and cut in quickly before he could come up with any further derogatory remarks.

'On the question of Lupin's dysphoria,' she said, 'I thought there was a surgical procedure nowadays that could sort out the sort of gender problem you are talking about?'

Falls nodded. 'You are referring to gender reassignment surgery?' he suggested.

'Or slap-a-dick-to-me,' Roscoe muttered unhelpfully, attracting another scathing glance from the DCI.

Falls ignored him this time and addressed his boss instead. 'It is not that simple, Chief Inspector,' he went on. 'I won't bore you with the clinical details, but gender reassignment is a procedure that is not suitable for every patient. The problem is that transsexualism arises from a combination of biological, psychological, and emotional factors. As I have already indicated, transsexuals are absolutely convinced that they have been born into the wrong body. It isn't just a question of wanting to change from one sex to another for the sheer hell of it. Theirs is not a perverted whim or an attempt to shock social normality by making some kind of warped statement. In their minds they have been cheated by nature and they *are* the gender they identify with.'

He paused a second before continuing, as if trying to find the right words.

'It seems that Georgina underwent hormonal therapy several years ago, followed by a double mastectomy and a full hysterectomy and ovariectomy, but she suffered a relapse after the operation which nearly killed her, and the procedure for continuing gender reassignment had to be halted.'

'Pity it *didn't* kill her,' Roscoe butted in again. 'Then four innocent people would still be alive today.'

'Five actually,' Falls corrected grimly, 'counting my unfortunate friend and colleague, Dr Emrys Jones, whom she butchered at the hospital before escaping in his car.'

Roscoe simply shrugged, slipped some chewing gum into his mouth, and began chewing furiously as he pondered some issue known only to himself.

'Both physically and mentally, the situation left her in a kind of gender limbo – neither male nor female,' Falls added, 'and this accelerated the process of emotional deterioration, with the conflict in gender identity leading to, among other things, confusion, frustration, and psychosis. Over the years this has manifested itself in self-harm and violence, but at Larchfield we thought we had finally managed to arrest this behaviour through our individually targeted therapeutic treatment programmes.' He shrugged. 'Georgina – or George as she insists on being called – made exceptional progress, as a result of which she earned the trust of her psychiatric team and was rewarded with certain privileges—'

'You mean she had you over?' Roscoe put in again. 'You were conned by one of your own patients. Why doesn't that surprise me?'

Falls seemed unwilling to bite. 'We operate a much more progressive regime at Larchfield than elsewhere in the mental health sector,' he explained patiently. 'We believe in encouraging our patients to overcome their psychological problems by taking greater charge of themselves and their own behaviour, rather than treating them as sub-human and simply locking them away under constant sedation. Their progress is carefully monitored and although pharmacological and other interventionist therapies are employed where appropriate, these are strictly controlled and the more the patient can demonstrate their ability to manage their own condition, the more licence they are afforded within the hospital precincts. We have had considerable success with this approach too, but we have to accept that mistakes can be made on occasions—'

'Tell that to the victims,' Kate cut in, for once on Roscoe's side.

Falls closed his eyes briefly, then nodded. 'Okay, look, I am extremely sorry that innocent people have died at the hands of one of my patients, Sergeant,' he said, 'but you have to understand that Georgina is driven by inner demons she cannot control and we believe that their emergence and increasing influence over her behaviour harks back to her childhood.

'We have no information on her medical history as a child, but it is likely she would have exhibited some characteristics inconsistent with her assigned biological gender at an early stage and these would have grown more pronounced as she approached puberty. The help, understanding and support of a loving family would have been essential to enable her to cope with the conflict raging inside her. I have no information as to whether she got this, but the very evident deterioration in her mental health over the years and the violence and self-harm that has accompanied it – resulting in a lifetime of incarceration – suggests that she did not.

'Furthermore, it should be borne in mind that the time Georgina would have most needed understanding and support was in her formative years, as a child. But then we are talking about the fifties and sixties, when not only would any of the professional help society can call upon today have been unavailable, but her presentation of a more masculine identity would, like homosexuality, have been regarded as an obscene affront to public decency and dealt with as a heinous crime. People were actually put away for it, as in effect Georgina was by being sent to Talbot Court—'

'And all this is supposed to excuse her, is it?' Kate cut in. 'George tried that one herself when she unloaded on me. But forgive me for not feeling particularly sorry for this poor, misunderstood psychopath after seeing the corpses of her last two victims floating in the slurry pit yesterday.'

Falls shook his head. 'I am not seeking to excuse her at all, Sergeant,' he replied, 'merely to explain how a psychosis can develop and to reiterate that her apparent psychopathic illness is not a product of her transsexualism, but possibly a manifestation of the trauma she suffered earlier in life.' He broke off with a slightly apologetic smile. 'But enough of my burbling. You said just now that she unloaded on you. That has to be a plus. She has consistently refused to talk to myself or my colleagues about her childhood or her family, clamming up at the first mention of either. So, what did she tell you?'

Kate shrugged and, after a quick glance at Hennessey and Roscoe who were both now staring at her fixedly, she took them back to the previous night and George's ravings.

No one said anything for a few moments after she had finished, but then Falls commented, 'That was very illuminating, Sergeant, and it explains a great deal. We knew nothing about this abuse or about the paranoia from which she seems to have been suffering in relation to these so-called aunts of hers. We were aware that she had been sent to the orphanage at Talbot Court as a child after the death of her parents in a road accident and that she was then incarcerated for stabbing this man – Scarsfield – after he had sexually abused her, but we knew nothing about the abuse she suffered at the hands of the Quigleys.'

'Seems to me that you didn't know a lot about anything,' Roscoe cut in again. 'Even as head honcho.'

Falls noticeably coloured up this time. 'I was not actually in post when Georgina was transferred to Larchfield, Inspector,' he retorted defensively. 'I have only been there for two years. But she was handed over to our care from another secure unit as Georgina Lupin and the paperwork we still have on file includes her birth certificate affirming this fact. I suspect that the previous institutions to which she was sent, as well as the original sentencing court, had the same details and that the aunts – or one of them – offloaded her on to Talbot Court as Georgina Lupin to protect the Quigley reputation. Obviously, no one thought to check further. Incredible when you think about it, but Georgina didn't help matters by resolutely sticking to the Lupin name herself.

'Unfortunately, it was exactly because we at Larchfield were unaware of her past family affiliations that the possibility she might have been planning to head back here to Somerset did not occur to us – not until we were told about the recovery of Emrys Jones' car in that lake of yours, then subsequently found his body in his apartment at the hospital.'

'Unbelievable!' Roscoe burst in again. 'You're supposed to be running a secure psychiatric unit, Doc, yet one of your own shrinks is stiffed on the premises by a resident nutter who then manages to steal the shrink's car and piss off into the blue without anyone being the wiser. Even worse, rather than just a couple of hours, which would have been bad enough in itself, it takes days for it to finally dawn on you that you're one shrink and one psycho down. It's like something out of *Monty Python*!'

'That's enough, Inspector!' Hennessey rapped angrily, but Falls held up one hand in apparent submission, his face now pale and a haunted expression shadowing his eyes.

'No, he's quite right,' he said, 'and I take full responsibility for what has happened. All I can say is that, like other public services, we are very short staffed and critically underfunded at Larchfield, and this happened on a weekend when we were operating a skeleton crew. To compound the problem, as I have already indicated, Lupin had earned the sort of privileged status that is afforded to trusted patients, so would not have been subjected to the more rigorous checks that would otherwise have been required. As for Emrys Jones, he should have been on holiday from that Friday evening and gate security saw what they thought was Emrys driving away in his distinctive VW. As a result, it was assumed by everyone that he had actually gone away. His body was dumped in his private apartment behind a locked door, to which no one else had access, and it wasn't until a cleaner detected an unpleasant odour coming from inside that entry was made and his remains found.'

'But even allowing for the fact that Lupin went AWOL on a bank holiday weekend when you were understaffed,' Kate put in, 'that's just three to four days. Why has it taken until now for it to be reported to us? Surely the breach in security should have been discovered as soon as you were back to full staffing on the Tuesday, the moment everyone returned from the bank holiday break?'

Falls fidgeted and looked down at his feet. 'It was,' he replied simply. 'But we had to carry out a full search of the hospital and grounds to ensure Lupin was not just hiding away somewhere – it is a very big site. Then we had to alert the local police and have a search of the external area carried out—'

'You mean you pissed about,' Roscoe came in again. 'Went into panic mode at the thought of the likely repercussions and sat on it, in the hope that this crazy arsehole would turn up again?'

Falls winced, but didn't try to deny the allegation.

'We have to accept that Lupin deceived us all,' he said instead. 'Seemingly taking her medication, going along with the treatment programme, and successfully combating her psychosis after years of violence and disruptive behaviour in different institutions, when all the time this was a ploy to gain our trust and earn those privileges that would give her the necessary freedom within the precincts of the hospital. We were fooled – I admit it – but hindsight is a wonderful thing. Nevertheless, this security breach should never have occurred and a rigorous internal inquiry is already underway to determine how it could have been allowed to happen.'

'After the bloody horse has bolted,' Roscoe muttered.

'We all make mistakes, Doctor,' Hennessey said quickly, 'and it's apparent that we are dealing with a very clever and resourceful psychopath. But what I cannot fathom is why she suddenly decided to break out and embark on her vendetta now after all these years of incarceration.'

'Oh, she did try to get out before,' Falls replied, 'many times at different institutions, but each escape was foiled. Obviously, it eventually dawned on her that subterfuge was the only way she was going to be able to achieve her aims and she must have been planning her escape from Larchfield for quite some time.' He hesitated. 'There is possibly another reason too.'

'Go on.'

'She is dying.'

'Dying?'

'Yes, some weeks before her escape she was diagnosed with an aggressive tumour, which is untreatable. She knows she doesn't have much time left and this may have given her the impetus for her escape plan and the launch of her vendetta.'

'With nothing to lose one way or the other,' Kate breathed.

Falls nodded soberly. 'Precisely, and you should not assume that the tumour, which is eating away at her tissues, will make her any the less dangerous. She is otherwise very fit and in her time with us at Larchfield was a regular visitor to our well-equipped gym, carrying out gruelling workouts to develop her physique. Consequently, she is the match for any woman ...'

'Or man,' Kate finished for him, throwing a quick glance at Roscoe as the office telephone rang and he picked it up and clapped it to his ear. 'And she has just one more target to find—'

'Who we may have found first,' the DI cut in triumphantly, covering the mouthpiece of the phone into which he had just been speaking. 'That was the front desk. We have a Mrs Iris Naylor downstairs, who wishes to speak to us.'

CHAPTER 21

Iris Naylor was a short, sprightly woman, who had to be in her early to mid-eighties. She reminded Kate of the late Joan Hickson in her role as Agatha Christie's Miss Marple. Dressed in a grey jacket and matching skirt, she wore her grey hair in a bun under a green hat and carried a large, brown handbag in one hand. The grey eyes were sharp and watchful behind the rimless spectacles and they narrowed slightly when Hennessey, Roscoe and Kate entered the interview room where she was standing with her back to the radiator, a cup of tea – evidently untouched – on the table in front of her.

Hennessey introduced the three of them and indicated a chair, inviting her to sit down, but she made no effort to accept the offer.

'Takes all of you to see me, does it?' she snapped. 'I would have thought one would have been quite sufficient?'

Roscoe seemed taken aback by her unexpected directness and Kate noticed his discomfiture with a faint smile, since it was rare for him to be thrown by anyone.

Hennessey, however, did not appear to be unduly put out by their visitor's approach and also smiled.

'We are very glad you are here, Mrs Naylor,' she said. 'We have been trying to get in touch with you.'

The old woman snorted. 'Yes, so I gather, but you didn't make a very good job of it, did you? I've been living at the same address in Wiltshire for twenty-odd years. Local vicar here got hold of me easily enough.'

Kate frowned. 'Local vicar?' she queried.

The grey eyes fastened on her. 'Yes, the Reverend Glover. He was my late sister Beatrix's parish priest and my other sisters, Elsie and Mabel, attended his church from time to time too.'

She made a grimace. 'I was originally married in that church, so I suppose he felt he had an obligation to try and find me to tell me what had happened to poor Elsie and Mabel.'

Kate raised both eyebrows, surprised not only by her revelation that the clergyman had pipped them at the post, but by the apparent absence of grief in her demeanour at the loss of her sisters.

'Reverend Glover didn't happen to tell us he'd found you,' she retorted. 'When I last spoke to him, he said he had no idea where you'd gone.'

She was treated to a thin, humourless smile. 'Good detective is Reverend Glover – better than you lot anyway,' their visitor retorted. 'He went through some old church papers apparently and came up with a letter I'd written to his predecessor about my late husband's death. Quite a simple exercise really.'

The cunning, duplicitous old bastard, Kate mused, thinking of the priest and the way he had reneged on his promise to let her know if anything turned up. Nevertheless, she kept her thoughts to herself.

'We're really sorry about your sisters,' Hennessey said, clearly relieved that Iris Naylor already knew about their deaths, absolving her of the responsibility of breaking the news personally. 'We are doing all we can to catch the perpetrator.'

The grey eyes focused on her now, still empty of tears. 'And it wouldn't be difficult to guess who that so-called perpetrator might be, would it?' the old woman said.

Hennessey quickly pulled out a chair and nodded to Roscoe and Kate to do the same.

'Well, I'm going to sit down, Mrs Naylor,' she said firmly, 'and it would be easier for us to talk if you would do the same.'

Their visitor hesitated for a second, then shrugged and eased herself into a chair on the opposite side of the table, taking a sip from her cup of tea after she had done so.

'Georgina managed to break out of that place at last, has she?' she said, setting the cup down with one trembling arthritic hand. 'I knew she would one day. I told my sisters to expect that and to be careful. Obviously, they weren't careful enough.'

'I admire your fortitude, Mrs Naylor,' Kate commented. 'You seem to have coped well with the tragic news of your sisters' deaths.'

There was a brief nod and the grey eyes blinked a couple of times.

'At our time of life, Death's shadow is a constant companion, Sergeant,' the old woman said in a much more sombre tone. 'And it should come as no surprise to us when he claims his bounty. Elsie and Mabel are safely in the care of the Lord now anyway – as I shall be soon – so grief is a pointless emotion.'

'Tell us about Georgina,' Hennessey put in gently, 'and why she would want to kill her own aunts.'

Another snort greeted the question. 'She was the devil's child, that's why. We tried to drive his demon out of her, but he was too strong for us.'

Kate stared at the large silver crucifix suspended on a chain around her neck.

'I assume from the cross you are wearing and your expression of faith just now that you are a strong Christian?' she said.

Iris Naylor gave her a defiant glare. 'The Lord is my life – always has been and always will be,' came the sharp reply. 'It was the same for all my family. Without Christ we are nothing but clay.'

‘So, what made you think Georgina was the devil’s child?’

‘Because she was. She had his mark. Even from the beginning, it was there.’

‘And what form did this mark take?’

A tight grimace. ‘It was in the way she looked, the sinful way she behaved,’ came the bitter reply. ‘She was an affront to decency. And her wicked ways grew worse as she got older. We all knew there was a demon inside her, mocking the ways of the Lord, and that he needed to be cast out.’

Hennessey glanced quickly at Kate, but seeing that her DS was getting somewhere, she allowed her to continue without interruption. As for Roscoe, he just stared at their visitor in stony silence, plainly out of his depth.

‘What did she do to mock the Lord?’ Kate went on.

‘Do? She was an abomination, a freak of nature that should never have been created.’

‘And why is that?’

‘You know very well why and I refuse to name it.’

‘You mean because she was a transsexual?’

The old woman gripped the crucifix around her neck for a moment.

‘I wouldn’t let that filthy word pass my lips,’ she said tightly. ‘She disgraced the whole family with her degenerate behaviour.’

Kate nodded. ‘Is that how you and your sisters saw things at the time?’ she went on. ‘Degenerate behaviour? And is that why you persuaded Georgina’s parents to punish her so severely?’

Iris Naylor’s lip quivered with suppressed emotion.

‘It was the only way,’ she said. ‘She refused to abandon her sinful conduct and seek the Lord’s forgiveness.’

‘Maybe she didn’t see that there was anything to be forgiven for. Have you considered that your efforts to drive the demon out of her could actually have had the opposite effect and turned her into the psychotic she became?’

'Rubbish! She was born evil. Was it our fault that she stabbed that man to death in the orphanage? Of course it wasn't. She chose the wicked path she followed.'

'Apparently she killed the man because he was abusing her.'

'And that makes it right, does it?'

'No, it doesn't, but it explains her motive, doesn't it?'

There was a sharp hiss.

'And I suppose the next thing you're going to say is that because my sisters and I had Georgina sent to the orphanage at Talbot Court, it was our fault that she became a cold-blooded killer – we were responsible for what she did?'

Not directly, Kate mused grimly, without answering her question. But she felt tempted to quiz her as to what, apart from her so-called deviant behaviour, had motivated the old woman and her sisters to have their niece packed off to Talbot Court so soon after the deaths of the parents – and whether, as alleged by George herself and hinted at by Leslie Brookes, it might have had something to do with the inheritance due on their estate.

Certainly questions that needed answers, but maybe, Kate decided, not at that precise moment in time. As yet, there was no proof that anything fraudulent had actually occurred. Furthermore, there were far more important priorities to attend to than worrying about the veracity of Iris Naylor – like, for example, apprehending a dangerous psychopath before she killed again. So, she simply bit her lip and said nothing at all – which, ironically, had an adverse effect on Irish Naylor, who apparently took the detective's non-response to her question entirely the wrong way.

Leaning forward in her chair now, shaking with righteous indignation, she blazed defensively.

'We did everything we could for that ungrateful girl. Everything—'

'Including packing her off to Talbot Court, so you could wipe your hands of her?'

'That's a malicious slur! She was beyond help and none of us was prepared to take on responsibility for her when her parents died in that tragic car crash. Talbot Court should have provided the guidance and support that we couldn't. They were the professionals after all. How could we have been expected to know what was going to happen there?'

'But why pretend her surname was still Lupin, when in fact her mother had remarried and it should have been changed to Quigley? Was that to protect your family's reputation?'

'Absolutely not. It was Georgina herself who insisted on keeping that name. She refused to have it changed to Quigley—'

'What, a child of – what was she then – nine or ten?'

Perhaps sensing that the interview was fast becoming an interrogation, Hennessey quickly held up a hand in an apologetic gesture before the old woman could reply.

'Please, Mrs Naylor,' she said hastily, 'we are not seeking to criticize you or your sisters. We are simply pointing out what seems to be behind Georgina's murderous vendetta – what twisted thoughts are motivating her – and the key issue here is that, whatever the rights and wrongs of the situation, you are in the gravest danger.'

The warning prompted a short, cynical laugh. 'What, from the devil's child, you mean? I'm not afraid of Georgina Lupin, Chief Inspector – God's power will protect me.'

'It didn't do much for your two sisters,' Roscoe cut in, abruptly surfacing from the reverie that seemed to have occupied him since her arrival. 'They're both in the morgue.'

Hennessey threw him a sharp sidelong glance. 'We must find you some sort of safe house until we bring her in,' she said. 'You're welcome to remain here for a few hours until we can fix something up for you.'

There was an obstinate shake of the head. 'You'll do no such thing, Chief Inspector. I intend staying at Elsie's bungalow until everything is sorted out. I presume you'll want me to carry out a formal identification of my two sisters' remains, as I am their sole surviving relative, and there are funerals to arrange. I am determined both Elsie and Mabel will be given proper Christian burials and I will be speaking to the Reverend Glover about it as soon as I can get hold of him again.'

Hennessey sighed heavily. 'I'm afraid that, apart from the usual opening inquests, nothing else can be arranged until Georgina has been caught and the whole murder inquiry concluded,' she said, 'and actually catching her could take quite some time.'

The grey eyes appraised her again. 'There is one way to shorten the process.'

Hennessey frowned. 'I don't follow you.'

'Don't you? Well, it's quite simple really. You use me as a lure.'

'A what?'

A watery smile greeted the question. 'Bait, Chief Inspector, bait. We make sure my *darling niece* finds out that I am staying at Elsie's house. Then you and your officers lie in wait for her to come for me.'

For several seconds, all three detectives stared at her, plainly aghast at such an outlandish suggestion, especially coming as it had from a frail-looking old woman who seemed to have difficulty holding a tea cup steady in one hand, let alone confronting a dangerous psychopath.

'You've got to be joking?' Hennessey finally exclaimed. 'There is no way that that will happen.'

An ambivalent shrug. 'Please yourself. I shall be staying at Elsie's home anyway and I've already spoken to a reporter from the local newspaper, so Georgina is bound to find out sooner or later.'

'You've done *what*? Are you mad?'

'Now you're being insulting.'

'You're telling us you tipped off the press?'

The old woman tutted irritably and shook her head several times. 'I didn't tip anyone off. I just happened to run into a reporter outside your police station when I arrived here earlier. He seemed a pleasant enough young man and was obviously bored, so we had a nice little chat about things.'

'What sort of *things*?' Hennessey asked cautiously.

Their visitor hesitated, as if sensing that she had said too much. 'Well, you know – about the callous murder of my sisters and the fact that the … er … daughter of our late sister-in-law was responsible.'

'You said what?' Hennessey closed her eyes in resignation. 'Do you realize what you've done, Mrs Naylor? We've managed to keep all that information from the press so far and now you've blown it for us. This will be headline news in the daily newspapers this evening and it will almost certainly be on the radio and television news by lunchtime.'

Mrs Naylor tried unsuccessfully to feign innocence. 'Well, I wasn't to know that, was I?' she said with a cultivated humility.

The DCI's stare was cold and angry now.

'Whether you were or were not is irrelevant, but you're certainly not going to stay at your sister's home after this,' she said, 'and that's final – I won't allow it.'

'You're not in a position to stop me. Elsie was my sister and I have every right to stay at her home if I wish to do so. There's nothing you can do about it. Oh yes, and you needn't think you can scare Georgina off by sticking a uniformed policeman outside my door – *I* won't allow that!'

'It's a bloody crime scene,' Roscoe blurted suddenly. 'That means, it's a prohibited area.'

'No, it isn't. I happen to know that your people have already finished there.' The old woman climbed slowly to her feet. 'Anyway, perhaps you would like to argue the point with my solicitor? I'm quite sure she would see things very differently.'

For the first time Hennessey looked totally flummoxed, glancing quickly at both Roscoe and Kate, as if seeking some sort of support from them.

Their visitor gave a triumphant little smile. 'So, there it is, Chief Inspector. You either go along with my proposal or risk the public outcry that will follow if I suffer the same fate as my two sisters as a result of your intransigence.'

'Which could still happen if I were to agree to such an impossible madcap scheme,' the DCI retorted.

'It wouldn't if you were to set up an effective – what is it they call it? Oh yes, "stake-out", that's the phrase.'

'You've been reading too many detective stories, Mrs Naylor,' Kate put in grimly.

The old woman smiled. 'Maybe I have, Sergeant, but I do believe the three of you have reached one of those fait accompli moments and while you have a little chat about my suggestion, I think I would like to try some lunch in your police canteen, which I'm told is upstairs. I've had rather a long journey on the train, you see, and I am quite peckish.'

CHAPTER 22

Roscoe pulled out a packet of cigarettes. Then, under the DCI's admonishing frown and conscious of her meaningful glance at the 'No Smoking' notice on the wall, he slid them back into his pocket and selected a strip of chewing gum instead.

'So, where do we go from here?' he growled. 'Four bleedin' corpses in the local morgue, a dead shrink in another morgue up north, the killer still on the loose and the press camped outside the nick, demanding answers we can't give 'em – and now, just when we thought it couldn't get any worse, that old biddy pops up like a bad smell to give the screw another turn.'

Hennessey made a face. 'Well, that "old biddy" is out of luck if she thinks I'm going to agree to what she proposes,' she said. 'First, I don't have the manpower resources for such a labour-intensive commitment and secondly, if she imagines for one moment that I would ever agree to the sort of insane scheme she has come up with, then she's even more senile than she appears.'

'She's hardly senile,' Roscoe corrected. 'Strikes me she's a pretty tough cookie who couldn't be more switched on than she already is and whether we like to admit it or not, she's got us by the short and curlies. If we go along with her daft plan and that nutter manages to get past a surveillance team to stiff her, we'll be hung out to dry for using a frail old woman as bait. If we turn her down and she gets totalled anyway, we'll be pilloried for denying a vulnerable pensioner proper protection. It's a lose-lose situation.'

'Maybe Lupin wouldn't take the bait anyway?' Hennessey went on. 'After all, the whole thing is a bit obvious, isn't it? She's bound to smell a rat.'

'She can't afford *not* to take it,' Kate said. 'She's put too much effort into her bloody vendetta already and she's unlikely to pass up on the opportunity of one last hit, even if she does suspect she might be walking into a trap.'

'So, what *do* we do?' Roscoe snarled. 'Seems to me that whichever way we jump, we're right up shit creek without a paddle!'

Kate pursed her lips thoughtfully for a moment before commenting further.

'Maybe not,' she said. 'Maybe there is a way we could set a trap for Lupin baited with Iris Naylor, but at the same time minimize our exposure to any criticism that might result afterwards.'

'I'm all ears,' Hennessey encouraged cautiously.

Kate smiled. 'The media will, of course, be certain to release the information they have been given by Mrs Naylor,' she pointed out, 'especially after the double murder at the farmhouse, which has really raised the temperature of the water. But if we were quick enough with a general press release, naming Lupin as a person of interest to the inquiry and asking the public to report any sightings of her, the local media would be sure to marry that up with their own story. That means we wouldn't actually be the ones disclosing the information about Iris Naylor – thereby running the risk of being seen as deliberately placing her in jeopardy – but simply doing our duty by warning the public about Lupin being at large.'

'Bit dodgy giving out a suspect's details before we nail them, isn't it?' Roscoe cautioned. 'Could cost us a prosecution on the grounds of pre-trial prejudice.'

Kate shook her head. 'There is a precedent for this kind of release where it is considered that the risk to the public that a killer represents outweighs the usual legal considerations.'

Hennessey considered her comments, then nodded slowly. 'It could work too, Sergeant, but it would mean confirming the identities of Elsie Norman and Mabel Strong to the media prior to formal identification.'

'Yes, but that would be more of a technical breach of procedure than anything else at this stage as there is no doubt as to who they are and Iris Naylor is obviously their sole surviving relative, so no one else has to be informed first. Furthermore, the old woman will almost certainly be able to carry out formal ID for us shortly anyway, so the whole issue is now academic.'

'Okay, but what about the rest of what Mrs Naylor suggests? We still have to find a way out of that.'

'We could always adopt a halfway-house position.'

'And what's that when it's at home?'

Kate hesitated, conscious of Roscoe's narrowed gaze. 'Put a plainclothes officer in the bungalow with her,' she suggested. 'Another woman perhaps – a sort of companion – who would remain hidden from view the whole time and be ready to call in on a dedicated radio channel if she spotted anything suspicious.'

'That's just another sort of surveillance,' Roscoe growled dismissively. 'No difference.'

Kate shook her head. 'I disagree. This would be an observation role and could be set up without risking the kind of attention that a full surveillance operation would attract.'

Hennessey frowned. 'That would put one hell of a responsibility on your obs officer and place her in considerable danger.'

Kate shrugged. 'That's the name of the game for all of us, isn't it?' she said. 'But I would assume that the officer in question would be armed anyway, just in case, so the danger would be minimized.'

The DCI shook her head firmly. 'An armed officer would be out of the question – ACC Operations would never agree to it under the circumstances. Too much risk to Iris Naylor and other local residents, which couldn't be justified, especially as the target in this case is not thought to be armed.'

'She was armed with a shotgun at the farmhouse where I was held.'

'Yes, but she abandoned the weapon and we have no reason to believe that she has got hold of another one.'

Kate capitulated with a resigned nod. 'The important thing is that Mrs Naylor would be provided with a measure of protection, while at the same time we couldn't be accused of deliberately using her to ensnare our killer – which is, in fact, exactly what we *would* be doing.'

Hennessey treated her to a grim smile. 'Overall, what you are suggesting seems to be a good compromise, Sergeant,' she said. 'And to satisfy your other concerns, I will arrange for a back-up team to be deployed at a suitable location close to but not actually at the scene.'

Her smile broadened. 'So, a press release first then and, while I'm on to the Press Office about that, I suggest you nip home to get your toothbrush and nightie, ready for when Mrs Naylor is about to leave.'

'Me?'

'Who better to be her companion than the brains behind it all?'

Roscoe chuckled. 'You know what they say, Kate,' he taunted. 'When in a hole, stop digging – but think of this as a plus. At least you won't have to spend another night at home with dear old hubby.'

Hennessey threw him a curious glance, but Kate cut in before he could qualify his comment.

'Don't ask, ma'am,' she said tightly. 'Don't even ask.'

*

Georgina Lupin heard the news on local radio as she was buying a burger and a Coke from a van parked on a factory estate just outside Highbridge. The chubby man inside the vehicle had his radio on beside the fat fryer and it had been blasting out pop music until this was interrupted by the broadcast, and she wouldn't have paid much attention to it had the newscaster not come out with her name. When he did, she froze with the bun halfway to her mouth, the juices from the meat and fried onions running down the back of her hand on to her wrist as she listened intently to the news flash.

'Avon and Somerset Police have confirmed that they are currently investigating the deaths of a local farmer and his daughter whose bodies were found in a slurry pit on their farm last night. At present the names of these deceased are not being revealed, but we understand that their deaths are being treated as murder and that, in connection with the crime, a police manhunt is currently in progress to locate the whereabouts of a missing mental patient whom police have taken the unusual step of naming as Georgina Lupin. Lupin apparently escaped from the Larchfield Secure Psychiatric Hospital in Lancashire several days ago. She is also wanted for questioning in connection with the brutal murder of a senior hospital psychiatrist, Dr Emrys Jones, and the murders of two elderly sisters from the Highbridge area, who have now been named as Elsie Norman and Mabel Strong. A police spokeswoman has warned that Lupin, who is understood to be suffering from a serious mental illness, is extremely dangerous and should not be approached under any circumstances …'

There followed a description of the wanted patient and the usual emergency telephone number for the public to call in the event of a sighting, but George was no longer interested in the broadcast. Moving casually away from the van to avoid attracting unwelcome attention, she sat down on a low wall nearby, close to the bicycle she had stolen from outside Highbridge railway station. But she was still within earshot of the radio and the next instant some of the bun she was eating jammed momentarily in her gullet as the newscaster added to his broadcast.

'In a further twist to this case, crime correspondent for this channel, Jason Durrell, has this morning interviewed a Mrs Iris Naylor, who

is apparently the sister of the late Elsie Norman and Mabel Strong. Despite her age and infirmity, she has come forward to try to help the police bring this tragic case to a successful conclusion. Here is what she had to say …'

George's lip curled as she listened to the short interview, in which her aunt pleaded with her to give herself up. 'God will forgive,' the old lady promised, but Patient 174 was less interested in the Almighty's forgiveness than the revelation that the 'old bitch' would be staying on at Elsie Norman's home until she had sorted out her sisters' affairs.

George finally managed to swallow the remains of her bun and wipe her mouth on the back of her hand. So, Iris was back, was she? And staying in Aunt Elsie's home just a couple of miles away? Couldn't be better – or was there more to it than that? She frowned as she flicked open the tab of the Coke can. The whole thing smelled like rancid meat. It was as if it had been deliberately rigged. Maybe there was no Iris at all and the police had colluded with the radio station simply to set a trap for her to walk into? After all, she had not heard her aunt's voice since she was a child, so how could she know whether or not the speaker was the genuine article?

She took a long pull on the Coke can and idly watched a couple of workmen walk away from the burger van, clutching their dripping buns as they headed for one of the factories on the far side of the concrete apron that the burger van had chosen for its parking place.

But what if Iris really was back and staying at her sister's house? What if the news broadcast was just a case of the media getting a bit too cute on things? In any event, an opportunity had presented itself that was too good to miss. It had to be pursued, whatever her suspicious. She smiled grimly. Yes, but not without a very careful reconnoitre first. Draining the Coke can, she crushed it between both hands before dropping it over the wall. Then, picking up the bicycle, she pedalled out of the site towards the main road.

*

The stars were out, but the full moon was now partially obscured by scudding clouds. Not for the first time since commencing her observation duty, Kate peered through a chink in the curtains of the unlit front room, looking for any sign of movement outside. But the street beyond the tiny front garden was deserted and the windows of the other bungalows in immediate view were either displaying dim, ghostly lights behind their heavy curtains or were blacked out completely.

That was hardly surprising under the circumstances, since it was already well after eleven and most of the residents on this small development were known to be elderly and, like Iris Naylor herself, habitually turned in early. Nevertheless, it left Kate with a strange sense of isolation and a keen awareness of her own vulnerability. This was in spite of the fact that a second woman officer, Jenny Grey, was sleeping in the spare room upstairs. Unlike Kate, Grey was Taser trained and equipped, and had been reluctantly assigned to the OP at the last minute by Hennessey to provide a measure of additional protection, plus the four hours on-off cover necessary on such operations.

'Babysitting' Iris Naylor was not one of the easiest jobs Kate had been given and she felt that she had been handed a real poisoned chalice this time – especially as the old woman had been bristling with hostility from the first moment the DS had been assigned to protect her.

'What good is *she* going to be?' the eighty-something year old had sneered. 'Georgina will eat her for breakfast. I want a real policeman to watch over me, not some slip of a girl still wet behind the ears.'

Kate's mouth tightened as she recalled the old woman's bruising comments and Roscoe's broad smirk in response. The barbs had not stopped there, either, but had kept coming even after they had left the police station in the CID car. Without a doubt, Iris Naylor was a proper bitch and if her sisters had been anything like her, small wonder that

Georgina Lupin had developed such a pathological hatred of her aunts. So much for Christian values. It seemed that the Lupin family had been more like a witches' coven than anything else. Kate was almost tempted to walk out on the old woman altogether and actually let her homicidal niece finish her off like she had the others. Pity that could only be a pipe dream.

Turning into the room, Kate let the curtain fall back into place, making a wry face as Iris Naylor's snores filtered through the ceiling from the main bedroom upstairs.

She had already scrutinized the alleyway at the rear of the bungalow again and checked to make sure all the doors and windows were secure, but even though she had spotted nothing untoward, she was still uneasy, unable to shake off the feeling that the place was being watched.

Georgina Lupin was out there somewhere, she was sure of it; she had no option but to wait for her to make the first move. That ball was very firmly in George's court.

She glanced at her watch. Another couple of hours to go and it would be her turn to get her head down while her colleague did the honours, but while she felt dog-tired already, she knew she wouldn't be able to sleep properly. There was just too much on her mind – and not all of it related to Georgina Lupin either.

She had bumped into Hayden at lunchtime while returning to their cottage to pick up a change of clothes and some toilet requisites. He had been in the process of leaving for his late cover duty as she'd been about to turn into their driveway and his Jag was already belching smoke as it reversed out into the road. For a moment they stared at each other through closed windows and she saw his face crease into a surprised frown to see her coming home, but he made no effort to wind down his window to speak and before she could say anything, he had ducked his head and accelerated away. A man weighed down with guilt, she mused through gritted teeth, but one without the guts to face her and admit to his infidelity.

Swaying slightly, she simply stood there in the middle of the room, gripping the back of a nearby armchair and trying to hold back the tears.

*

Georgina Lupin stood up slowly and stretched the muscles of both legs to ease the painful cramp in her calves. She ruefully acknowledged that taking to bicycle power again after so many years incarcerated in Larchfield and other institutions may not have been the best idea she had ever had.

The overgrown rear garden of the small, apparently empty cottage backed on to the lane behind Elsie Norman's chalet bungalow where George had previously parked the stolen Land Rover. It provided an ideal observation point and a perfect place to conceal the stolen bicycle. From the all-embracing gloom of the broken-down gateway, she had an uninterrupted view of the bungalow opposite and had spotted the two plainclothes policewomen sneaking in via the back door just before it got dark – one she immediately recognized as the detective she had earlier held captive.

So, Iris had a couple of minders, had she? No doubt equipped with state-of-the-art personal radios, linked to the police station. She affected a sneer. *Stupid bastards!* Did they think she would swallow the whole rigged set-up just like that? She'd already suspected the thing was a trap, so she wasn't surprised to have it confirmed by the arrival of the two coppers. But it wouldn't stop her finishing what she'd started anyway, that was for sure. Aunt Iris had been the ringleader throughout George's years of misery, influencing all the others with her poisonous religious claptrap, and there was no way she was going to escape the very special punishment the twisted brain of her psychotic niece had in store for her.

The problem was how to get to the old woman without bringing half of Avon & Somerset's finest down on her head. George was not put off by the presence of the two policewomen. In a physical confrontation, she knew they would be easy meat and they hadn't appeared to be armed when she'd seen them. But at the same time, it needed to be borne in mind that it would only take one press of a panic button to foul everything up and there might never be another opportunity for a crack at the old woman.

She frowned, tapping her front teeth with her fingernails as she tried to come up with a solution. What she needed was a diversion of some sort – something to distract the police long enough for her to get into Elsie Norman's bungalow and out again with her 'prize' before anyone was the wiser. But what? Then she glimpsed the orange flicker of an open fire in the window of the property next door and remembered the industrial site where she had bought her burger only that morning. Yes, that was it. And it was within easy pedalling distance of where she now stood too. She felt her heart jump. Of course. So simple and yet so effective. It just couldn't fail. All she needed was a little more time to set things up.

Seconds later, she mounted her bicycle again and slipped away into the night.

CHAPTER 23

Daniel Tomlinson had been working for Lester Security for what seemed like forever – ever since his retirement from the Metropolitan Police. Now just short of sixty-two and not in the best of health – mainly because of his beer-induced weight and forty-a-day smoking habit – he was actively looking for a way to pack in the job early and spend more time with his lively grandchildren, whom he adored.

Pullman Paints was just one of any number of factories on his list of nightly checks – an ugly, rambling site of concrete and corrugated iron in an industrial estate just outside Highbridge. Why it was actually on his list of vulnerable premises he couldn't fathom, as the site had nothing of real value to criminals – just sheds full of tins of paint produced by Pullman's monster machines for the building trade – but it wasn't his place to question the wisdom of those who had hired the company he worked for. They had to have their reasons and he happened to know that there was a nice wooden hut just inside the double gates where he could shelter from the cold and the wet with his whisky flask and a roll-up, so who was he to complain?

'Just go with the flow, Dan,' he'd often said to himself. 'Go with the flow and be thankful for small mercies.'

But that was until he made his discovery during his rounds on what had to be his hundredth visit to the factory, a discovery that rooted him to the spot with shock for several seconds. The chain-link fence to one side of the main padlocked gates had been cut and peeled right back.

'Bloody Nora!' he breathed, following the trail of moonlight with his eyes as it flowed through the gaping hole and along the service road into the site.

Automatically, he reached for the button of the personal radio clipped to the lapel of his uniform jacket to alert Lester Security's control centre, but then he paused, thinking quickly as he glanced around him. He'd reported what had turned out to be false alarms on two other premises the previous month and a third would do him no good at all – especially as some of his younger colleagues were already poking fun at him behind his back, suggesting he was heading for the funny farm. Maybe he should check around first before sending the balloon up. After all, the site was in a pretty poor state, with much of the chain-link already rusted and bulging in places, and the damage could easily have been the work of mischievous kids from the nearby housing estate, looking for somewhere quiet to roll a joint. Anyway, why would anyone want to screw a paint factory? It didn't make sense.

Mind made up, he unclipped his flashlight and bent down to duck through the hole, swearing as he caught the back of his hand on one of the severed strands of the fence.

The river of moonlight led him between a couple of long, corrugated-iron sheds he assumed to be paint stores, to a large, brick building, which faced him across a tarmacked apron divided up into white-painted parking bays. He'd done the rounds of the site before and knew that the building he was looking at housed the factory and administrative offices, so was no doubt a hive of activity during the day. It was dead now, of course, and the only light visible in the windows of the building was that provided by the reflected light of the moon.

He shivered slightly. There was something about the place on this brilliant moonlit night that gave him the creeps and he glanced quickly around him, sensing without any tangible reason that he was being watched.

'Get a grip, you old fool,' he muttered to himself, thinking of his thirty-year police career. 'What are you, some kind of bloody wimp?'

Forcing himself across the car park towards the factory block, he checked the double doors but found them to be securely locked. Then, moving slowly along the wall to his left, he turned his attention to the transom windows. Nothing. Everything seemed secure. He was on the point of taking a look at the back of the place when he heard it – a loud 'clang' coming from the paint sheds on other side of the car park.

He wheeled around, the hairs stirring on the back of his neck. Immediately he saw the light. It seemed to be framed in the side window of one of the sheds. An intense flame that blossomed into an angry glare even as he looked. Fire!

Depressing the button of his personal radio, he shouted his call-sign and location to the control room as he ran towards the shed, which in the space of those few seconds had erupted into a mammoth blaze.

Georgina Lupin emerged from the rear of the building even as Daniel reached it. But the security officer was hardly conscious of the figure heading for the front gates at a characteristic loping run. At that moment the thousands of litres of paint, thinners and other corrosive substances stacked in 5-litre cans on the steel racks exploded in a massive fireball, engulfing both him and the adjoining shed and providing Daniel Tomlinson with a much more dramatic, though terminal, exit from his job than the early retirement he had envisaged.

*

Kate couldn't sleep. Jenny Grey had reluctantly taken over from her an hour before and was somewhere downstairs, keeping vigil, but this didn't give Kate any real sense of reassurance, despite the fact that her colleague was equipped with a Taser. She knew from personal experience what Georgina Lupin was like and how dangerous the woman could be, Taser or not. As Kate herself was not so trained and therefore not authorized to carry the immobilizing weapon, she felt very vulnerable with just her police issue CS gas spray for protection. She could practically feel George's presence nearby and was jolted into instant wakefulness at every creak and groan of the old sixties' bungalow, every grunt and snore of the old woman sleeping in the next room, visualizing the bald-headed psychopath creeping up the stairs from the hallway.

In the end, she got up and left the room to check around – and it was just as well that she did. She found Jenny curled up, fast asleep in one of the armchairs in the sitting room downstairs and shook her roughly by the shoulder.

'What the hell do you think you're doing?' she hissed. 'You're supposed to be keeping watch.'

'Sorry, skipper,' the young woman mumbled. 'I just couldn't keep my eyes open. What time is it?'

Kate moved to the window and peered out through the tiny gap in the curtains, glancing briefly at the luminous dial of her wristwatch in the process. 'Just after three,' she replied, scrutinizing the small front garden and empty street. 'Go and get your head down. I'll continue this watch.'

'But I should be doing that. It's my turn.'

Kate grunted. 'Forget it,' she retorted. 'I can't sleep anyway. Have you called in a "sit" report to control, as per schedule?'

'Ten minutes ago. Told them nothing was happening.'

Kate nodded grimly. 'Let's hope it stays that way.'

But it didn't. Within twenty minutes of Jenny disappearing in the direction of the stairs, Kate heard the dull and not too distant 'whoomph' of an explosion and, returning quickly to the front window and pressing her face against the glass, she saw the fiery glare lighting up the night sky beyond the bungalows towards the end of the street. It was a major fire obviously and she guessed it was located on the other side of the fields she had checked out before, following Elsie Norman's murder. More explosions followed and this was closely followed by the scream of sirens.

'What's going on?' she demanded on her radio's dedicated channel.

'*Major fire,*' the control room operator replied tersely. '*Paint factory on an industrial estate. Outskirts of Highbridge. Fire brigade and all available units en route.*'

'Cause known?'

'*Too early to say.*'

Kate frowned, feeling distinctly uneasy. But she didn't communicate the fact to the operator.

'Keep us in the loop,' she said before signing off.

A grunt sufficed as an answer and the phone went dead, leaving her to the stillness of the night.

For a few moments she stood in the middle of the room, chewing her bottom lip and thinking. Fires on industrial sites were not uncommon and most of them turned out to be due to electrical faults, but it seemed a bit coincidental that one should break out on this night of all nights and just a few fields away from the little bungalow development. Maybe she was getting paranoid, but it occurred to her that an incident of this nature was almost certain to suck in every available resource from miles around – including some, if not all, the potential back-up she had been promised in the event of George paying Iris Naylor a visit. Lupin might be crazy, but she was also highly intelligent and would have known only too well what the consequences of such a serious incident would be. As a diversionary tactic, a major fire with all the risk to life and property that it posed – not only from the flames themselves, but also from the toxic cloud that it generated – had no equal and that bothered Kate more than she cared to admit.

As a reflex action, she abruptly turned on her heel, heading back along the short hallway and upstairs to the front bedroom where Iris Naylor was sleeping, her torch lighting her way but masked in one hand. Loud snores still emanated from the room, but she poked her head inside anyway, just to make sure all was in order. The old woman was lying on her back in a sliver of moonlight, propped up by three or four pillows. Her mouth was wide open and her slight frame in the flannel nightdress trembled with each reverberation that issued from the back of her throat.

Kate gave a slightly amused smile and, crossing to the window and carefully closing the narrow gap in the curtains, she returned to the landing and shut the bedroom door quietly behind her.

For a few moments more she stood there, with her head on one side, listening intently. Above the snores she could hear the sound of more sirens on the main road perhaps 2 miles away, almost certainly heading for the blazing factory. But otherwise there was nothing.

Next, she checked on her colleague and found that she was also out for the count. Peering round the door of the spare bedroom, she just managed to make out the hump on the single bed under the window and marvelled at Jenny's ability to sleep so soundly in such circumstances. She hesitated for a second, wondering if she should wake her with her apprehensions, but then thought better of it. They would almost certainly turn out to be groundless and she would end up looking a complete fool.

The floorboards creaked as she withdrew from the room and made her way back downstairs, but it was the only sound to disturb what now felt like an unnatural stillness. The prelude to something perhaps, or maybe just her paranoid imaginings?

The beam of her torch glinted on the stainless-steel kettle standing alone on the cooker hob in the kitchen and she jumped involuntarily as something suddenly passed in front of it. But it was only the black cat Iris Naylor had brought with her and she gave a relieved chuckle as she bent down to ruffle its ears.

'Out on the razzle, are you, puss?' she breathed. 'Let's hope you're the only one.'

Switching off her torch, she crossed to the small window and parted the Venetian blinds to peer out into the back garden – spending a few moments studying the patchy shadows where the moonlight failed to reach. But she saw no one and finally allowed the blinds to fall into place again.

Turning back into the kitchen after testing the handle of the rear door to make sure it was securely locked, she filled the kettle from the kitchen tap and switched it on. After making herself a black coffee she returned to the sitting room, sipping from the china mug as she went.

The night retained its composure after the earlier disruptions, the sirens no longer screaming out their warning, but the curtains were touched by a faint orange glow. She peered through a chink and saw that the blaze on the other side of the fields had strengthened considerably, lighting up the whole horizon and spilling out clouds of heavy black smoke, tendrils of which had already begun to reach across the face of the moon.

She let the curtain drop back into place and was on the point of dropping into an armchair to finish her coffee, when she heard a loud 'crack' like glass breaking, apparently coming from the rear of the house. Dumping her mug on a coffee table, she tiptoed across the room to the hall and stared into the gloom, pulling her torch back out of the pocket of her coat as she did so but without switching it on.

Silence. She could feel it pressing down on her like a tangible thing. She fancied she heard movement in the hall and on sudden impulse, flicked on the torch.

The cold, green eyes met hers in an unwavering stare and she inhaled sharply. It was the cat again, no doubt seeking company, and it continued playing with what seemed to be some sort of small medicine bottle it had picked up somewhere, pouncing on it and seizing it with its jaws before rolling over on to its back with its claws trapping the thing between them as if it were a mouse.

Kate took a deep breath. No doubt the sound she had heard was the bottle striking the kitchen tiles in the course of pussy's game. The damned animal would give her a heart attack if it carried on like this – if it didn't cut itself on the glass first. She directed her torch down the hall towards the kitchen she had only just checked. Everything looked fine.

She shivered, thinking of the horror films she had watched as a teenager. It was always the cat that would first startle the teenage girl in the creepy house, wasn't it? Usually in the cellar, the attic or the outside washroom. And then, just after it had materialized and the girl had relaxed with a sigh of relief, the psychopathic killer would jump out on her from the shadows and cut her throat. She scowled, glancing quickly behind her.

'Nice one, Kate,' she murmured to herself. 'Just what I need right now.'

Returning to the sitting room, she checked the street outside again, then dropped into the armchair she had just left.

As she did so, Hayden's chubby smiling face appeared in her mind's eye. She wondered where he was at that precise moment – still on late duty perhaps? Maybe he was at the fire with everyone else? There could be evacuations underway from nearby houses, which was standard practice if dangerous, toxic fumes were present, and CID as well as uniformed officers would be deployed to knock on doors. Furthermore, if the incident turned out to be suspect, there would be a crime scene to preserve after the fire service had done their stuff and an investigation to undertake.

She scowled. Yeah, but it was more likely that he had already gone off duty and was at that very moment tucked up with his new love in Uphill. The creep.

The thought of him in bed with another woman conjured up some very unpleasant visions, but despite closing her eyes tightly for a few seconds, these refused to go away and they would have plagued her for a lot longer had she not been abruptly shaken out of her reverie by a more immediate concern – what she thought was a series of dull thuds coming from somewhere not too far away from where she was sitting.

She held her breath and leaned forward in the chair, ears straining for a repeat of the sound, eyes fixed intently on the dark, oblong slash of the sitting room door. But she was unable to detect any furtive movement outside in the hall and the sounds were not repeated. Frowning, she climbed slowly to her feet and crossed the room to peer round the edge of the door, thinking that maybe the cat was up to its tricks again or either Iris or her own police colleague had got up to use the toilet upstairs. But nothing now stirred, upstairs or downstairs.

She stepped carefully into the hallway, switching on her torch but masking the beam in one hand, as before. Through the open kitchen door, she could see a trace of moonlight on the quarry tiles, but there was no sign of anyone when she directed the full beam of her torch into the small room and certainly nowhere to hide. But then she saw the broken glass – a few glittering shards lying close to the back door – and felt an immediate adrenalin rush.

Striding swiftly into the room, she saw that the back door was ajar and one of the six glass panels in the upper part of the door – the one nearest to the lock, which had been repaired after Georgina Lupin had previously broken in – had been smashed. Much of the glass, which seemed to have been taped up before being broken, was lying on the grass outside, with tape still attached to some fragments. It was obvious to Kate's trained eye that the pieces had been carefully removed from the frame and deposited there to enable the insertion of a hand to turn the key and unlock the door. Georgina Lupin was inside the bungalow.

Depressing the transmit button of her personal radio, she blurted the pre-arranged coded emergency call to the control room. Then, without waiting for a reply, she jerked the CS gas spray from her pocket and headed for the stairs, her torch blazing a path through the gloom as she took them two at a time.

The door to the spare room was wide open and, despite the gloom, the figure draped across the bed was clearly visible.

Snapping on the light, she took in the horrific scene in a split second. Jenny was lying on her back, half in, half out of the bed, her tousled curls practically touching the floor, her eyes bulging from their sockets and lips drawn back in the grotesque, rictus grin of strangulation. From the state of the bedclothes, it was obvious that she had put up quite a fight before she'd died, but the policewoman hadn't stood a chance against her much more powerful adversary. Kate now knew the cause of the thudding sounds that had alerted her and she felt the guilt all but consume her at the thought that, while she had been rooting around downstairs, just feet above her head her young colleague had been fighting for her life. But she was left with no time for self-recriminations. Even as she choked back the bile surging up into her throat, a shrieking cry, followed by the unmistakable blast of a firearm, erupted from the room opposite, spinning her around and sending her charging across the landing.

Wrenching open the main bedroom door, she was presented with an unbelievable sight. Iris Naylor was sitting upright in bed, her back against the pillows and a heavy-looking revolver grasped in both hands. Just feet away, Georgina Lupin was backing away, one hand held out in front of her, palm raised in an apparent defensive gesture and a twisted expression on her face in which anger and disbelief were clearly mixed.

That the bullet had missed its mark was apparent from the gaping hole in the wall plaster above the psychopath's head, but the old woman's finger was already tightening on the trigger and the gun was shaking in her unsteady grip.

'Devil's child!' she admonished in a high-pitched theatrical voice. 'I cast you back from whence you came!'

But even as she pulled the trigger, it was already too late. Moving with surprising speed, her would-be target hurled herself to one side, slamming into Kate before she could employ the CS gas spray and bowling her over. At the same moment the revolver blasted another hole in the wall where the killer had been standing. Then George was gone, lunging through the bedroom doorway and hammering down the stairs like some grotesque creation from a Gothic horror story, before merging with the patchy shadows of the moonlit street.

CHAPTER 24

'I'll take that,' Kate snarled, relieving Iris Naylor of what turned out to be a Webley revolver. 'Where the hell did you get this?'

The old woman gave a slow, secret smile. 'My hubby was in the army once,' she replied simply. 'He kept it as a souvenir after demob.'

Kate took a deep, trembling breath, feeling the room swaying around her as she tried to stay in control.

'And you thought you would use it to execute your niece?' she choked through the bile once more rising in her throat.

An unrepentant shrug. 'I knew she would come for me, so I slipped the gun under my pillow and waited for her to appear.'

Kate stared at the hole in the wall where the first shell had ended up and closed her eyes tightly for a second to shut out the vision of Jenny lying on the bed.

The old woman made a face, seemingly unaware of the policewoman's distress.

'Well, I did manage to load it all right with some spare bullets hubby left in a drawer, but I thought it would be easier to use than it was. I've never fired a gun before.'

Kate placed one hand against the wall to help her to keep her balance as waves of nausea swept through her.

'So … so all this talk about a police surveillance operation was just rubbish?' she grated in a voice that did not seem to belong to her. 'You … you were using us as back-up in case anything went wrong?'

Another shrug and the old lady eased herself out of the bed and felt for her carpet slippers before staring up at Kate defiantly.

'She is an abomination and has to be destroyed,' she said. 'I have a duty to my faith and my poor sisters to send her back to the demon that created her.'

Kate came off the wall and shuddered as she stared back through the open door to the body of her colleague still lying crosswise on the bed in the next room.

'A *duty* which has now cost the life of a dedicated police officer,' she rasped, making no attempt to conceal the disgust in her voice as she tore her gaze away from the grisly sight. 'An officer who was put here to protect *you*.'

The old woman peered round her, across the landing, and instantly paled, raising a hand to her mouth.

'God help us,' she gasped. 'Are you saying she's … she's dead?'

Kate turned away from her and headed unsteadily for the door as flashing blue light suddenly washed across the walls through the thin curtains, announcing the arrival of the back-up she had been shouting for.

'As she'll ever be,' she threw back over her shoulder. 'Dead at twenty-four years of age – and all because of your stupid underhand plan.'

The ambulance crew were up the stairs first, a man and a woman in their green paramedic uniforms. Kate waved them into Jenny's room as a uniformed police constable thumped up the stairs, closely followed by a furiously scowling Roscoe.

Kate lowered her gaze as he brushed past her into Iris Naylor's room where she was sitting on the edge of the bed, wringing her hands and sobbing quietly. He threw her a scathing glance, then turned and stared at the revolver still grasped in Kate's hand.

'She … she had it under her pillow,' Kate said tremulously in response to his unspoken question. 'Tried to waste George. It was what she was up to all along.'

He took the weapon from her and handed it to the uniformed officer standing awkwardly on the landing behind him.

'Bag it,' he rapped, then turned sharply to push past Kate to the threshold of Jenny's room, where he paused, taking in the scene with one sweeping glance and noting the ambulance woman's helpless shrug with a grunt.

'Get hold of the Home Office pathologist,' he shouted at a plainclothes officer who was just starting up the stairs, 'and we'll need to secure this crime scene and get SOCO here pdq.'

As the ambulance crew left, the DI treated Kate to a hard stare.

'You okay?' he said, studying her face intently, and when she nodded, he jerked his head in the direction of the stairs, adding, 'We need a private talk.'

Joining him in the sitting room a few moments later, Kate waited for the outburst she was expecting. Instead, he sank on to the arm of the settee and ran the palm of his hand over his face. He looked about ten years older than he actually was and his eyes seemed to have shrunk into their sockets.

'No trace of the bloody psycho,' he said. 'Pulled four units off the fire as soon as I could after control sent out your call, but by the time we managed to get 'em mobile the bitch was away on her toes.'

He scowled. 'Turned up a stiff at the blaze too – security officer, looks like. What a bleedin' mess!'

Kate sat down carefully on the edge of an armchair, feeling a sudden weakness in her legs, which had also begun to shake.

'Have … have we called for a dog unit?' she queried a little too abruptly, her desperate attempt to maintain a professional stance after the awful shock she had received betrayed by the faltering tone of her voice.

He threw her another keen glance, but kept any observations he'd made to himself and nodded.

'No dice. Apparently, any dogs that were available have been sent to a major incident – triple stabbing and near riot at a biker's so-called convention near Bristol. Waste of time anyway. Our killer will already be long gone by now.'

She clenched her teeth briefly, feeling hot and clammy as waves of nausea threatened to engulf her.

'Do you think Lupin started the fire as a diversionary tactic?' she said, still trying to sound as normal as possible, but acutely aware of the fact that she sounded anything but.

'Highly likely, I would think – and it friggin' well worked too.'

'At least she … she didn't succeed in adding Iris Naylor to her hit list …' she blurted on impulse, then broke off with a gulp as she thought of Jenny Grey lying dead upstairs, but he seemed not to have heard her.

'Don't suppose the old girl managed to wing the bitch, did she?'

She swallowed hard, then shook her head. 'Put holes in the wall, that's about it.'

'So, Lupin is uninjured then?'

'I think so, yes.'

'Must have nine lives, that one – like a soddin' cat – number of times she's got away.'

'They say the devil looks after his own,' she said bitterly.

He gave her an old-fashioned look, then stood up quickly, some of his old vigour returning.

'Yeah, well let's hope the guv'nor thinks of it that way when she gets here. Meantime, we need to get Naylor away to a safe house.'

Kate made a supreme effort to get a grip on herself and cleared her throat to strengthen her voice.

'Could be risky – moving her, with Lupin still out there.'

He slipped some gum into his mouth and shrugged. 'No choice. She can't stay here after this and it's a crime scene now anyway, which will have to be preserved before every hairy-arsed plod walks all over any evidence that may be present.'

'Anywhere in mind?'

'Nope. But the boss might have when she deigns to arrive. If I had my way, though, it would be somewhere like Afghanistan.'

*

Georgina Lupin studied Elsie Norman's bungalow from just inside the broken-down gateway with a keen intensity. After fleeing the crime scene, she had brazenly doubled back, returning to the very observation point she had used before breaking into the bungalow and strangling the woman police officer.

The spot suited her purposes admirably. She had a clear, unobstructed view of the rear of the bungalow, from the gateway of the small cottage, with its high, ivy-clad perimeter walls completely shielding it from the moonlight on the other side of the lane. She was confident that the comforting gloom kept her well hidden from prying eyes, particularly those of nosy neighbours and the police – though it was unlikely it would occur to the latter that she'd have the gall to return to the crime scene anyway. They would assume she was at least a couple of miles away by now and still running – which was exactly what she was counting on.

It would have been better, of course, to have found somewhere at the front of the bungalow where all the action was, but that had presented too much of a risk and, from what she'd remembered of the cul-de-sac, it offered no suitable places of concealment anyway, so it was not worth considering.

No, she was in the best possible spot, she was sure about that. The only problem was what to do next. There was no way she was going to abandon her vendetta and let Iris Naylor off the hook – not when that evil old crone was the principal cause of the misery inflicted on her throughout all those long, nightmare years. The other three sisters had been guilty too, of course. After all, they had gone along with everything Iris had proposed and, although this had probably been due to their own spineless reluctance to stand up to their more dominant sister, they were still complicit, so it didn't lessen their culpability. But it was Iris who had been the prime mover in it all, so it was Iris who had to face the most elaborate punishment.

How to get to the old woman, though? That was the point. In her present position, George obviously had no real idea what was happening inside the bungalow – exactly where Iris was and whether or not she was now under even tighter police protection. She knew from the multitude of news and documentary programmes she had watched on her bedroom television during her long period of incarceration at Larchfield that the bungalow would now have been made a crime scene. That meant it would have been put under heavy police guard to await the arrival of the Scenes of Crime forensic teams, so not even a mouse would be able to slip in unnoticed. It also meant that no one, save the SOCOs, would be allowed to remain inside and that would include Iris Naylor. In fact, there had been the sound of doors banging and vehicles pulling away at the front of the place a short time earlier, which suggested that the exodus had already begun, and a marked police car had now been parked across the bungalow's back entrance, just feet away from her, almost certainly as a very visible security measure.

She scowled in the darkness. So, where the hell *was* Iris Naylor? Had the old woman already been spirited away to some secret address by one of the police cars that had just left or was she still in the bungalow, waiting to be escorted out? And if the bird had already flown, how would it ever be possible to find out where she had gone?

George's frustration was reaching boiling point – the memory of decades of childhood abuse and institutionalized misery once again burning a lava-like path through her brain as she thought of all that she had been subjected to, all that she had lost, and all that was to be denied her because of the cruel, agonizing death soon to cut short the remainder of her wasted life.

There would be no last-minute reprieve because of past sufferings or injustices. No review or reconsideration. Not even a temporary stay of execution. The clock was already set and ticking and its progress could not be reversed or halted. Death was inevitable – yet obscurity was not and George was determined that, with her last act, the world would know the truth and be ashamed. But to achieve that end, she needed to get to Iris Naylor and the prospect of locating her looked to be fading by the minute.

George was so wound up that at first, she took little notice of the second police vehicle – a long wheelbase Ford Transit van – turning into the back lane. But she was jolted out of her self-pitying reverie when she saw the uniformed police officer climb out of the patrol car parked across the bungalow's rear gate and step into full view of the Transit's headlights. The police officer in the big vehicle flashed his lights, then accelerated past the patrol car to another gateway further along the lane. George watched as the Transit reversed into the gateway, turned, and drove slowly back to the patrol car to park a short distance in front of it.

The driver climbed down from the vehicle, nodding briefly to his colleague as he sauntered towards him with his hands thrust deep in his pockets and George stiffened, her heartbeat suddenly accelerating, when she heard him announce loudly what he was there for.

'Sent to pick up some old biddy – an Iris Naylor?'

'Yeah,' the patrol car driver replied. 'She's just packing her stuff. Guv'nor wants her out of here asap. I'll take you to her. She might need a hand with her suitcase.'

He led the way round the patrol car and through the bungalow's back gate.

'Any trace of the bleedin' psycho what did poor little Jenny?' George heard the Transit driver query.

'Nah,' the other replied. 'Guv'nor reckons she'll be halfway to Taunton by now.'

And as their voices faded, just thirty feet away in the gloom of the ruined gateway, 'the bleedin' psycho' gave a triumphant smile.

CHAPTER 25

DCI Hennessey was in a foul mood when she arrived – pale, tight-lipped and radiating aggression. And she was in an even worse mood once she had climbed the stairs to see Jenny Grey's contorted body laid out on the bed in the upstairs bedroom, beyond the crime scene tapes.

But she said nothing there, merely issuing a sharp explosive hiss before leading the way back down the stairs to the front room.

'How could this have happened?' she demanded harshly, studying Kate with undisguised hostility.

Kate swallowed hard, tears still evident in her blue eyes. 'Lupin forced her way in through the back door while I was on watch in here,' she said. 'I heard nothing, until … until …'

To her surprise, Roscoe quickly came to her rescue. 'Lupin taped up the window to deaden the sound of the breaking glass, then reached through to turn the key,' he said. 'No one would have heard anything from in here.'

The DCI closed her eyes briefly in resignation. 'We left the *key* in the door?' she exclaimed. 'Why didn't we just put a notice outside inviting the murderous swine in?'

Kate had no answer for that and simply stared at the floor.

Hennessey shook her head in disbelief to reinforce her point, but didn't pursue the issue any further.

'So, what made Lupin take off without first wasting Iris Naylor?' she went on and cast Kate a cynical glance. 'It seems unlikely that Sergeant Lewis here managed to put the fear of God into her on her own.'

'The old girl had us over,' Roscoe explained. 'Her whole purpose was to lure the nutter to this place, then top the cow herself. She had her dead husband's revolver hidden under the pillow in her bedroom and went for a couple of pot-shots.'

The DCI raised an eyebrow. 'And?' she said tersely.

'She missed,' Kate replied.

Hennessey shook her head and uttered a short unamused laugh. 'Why doesn't that surprise me?' she said, then after a brief pause, released a heavy sigh, adding, 'Well, for the information of both of you, I've just had ACC Operations on the blower and he's not a happy man.'

'Object to having his beauty sleep disturbed, did he?' Roscoe commented drily.

Hennessey scowled at him, but ignored the remark. 'SOCO been called?' she went on tersely, changing the subject.

The DI grunted. 'And the pathologist. ETAs of both around half an hour, we've been told.'

'And our "sharp-shooter"? Where is *she* now?'

'Shut in her bedroom,' Roscoe replied. 'But we need to get her out of here pdq. I've got a unit coming to pick her up and take her back to the nick.'

'To go where?'

'I thought you might want to decide where we should place her for the rest of the night.'

A curt nod in response. 'The nick will do for the time being. Any news on Lupin?'

Roscoe shook his head. 'Got all units out looking. Nothing so far. She seems to have completely disappeared.'

'But it's possible she might have gone to ground somewhere close by, with the intention of having another go at her target when the opportunity presents itself.'

'Unlikely, but yeah, I suppose that's feasible.'

'So, we'll need to make sure Iris Naylor is kept under close protection until we can feel Lupin's collar.'

'Already in hand. We're going to move her out the back way under escort to avoid attracting attention.'

Hennessey grimaced. 'Press will be all over this thing at first light,' she pointed out. 'We'll have to have an official statement prepared before some eagle-eyed stringer pips us at the post and calls the story in.'

She raised her gaze to meet that of the DI. 'And what about Grey? Was she married or what? Close relatives will need to be informed before this gets out.'

'She was single, I believe,' Roscoe said gruffly. 'But I'll see to it.'

'You do that, and in the meantime, Sergeant Lewis here will go in the escort wagon to the nick with Mrs Naylor and stay with her until I decide what we do with her – got that, Sergeant?'

Kate nodded.

'Good. And this time you will not allow her out of your sight. Capiche?'

Another nod, but Hennessey was determined to ram her message home. 'And that means even if she wishes to go to the toilet or wash her hands, you will go with her, like a bloody shadow.'

Roscoe snorted. 'I can't see that being necessary in the nick,' he growled. 'Lupin wouldn't have the nerve to try something there.'

Hennessey's face was grim. 'Is that right? Well, I for one wouldn't like to put money on it,' she replied.

*

Police constable Bill Adams had been in the force for twenty-eight years. A tough ex-army man, he had a reputation for a no-nonsense approach to his job and he was not averse to dishing out summary justice when the situation warranted it. His short fuse had given rise to a number of complaints from disgruntled, badly bruised 'clients' over the years, two of which were still being investigated, and he was certainly not a strong contender in the popularity stakes at police headquarters. But despite his track record, he did have other uses, a fact which the ever-pragmatic Ted Roscoe had recognized in detailing him to act as Iris Naylor's unofficial minder.

As for Iris Naylor herself, while she could not possibly have known anything about Adam's reputation or his past history, his comforting bulk would have been enough on its own anyway and, as Kate followed the comic ill-matched pair through the back door of the bungalow and along the moonlit path – the tiny woman completely submerged in the shadow of her muscular escort – she could not help but appreciate the humour of the moment and she was unable to hold back a smile in spite of the situation.

Her smile did not last long, however. Just as they got to the garden gate, Iris Naylor suddenly stopped dead and swung round to face her.

'I've forgotten my vanity case,' she exclaimed. 'I can't leave without that.'

Kate threw a quick glance past her at her colleague, who had also stopped and had set down the suitcase he was carrying for the old woman.

'I'll bring it to the station for you later,' Kate said with undisguised irritation.

'No, no, no,' the other wailed. 'I have to have it with me now. It has all my toiletries in it – plus all my money. I must have left it on the bed.'

Kate took a deep breath and once more stared past her at her colleague, only to be treated to a resigned shrug.

'All right, all right,' she snapped. 'Go with this officer and I'll get it for you.' Then to Adams, 'I won't be a minute, Bill.'

In fact, it was ordained that she was going to be a lot longer than a minute. The case was certainly where Iris

Naylor had said she'd left it, but Kate never got to take it out to her. The heavy-set figure in the ill-fitting coat that suddenly materialized at the bottom of the stairs, barring her way, put paid to that.

Hayden's face was flushed and perspiring, his hair even more awry than usual, his blue eyes wide and staring.

'What on earth are you doing here?' she exclaimed, making to push past him. 'This is a crime scene. You shouldn't even be in the place.'

A hand seized her arm in a surprisingly strong grip.

'I heard a wopsie had been … had been—' he blurted. 'I thought—'

She glared at the hand clasping her arm, angered by the attempt at restraint and also the use of the long-outdated colloquialism for a female police officer.

'No, it wasn't me, Hayd,' she grated. 'Disappointed, are you?'

He released her arm and shrank back from her as if she had struck him. 'That's a horrible thing to say,' he choked.

'Is it?' she retorted. 'What did you expect me to say?'

'But there is no other woman. You have to believe me.'

'I don't *have* to do anything, Hayden,' she replied. 'So, why don't you just clutter off back to your bit of spare?'

She was conscious of him shambling after her and desperately calling on her to 'wait' as she headed for the back door. But she ignored his entreaties and instead quickened her pace as she strode up the garden path to the gate.

Once there, however, she had a lot more to think about than Hayden and his other woman. The patrol car, which had been parked across the back gate, was now gone – called to a fatal accident she later learned – and a few feet away, lying in the space previously occupied by the long wheelbase Ford Transit, was the prostrate figure of Bill Adams. As for Iris Naylor, she was nowhere to be seen.

*

Bill Adams was swearing like a trooper as Kate and Hayden helped him to his feet and he shook them both off angrily.

'I'm fine,' he snarled. 'Just a crack on the head, that's all. Bastard was crouching in the shadows by the side of the Transit. Belted me with something, then nicked the wagon—'

'And Iris Naylor?' Kate demanded, peering about her in the moon-splashed shadows.

'Dunno, I was away with the ruddy fairies, wasn't I?'

'Shit!' Kate breathed. 'George must have her.'

Spinning round, she shouted a quick instruction to Hayden – 'Stay with him,' she said,– then headed back towards the bungalow at a stumbling run.

She almost bowled Roscoe over as she ran down the hallway.

'What the hell's going on?' the DI yelled after her.

'George has snatched Naylor,' she threw back over her shoulder, 'and nicked the Transit.'

Then before he could say anything else, she was out through the front door – scattering a small crowd of local residents and reporters being kept at bay by a couple of uniformed policemen on the front gate. But even as she tore open the door of her CID car parked a few yards away and scrambled in behind the wheel, the passenger door was flung open and Hayden piled in beside her.

'Get out!' she ordered, starting the engine and hovering in first gear, with repeated revving. 'I told you to stay with Adams.'

'No way,' he retorted. 'You're not going there on your own.'

'You have no idea where I'm going. So, get out of the car.'

'There's only one place you could be going.'

'I said out!' she yelled. 'I don't want you anywhere near me.'

'Tough, because I'm staying where I am.'

'Then on your head be it!' she blazed and took off with a screech of tyres.

CHAPTER 26

Iris Naylor was terrified. The confident, hard-nosed attitude she had adopted since turning up at Highbridge police station was now no longer in evidence. Clinging to the front passenger seat of the Transit listening to the staccato bark of the police radio, she was shaking fitfully as the van was powered through the empty streets at breakneck speed, with a succession of crunching gear-changes and sudden braking – mounting the kerb at one point and demolishing a number of traffic bollards as they went.

George had said nothing since attacking the police escort, roughly bundling her into the vehicle and driving off, but the old woman was acutely conscious of her abductor darting glances at her as they drove, the moonlight highlighting the grotesque bald head and revealing the thin lips drawn back over bared white teeth in a grin of malevolent satisfaction.

She had made no effort to resist or try to escape – it would have been futile at her age anyway – but she was mystified as to why George had not killed her straight away, as she had poor Elsie and Mabel, and now they seemed to be heading out into the countryside without any slackening of speed.

George seemed to read her thoughts and laughed suddenly, but without humour.

'Wondering where we're going, Auntie, are you?' she mocked. 'Well, you'll have to work that out for yourself, but I'll tell you one thing, it's somewhere very special, for I've got an equally special punishment reserved for you.'

'Please don't do this,' the old woman pleaded. 'At my age, I have very little time left to me now anyway.'

The Transit swerved again, clipping a hedgerow under heavy braking that, but for the seatbelt, would have put her through the windscreen.

'So, I should wait for you to die peacefully in bed, is that it?' George snarled. 'After everything you and those other bitches did to me, I should just let the Grim Reaper do the job in his own time?'

'Believe me, what we did was for your own good. We … we all thought we were doing God's work and could save your soul …'

George laughed, a high-pitched, unbalanced sound. 'Save my soul? Is that why you said I was the devil's child a few hours ago and tried to put a bullet in me?'

'I … I was frightened. I was just trying to protect myself.'

'Set me up, you mean. Well, it didn't work did it? And now you're going to pay for all the years of misery you subjected me to – and pay in full.'

George emitted an unexpected sob. 'All I ever wanted was to be understood,' she choked. 'To be treated as the person I knew I should have been. I was never a girl, I had been born into the wrong body and my real self was screaming to be let out – but you,' and she hammered the steering wheel violently with the palms of both hands, sending the Transit careering across the road towards the double gates of a large house before managing to haul it back on course, 'you and your bloody harpy sisters treated me as some kind of unclean weirdo, to be reviled and tortured.'

'It … it was your father and mother who made us do it. They said it was the only way. We were trying to help you.'

'Help me?' George shrieked. 'The only thing you helped was yourselves – to my inheritance. What did you do with all the money and the proceeds from the house sale when I was orphaned, eh? Put it towards nice bungalows for each of you?'

'No, I set up a trust fund for you—'

'You did that all right, but as a solicitor, you knew all the wrinkles, didn't you? Like how you and Edward Grace could milk it without getting caught, while all the time I was being screwed every which way by him and his pervy cronies.'

'I ... we didn't know what they were doing to you. Edward was a committed Christian and—'

'Shut it, you evil old cow. I don't want to hear any more of your lies.' George leaned towards her for a moment, her eyes smouldering with hate. 'Just enjoy the ride – it's the last one you're ever going to have!'

*

'So, where's the Transit?' Hayden challenged as Kate pulled up in front of Talbot Court with a swirl of gravel. 'I see no cars.'

She treated him to a contemptuous glance, ignoring his facetious play on the words of Horatio Nelson at the Battle of Copenhagen.

'Could have dumped it somewhere close by,' she muttered, scanning the surrounding woodland, but seeing only trees. 'Doesn't prove anything.'

The derelict building towered over them, its broken windows like dark, haunted eyes that had already borne witness to decades of the unspeakable and now anticipated the tragic sequel.

Hayden was so close behind her when she pushed through the front door that she could feel his breath on her neck.

'Be careful,' he said unnecessarily, wincing as he crunched on the broken glass that the beam of her torch had picked out and she had avoided.

The house seemed to be holding its breath and the silence hung heavy in the air, its ethereal weight almost tangible.

Kate moved forward, her torch probing every room in turn, but without success. 'Next level,' she snapped, heading for the wide staircase. 'Maybe George took her up to the dormitory.'

But she was wrong. The dormitory was empty, as were the rest of the rooms upstairs, and a visit to the basement shortly afterwards found nothing but rubbish-strewn rooms, dripping walls and the same eerie silence.

Demoralized and fearful for Iris Naylor's welfare, Kate returned to the hall, with Hayden hard on her heels desperately trying to offer her words of reassurance. They were met by a confusion of flashing blue light and armed uniformed figures pouring into the hallway through the open front door.

'Great minds think alike,' Roscoe growled as they finally joined him on the forecourt outside. 'Guessed you'd head here.'

Kate emitted a strained laugh. 'Mind not so great, it now seems,' she said. 'Place is empty.'

The DI scowled. 'Shit!' he said. 'Then our nasty neighbourhood psycho could be anywhere.'

'Not *anywhere*, guv,' Hayden corrected drily, receiving a scathing glance from Kate. 'Everyone has to be somewhere.'

Roscoe ignored him. 'So, where the hell could she have taken Iris Naylor?' he said savagely. 'Time's running out for her.'

'May already have run out,' Kate retorted grimly. 'All we can do is to keep searching.'

'Searching – where?'

Kate shrugged and turned away from him. 'I've left my crystal ball at home,' she muttered under her breath.

And as she climbed into her car, her heart felt like a cold lead weight.

*

The village was still fast asleep, despite the breaking dawn. The Transit passed through it at speed, then braked heavily to turn off the main street into a narrow lane.

‘Know where you are?’ George said, pulling up before a pair of high wrought-iron gates and climbing out of the vehicle to open them.

Iris Naylor felt the acid surge up into her throat and she stared at George in disbelief as she climbed back into the vehicle, then drove through the opening on to a long driveway.

‘You’ve brought me back *here*?’ she whispered. ‘What possible good can that do?’

George cut the engine and emitted a sneering laugh. ‘Oh, I don’t know – a bit of nostalgia, perhaps? After all, you had fun here, didn’t you? You and the other old harpies? You certainly must have looked forward to coming here to do your “Christian” duty all those years ago.’

‘You are so very sick,’ the old woman ventured softly. ‘You need help, you really do.’

George laughed again. ‘Oh, I’m sick all right,’ she said bitterly. ‘But no one can help me now. I’m already dying, you see. But at least I’ll see you go before me.’ She climbed out of the car. ‘Now, come on, let’s see if we can stir up a few happy memories.’

*

The answer hit Kate well before they reached the main road and she braked so hard that they were both propelled violently forward to the limits of their seatbelts. The doors separating subconscious thought from active consciousness had suddenly and unexpectedly flown open, producing a sense of clarity that took her a few seconds to articulate.

‘That’s it,’ she exclaimed finally, ignoring Hayden’s protests at the sudden braking. ‘George said it herself – a place that had come to symbolize the beginning of her mental and physical degeneration. Of course, that must be where she’s taken her – to where it all began.’

Hayden frowned. ‘Forgive me for a lack of clairvoyance,’ he said drily, ‘but I seem to have missed the point of your emergency stop.’

For the moment she forgot all about her antagonism towards him.

'When George held me at gunpoint in that farmhouse,' she explained excitedly, 'she went on about the fact that the aunts had turned her home into a place where nightmares were born and where her mental and physical degeneration had begun. Don't you see? We've been barking up the wrong tree. It wasn't Talbot Court she was taking Naylor to – it was her old family home.'

'Which is where?'

'I don't know.'

'Oh.'

'But I know a man who does.'

And this time Hayden was slammed into the back of the seat as she roared away with her foot hard to the floor.

*

Unsurprisingly, the Reverend Glover was in bed when Kate pounded on his door at the rectory.

'Goodness,' he exclaimed, poking his head out of the bedroom window, 'whatever's the matter?'

'Police!' Kate shouted. 'Can you come down? It's urgent.'

The minister opened the door just minutes later, concern etched into his lined face.

Kate didn't beat about the bush. 'When we chatted before,' she said breathlessly, 'you told me that, before their marriage, Elsie Lupin and her sisters all lived in a house out on the Levels and that they had a brother who inherited the place?'

He nodded, looking puzzled. 'That's correct, yes.'

'We need to know the address of the house – and it is a life and death situation.'

He took a deep breath. 'My, my,' he replied, without asking for any further information. 'Well in that case, you had better come in. The register of all marriages at this church are in the rectory for safekeeping. It should be easy enough to find the address you are seeking.'

In fact, it took a lot longer and several registers later to turn up the information, but then there it was, the name of the house and the village written in a neat, if slightly wavering hand.

'Down End House!' Kate breathed. 'And that village is only a stone's throw from here.'

'You said it was a life and death situation,' Glover said, closing the register with a frown. 'What did you mean?'

But Kate didn't answer. She had already thrust Hayden aside and was heading for the door at a run, en route to their car.

*

The sign on one of the open gates read 'Down End House', but a wooden notice had been attached to the other gate, warning 'Keep Out. Trespassers Will Be Prosecuted.'

Iris Naylor shivered. She had not been back to her old home for decades and she was surprised it was still standing. The property had been sold following the death of her brother, John, and George's subsequent removal to Talbot Court, and she and her sisters had been glad to see it go. She'd heard that there had been a succession of different owners afterwards, each bringing their own peculiar modifications with them, like the long Edwardian-style conservatory which had been erected along the front of the house before the big Victorian building, with its pseudo-Gothic embellishments, had finally been abandoned. Pity it had not actually been razed to the ground, she thought.

'Come on, Auntie, no dawdling,' George said, prodding her forwards none too gently. 'Lots to see, you know.'

The old woman stared across the overgrown garden at the ruin facing them as she stumbled along ahead of her captor. She could feel her flesh start to creep as her gaze took in the broken guttering, part-boarded windows and ugly attic room – George's old room – which had been added to the original structure by her late father. It seemed to be crouching there on the flat roof between the tall chimney stacks like some grotesque abomination, its single window peering at her over the stone gargoyles projecting from the crumbling walls in a kind of malevolent greeting.

'Memories coming back, Auntie?' George sneered, prodding her in the back again. 'All those *happy* times?'

'Why don't you just kill me and get this over with?' Iris said tremulously over her shoulder. 'I am going to die soon anyway and I'm not afraid to meet my Maker.'

'Oh no,' George mocked. 'Not before the grand tour. We have to have that first.'

'I think the police will be here well before then.'

George shook her head. 'Hardly, Auntie. They will be homing in on Talbot Court even as we speak and they know nothing about this place anyway, so we have it all to ourselves. Now, isn't that romantic?'

*

Hayden grabbed Kate by the wrist as she thrust the key in the car's ignition.

'Aren't you going to let control know about Down End House before we do anything?' he said as she started the engine.

She shook her head irritably. 'We'd only be told to wait for back-up and there isn't time for that. We're not even sure George has gone there in the first place.'

'Whether she has or not,' he persisted, 'strikes me that it would be better to wait for back-up anyway. This woman is dangerous.'

'No way,' she retorted, prizing her hand free of his grip with her other hand and slamming the car into gear. 'I'm not having Iris Naylor's death on my conscience.'

'Why would it be on your conscience any more than anyone else's? What happens to Iris Naylor is not just down to you.'

'No?' she threw back at him in a tone laced with emotion. 'Well, in case you hadn't noticed, this whole mess is down to me. It was down to me that Georgina Lupin was able to sneak into the bungalow in the first place. It was down to me that Jenny Grey died. It was down to me that Lupin was able to snatch a vulnerable woman we were supposed to be protecting from under our very noses because I was not where I should have been. And it's down to me now to make things right.'

'You won't do that by going off at half-cock, like some hare-brained maverick.'

She flared instantly. 'Is that so? Well, if you don't like it, you can always get out and walk back to the nick, as I told you once before. I didn't want you with me in the first place.'

He winced. 'Hey, steady on, old girl,' he protested hastily, 'I was just pointing out that—'

'Well, don't!' she snarled, pulling away with a familiar torturous squeal of tyres. 'I don't need advice from a two-timing arsehole like you!'

Her foul mood persisted over the next few miles and it was this that may have led to her loss of concentration. The farmer had no doubt intended to make an early morning start when he drove his Ford tractor out of the gateway on to the road. Dawn was breaking by then and, as he could see enough to drive, he hadn't bothered with lights, even though to others his tractor had only fractionally more substance than a heavy shadow. He should have looked first anyway, of course, but perhaps the early start itself had led to his own loss of concentration. In any event, he happened to choose to pull out on to the road at exactly the wrong moment. Kate saw the tractor all too late and, though her police training and quick reactions enabled her to take immediate evasive action to avoid a direct collision, the CID car still ploughed through the low hedge on the opposite side of the lane, coming to rest with its wheels embedded in a sea of glutinous mud and steam pouring from its fractured radiator.

CHAPTER 27

Down End House was clearly marked for demolition and the Victorian building looked distinctly sinister in the gathering dawn. There were notices nailed everywhere warning 'Danger. Keep Out', and most of the windows and doors appeared to have been boarded up. Getting into the house did not present a problem, however, for someone had earlier smashed the padlock and ripped off the battens securing the front door.

George emitted a short, humourless laugh as she pushed Iris ahead into the hallway, training the torch she had produced on a low door set in the panelling under the main staircase.

'Nostalgia starting to get to you, is it, Auntie?' she said, jerking the door open to reveal a flight of narrow stone stairs plunging steeply into near Stygian darkness. 'Let's see if we can give it some stimulus, eh?'

Distorted shadows opened up before the torch in the cellar beneath, the powerful beam touching on bits of furniture, rolls of carpet and a pile of old books.

Iris shuddered, shrinking back instinctively from its evil-smelling gloom, but George pressed against her, holding her there in a cruel vice-like grip.

'This is where I was dumped as a punishment, remember?' she hissed close to her ear. 'Stripped naked, beaten, and locked in here alone to face all the monsters you said lived in this awful place.'

The torch homed in on an even blacker hole within a circle of bricks in the far corner.

'See the well?' George breathed. 'You told me the monsters lived at the bottom of it, ready to devour me because of my wicked ways. Can you imagine what that was like for a small child? What terrors that child endured, waiting for those monsters to appear from the depths, dreading what form they might take and screaming all the time to be let out?'

'I … I'm so sorry,' the old woman whispered. 'I really am.'

'Are you, Auntie, are you honestly?' George sneered. 'Well, that must be all right then. After all, forgiveness is what Christianity is all about, isn't it? You say sorry and I absolve you of all blame. What is it you Christians call it? Turning the other cheek, that's it. It's so simple when you think about it. Pity it doesn't work for me, though. Now, let's move closer to the well, to see if any of the monsters are at home, shall we?'

*

Neither Kate nor Hayden stirred for several long seconds after the crash. They just sat there in a state of shock, staring unseeing through the spiderweb cracks in the windscreen at the steam rising in the early dawn light from under the CID car's buckled bonnet. Kate was the first to move, jerking suddenly out of her dazed state and fumbling with her seatbelt.

As it clinked open, she turned quickly in her seat to check on Hayden, who had released his own seatbelt and was sitting there, prodding his chest tenderly with the fingers of one hand.

'You okay?' she asked.

'Bruised my ribcage, I think,' he replied, then snapped on the interior light and stared at her keenly, noting the blood trickling down her face from a deep cut in her forehead where her head had struck the door pillar. 'What about you? You're bleeding.'

She seemed aware of her injury for the first time and wiped the back of her hand across her forehead, wincing at the sudden stab of pain from the open wound and staring at the blood on the back of her hand with a scowl.

'I'll live,' she snapped. 'Where's that bloody tractor?'

He peered through his side window over the hedge. 'Scarpered by the look of it,' he retorted. 'Probably never even saw us.'

She put her shoulder against her door and burst it open. 'We have to get going,' she said. 'We're wasting time.'

'Get going?' he echoed. 'Like where and how? This car's a write-off.'

She climbed unsteadily out of the vehicle, holding on to the door frame for support, and almost threw up in the mud into which her shoes had sunk.

'Down End House.'

He gaped at her. 'You've got to be joking? That job's out the window now. We're going nowhere.'

'But the village can only be just down the road,' she retorted. 'Maybe ten minutes on foot.'

He stared at her in total disbelief. 'Are you mad?' he exclaimed. 'We've totalled the CID car, we're both injured and suffering from shock, and anyway, we can't just abandon a police vehicle and walk away from the scene of an accident. Call up control, as we should have done before. Let them handle things – there's nothing more we can do to help Iris Naylor.'

'Balls!' she grated, stumbling away from the car towards the gap in the hedge. 'You call up control. I'm going to finish what I started.'

Grabbing the door handle, he wrestled with the lock, but it seemed to have jammed and even when he put his shoulder against the door, it refused to budge.

'Kate,' he shouted through the still-open driver's door. 'Don't be a fool!'

But she had already reached the lane and disappeared behind a line of trees, leaving him desperately trying to crawl over the gearstick and centre consul in an effort to get out of the car on the driver's side.

*

'You never liked wells, did you, Auntie?' George said softly, pushing the old woman ahead of her to the wall encircling the black pit. 'I remember Father saying how you had a phobia about them. Imagine falling down one full of all the monsters you used to talk about, eh? I wonder how deep this one is …?'

Producing a coin from her pocket, she leaned past Iris while still holding on to one skinny wrist tightly with her other hand, and flicked the coin into the gaping mouth. 'Listen!' she ordered.

For a few seconds there was nothing and then a soft but definite 'plop' from far below.

'Long way down, isn't it?' she said, smirking as she felt the thin frame she was pressed against shaking fitfully.

'Have a closer look,' she went on and suddenly thrust her aunt forward so forcibly that, but for the hand gripping her wrist, she would have pitched the old woman right over into the depths.

'Whoops!' George mocked. 'Nearly lost you that time, didn't I? But don't worry, Auntie, I'm not going to punish you that way. No one would ever know what had happened to you then, would they? It would defeat the whole purpose of what I'd planned to do. Oh no, I've got something much better and more public in store for you.'

The main staircase to the upper floor was uncarpeted, though the beam of the torch in George's hand caught the occasional glint of nails with bits of carpet still attached. There were ragged holes in places too where the wood had rotted, and some sections of the bannister rails were no longer in evidence.

'Careful now,' George said, shining the torch past her as she prodded her aunt forward with her other hand. 'Don't want you falling through and breaking your neck, do we? That would spoil all the fun.'

Upstairs, open doorways yawned at them and Iris jumped when a bat flew out of one room in a panic, grazing the top of her head.

George obviously knew exactly where she was going and she continued prodding her captive forward until they were at the end of the corridor and standing before a half-open door partially shielding another bare, though much narrower, ascending staircase.

George reached past her to pull the door wide. 'Up you go, Auntie,' she said softly. 'You'll know where you are now, surely?'

There was another door at the top of the staircase and George once more reached past her to pull it open.

Like the rest of the house, the tiny room beyond was devoid of furnishings of any sort, but unlike the rest of the house Iris had previously viewed from the outside, there was no boarding across the single window and it was immediately apparent that there was no glass there either. It had been knocked out completely and jagged shards were clearly visible on the floor below the low sill. In the strengthening grey light streaming into the room, the torch had become superfluous and time-faded, handwritten religious texts were visible on every wall, with a part-obliterated list of the Ten Commandments above the missing window.

'You must remember this room, Auntie?' George said. 'It was my attic bedroom – or cell, as I liked to call it – where I was confined most days and forced to sit at my little wooden desk, trying to memorize texts from the Holy Bible. You all used to test me on it, didn't you? And when I got something wrong, I had to be punished – because as a girl wanting to be a boy, I was unclean, wasn't I? What was it Father called me? Oh yes, "an aberration and an affront to the Almighty", that was it.'

'The devil had turned you and we needed to drive his demon out to … to bring you back on the right path,' Iris stammered. 'It was God's will.'

George glared at her. 'God had nothing to do with it, nor had the devil,' she hissed with vicious force. 'What you did to me all those years was not done in the name of God, but to satisfy your own sadistic desire to punish an innocent child you believed to have brought shame on the family name just by being different. But enough,' and the sneer was back in her voice. 'We are now almost at the end of the grand tour and this is the best part of it.'

*

Kate could feel a burning pain in her chest as she stumbled along the lane, but she pushed on regardless, soon passing darkened cottages and a shuttered, uninviting-looking inn. She cast quick, panicky glances about her in an effort to pick out Down End House. She had no idea exactly where the place was and the address the Reverend Glover had produced from the church register had simply given the name of the property – no street or anything else. She reached the outer limits of the village before she found what she was looking for, a dilapidated sign leaning out of a hedge and pointing up an even narrower lane to her left, bearing the faint, barely discernible name of Down End House.

Her throat was dry and her legs shaking from her exertions by the time she got to the end of the lane, following a high brick wall. When the austere Victorian house with its Gothic facade and totally out-of-place Edwardian-style conservatory finally materialized on the far side of an unkempt garden, she was forced to stand for a moment, drawing in ragged gasps of the cold, dank air before she could go any further. She saw the marked police Ford Transit as she stood there holding on to one of the gateposts. It was parked in the middle of the driveway, just beyond the open gate. Her heart gave a sickening lurch and she found her fingernails digging into the soft wood of the post as the gravity of the challenge she had single-handedly taken on now dawned on her.

She was not given much time to think about it either. The scream that punctured the stillness of the air was only faint, but it cut into her like a knife. As she started through the gateway, she caught sight of two figures on the roof of the house, dangerously close to the low wall bordering the edge, one of whom appeared to be backing away from the other.

CHAPTER 28

'So, what do you think I've got planned for you, Auntie?' George gloated.

Iris simply stared at the floor, her eyes dull and lifeless. She was no longer trembling and it seemed that her tears had completely dried up. It was as if, in the final numbing throes of shock, she didn't care anymore.

Her silence was greeted with a frown of feigned disappointment.

'Come on now, I've gone to a great deal of trouble here. The moment I got out of Larchfield – even before I went back to Talbot Court – I came here to set things up. You could at least show some interest.'

There was still no response and George sighed. 'Do you know,' she went on, 'I actually cut my hand knocking out that window so we would be able to climb through it on to the roof and I took my life in my hands demolishing one of the stone gargoyles – all just for you. You're so ungrateful.'

Very slowly Iris raised her head, a hint of life back in her eyes and her gaze now focused directly on her tormentor's face.

'Just do what you have to do,' came the low, weary reply. 'I know you're going to kill me anyway, so get on with it. I've already said I'm not afraid to die.'

'No, of course you're not,' George patronized, 'but you should be really proud of the efforts I've made on your behalf to give you such a spectacular send-off.' She tugged a dark-coloured bottle from the pocket of her coat. 'Look, I've even brought along some sherry, so we could have a last drink together before you go – just like the old days. You know, a sort of toast for the dying.'

There was no response and George returned the bottle to her pocket with a manufactured sigh.

'Ah well, we can talk about that again in a minute and anyway, you might be more interested in this.'

She slipped her hand inside her coat and produced a sealed envelope, which she waved in front of her captive's nose.

'My confession, Auntie – for the police, you understand. A testimony that should justify my actions and exonerate me from all blame. It will be left for them to read after you have joined your Maker and I have disappeared ... I thought I might go to Ireland, you know. Spend my last weeks or days in some wilderness location. Dying, you see, is a very personal thing and I have no intention of waiting for the Grim Reaper to take me. I shall end it all on a day and method of my own choosing. Cheat the Reaper, as well as the authorities, but ensure through this letter that my name will be written into the annals of criminal history for evermore. Brilliant, eh?'

'You will burn in the fires of hell,' Iris whispered.

There was a high-pitched, unbalanced laugh as George returned the envelope to her pocket.

'Maybe I will, maybe I will, but it will be with a smile on my face for what I will have done to you.'

George waved an arm towards the window. 'Did you see the gargoyles when I first brought you here? Well, you may or may not have noticed that one of them is missing. That's because I removed it with a hammer. Took me a while and I had to proceed very carefully too, because each of those heads is supported by an iron spike, and I needed this one to be left in place to accommodate *your* head after it has parted company with the rest of you. With me so far?'

Iris swayed a little, but retained her composure, meeting his gaze without flinching, and George grinned again.

'Sure, you are. The thing is, I felt that for such an evil cow like you, your head would be right at home on a spike among the gargoyles. After I've removed it, of course – with this.'

The large, slightly curved knife seemed to appear in the psychopath's hand as if by magic and Iris closed her eyes tightly for a second, her hands clenching and unclenching by her sides.

'God forgive you!'

'Somehow, I don't think He will, but *c'est la vie* – or *la mort*, if you prefer. Now out you go, on to the roof. It's only a low sill, so you should have no trouble climbing over it.'

Iris stayed exactly where she was, a new look of defiance on her face.

George sighed. 'Surely you don't want to spoil it all, Auntie? You see, it would be a lot easier for both of us if I did what I have to do out there, close to your final resting place. Carrying a decapitated head through the window would be rather messy, don't you think? It would spoil the overall effect.'

Iris still refused to budge and George sighed again. 'Looks like I shall have to help you then,' she said, returning the knife to her pocket. 'After all, that's what good nieces do for their aunties, isn't it?'

Iris tried to stand her ground, but fit as she was for her age, she was no match for the powerful killer and swinging the old woman round to face the window, George propelled her towards it with hardly any effort.

Left with no option but to do as she was told, Iris lifted one foot over the sill, crouching down to enable her to get her head under the top frame, and it was as she did so that she saw the shards of glass lying on the flat roof on the other side. At this point, George's view was temporarily blocked by the old woman's body and she failed to see the gnarled hand reaching down to pick up one of the shards as the other leg was lifted over the sill.

The first George knew about it was when she herself ducked her head to climb through the frame and the jagged piece of glass ripped across her face, opening up the cheek and cutting through one eye as neatly as a surgeon's scalpel.

Her screams were a mixture of demoniac rage and pure agony, and as she tottered towards her aunt, blood streaming between the fingers of the hand that she had instinctively cupped over her eye, Iris shrank back across the flat roof towards one of the chimney stacks, still clutching the bloodstained piece of glass. Her mouth worked silently as she saw the knife once more appear in George's other hand. Then her back was against the tall chimney and, glancing quickly over her shoulder, she saw that the roof ended just behind the stack and she could go no further. And at that moment she knew that she was dead.

*

Kate was through the front door of the house and racing up the stairs within seconds of hearing the screams. She had no idea how to get to the roof and only knew that there had to be a second staircase or a ladder somewhere on the floor above.

She spotted the stairs to the attic through the open door almost immediately after gaining the landing. By then she was near to exhaustion. Senses swimming. Lungs on fire. The pressure from her pounding heart like a road drill in her eardrums, competing with the high-pitched voice ranting and raving from somewhere above her head. Calling on her last reserves of strength, she managed to haul herself up the attic stairs and clamber out through the window on to the roof – but then she abruptly froze in her tracks.

Georgina Lupin must have heard her climbing through the window and was waiting for her just feet away, blood spurting from a horrific facial wound, which seemed to have obliterated one eye. Kate was vaguely aware of Iris Naylor pressed up against a chimney stack close to the far end of the roof to her right, but she was denied the opportunity of a more thorough assessment of the situation. Instead, her focus was concentrated on Lupin as the killer, screaming and mouthing obscenities, advanced on her brandishing a long, curved knife.

All the police training manuals would have had a textbook solution for this kind of situation but in the reality of that split second, Kate did not even have time to go for the CS gas spray in her pocket. Instead, she was left with no option but to focus all her attention on the knife and the homicidal intent of the mad woman as she backed away from her towards Iris.

She managed to sidestep the first rush, lurching sideways and actually managing to get behind her assailant as the knife ripped harmlessly through the sleeve of her coat. But despite suffering from such a horrendous facial injury and being temporarily thrown off balance, George quickly recovered and, before Kate could capitalize on her brief advantage and reach for her CS spray, the killer had swung round to confront her again – and this time Kate did not fare so well. She managed to avoid the blade lunging at her, but in doing so forgot how near the edge of the roof she had strayed. The next instant her heels had slammed into the low wall enclosing it and, after a second's desperate wobbling effort to regain her balance, she pitched backwards into space, plunging towards the Edwardian conservatory far below.

*

To Iris Naylor, watching the confrontation from a few yards away, it was all over and it seemed inevitable that her would-be rescuer would be smashed to pieces on the forecourt beneath. But Fate was not done with Kate Lewis yet.

Even as she went over the wall, her flailing arms struck and somehow instinctively managed to lock on to the stone head of one of the gargoyles. She ended up dangling from it, with both arms locked around the long neck, her booted feet treading empty air.

Miraculously, she had escaped what should have been certain death, but as she clung precariously to the ugly stone head, her stay of execution looked like being very temporary indeed when George's face suddenly materialized over the top of the wall, blood still pouring from the ugly wound she had sustained.

'Well, well, well, Sergeant, you *are* in a bit of a pickle, aren't you?' the psychopath crowed.

Kate felt the blood from the killer's wound dripping on to her. The next moment the disfigured face was very close as George leaned over the wall, her knife gently stroking the backs of Kate's hands.

'Nice hands, Sergeant. Shall I cut one of them off, do you think? Could you hold on with just one?'

The stone head Kate was clinging to made a distinct cracking sound and she felt it give slightly. Her weight was obviously too much for the ancient sculpture and at any moment it was likely to part company with the wall, this time sending her to her death. In a panic, the toes of her boots scrabbled against the sheer stonework, futilely searching for a hold of some sort, but there was nothing. The knife cut into her wrist and she could tell from the razor-sharp blade that just a little more pressure would sever the artery.

'Well, maybe just the fingers, eh?' George went on, obviously enjoying the moment in spite of her own pain and semi-blindness. 'One at a time, I think.'

The knife cut into her little finger now, pressing down very slowly. At the same moment the gargoyle gave another crack and seemed to pull away from the wall slightly.

George emitted another of her unbalanced laughs. 'You seem to be on the move, Sergeant. Well, let's lessen the load, shall we?'

Kate gritted her teeth, waiting for the agonizing pain as her finger was severed, making her lose her grip. But it never happened.

The next instant the knife was withdrawn and George was no longer in her face. Instead, there was a loud commotion on the roof above. As she looked up, George's face once more appeared over the edge. This time, however, it was different. For one illusory, surrealistic second the face actually seemed to be lunging at her. Then, with the one visible eye bulging with apparent terror and a shrill, rapidly fading scream issuing from the gaping mouth, the psychopath hurtled past Kate, arms desperately clawing at the air in a wild dive. The splintering crash that followed told its own story. Peering down, Kate saw that the shattered panes of the orangery canopy far below had turned a noticeable shade of red in the morning light.

Her gaze was still locked on to the grisly sight with a sort of horrible, mesmeric fascination when she saw the convoy of flashing blue lights racing up the driveway. At the same moment she heard the familiar voice calling her name from above her head.

'Come on, old girl, give me your hand.'

She tore her eyes away from the smashed canopy to stare back at the roof and saw Hayden leaning over the wall towards her, one arm outstretched, a cold, hard look on his face that she had never seen before. For a few seconds she just stared up at him in a state of shock, unable to release her grip on the gargoyle.

'Quickly now, Kate,' he said in a much sharper tone. 'You must take my hand.'

As he spoke, the gargoyle made a grumbling, grinding noise and finally parted company with the wall.

'Kate!' Hayden yelled. But she was already falling.

AFTER THE FACT

Georgina Lupin's departure from her earthly world had been a dramatic one. The impact of her body had demolished a large section of the orangery canopy and the blood from severed arteries not only still dripped from the remaining fragments of jagged glass in the roof's broken window frames, but with almost the same force as a perforated high-pressure hose had redecorated much of the inside of the derelict building a grisly red. Her corpse had finished up on its back, draped over a rusted, iron-framed table, amongst a litter of broken flowerpots, her single visible eye staring up at the hole in the canopy, as if trying to pick out the precise spot on the roof of the house from which she had fallen.

Roscoe studied the corpse for a few moments, then popped a strip of gum into his mouth.

'The pair of you don't do things by halves, do you?' he said drily, casting a critical glance at both Kate and Hayden standing together a few feet away. 'And we've certainly lost any chance of a nice, tidy confession now.'

Hennessey nodded in agreement, then grimaced. 'Plus the fact that there'll be lots of questions from the powers-that-be and the press as to exactly how this happened.'

'Let them ask,' Kate snapped, picking up on the underlying insinuation. 'If Hayden hadn't done what he did, *I* would be lying there instead of her.'

It had certainly been a close call and Kate knew it was something that would be indelibly etched on her memory until her dying day. Literally throwing himself forward as the gargoyle had finally torn itself free, Hayden had nearly pitched over the low wall himself in a desperate attempt to save her – only just managing to grab the collar of her coat at the very last moment. For several critical seconds he had hung on to her as she'd dangled over the sheer drop, using all his strength, with his thighs pressed against the wall for leverage, to pull her up far enough for her to grab the top of the wall and haul herself over on to the roof. Things certainly couldn't have got any closer than that.

'Strange how Lupin just fell, though, isn't it?' the DCI went on.

Hayden seemed unperturbed by the repeated insinuation and the same hard, unrepentant expression that Kate had glimpsed on her partner's face when he had first appeared on the roof returned with a vengeance.

'Easy to overbalance on the edge of a roof, ma'am,' he replied smoothly, 'especially when you've lost the sight of one eye. Dangerous places, roofs, you know?'

'There was no struggle then?'

The detective pursed his lips for a second. 'Not as such, no. She just sort of toppled over the edge.'

Roscoe made a face. 'And not a blow struck in the process, eh?' he added, plainly unconvinced.

'Look, what is this?' Kate snapped. 'Anyone would think Hayden is the villain here.'

Hennessey shook her head. 'It's not that at all, but there's bound to be an inquiry,' she pointed out almost apologetically. 'Professional Standards and the IOPC in particular will want chapter and verse on the incident, especially as the casualty was a vulnerable mental patient.'

'Vulnerable?' Kate exclaimed. 'She was a killer. She murdered seven people, including one of our own, and, as I've already told you, she was trying to cut my fingers off as I clung to that bloody gargoyle, with the intention of adding me to her list.'

Hennessey made a deprecating gesture with both hands. 'I understand all that, Sergeant, but you know how the cookie crumbles these days. Certain people will suspect that we carried out our own kind of summary justice.'

Hayden shrugged. 'Let them suspect what they want. If they have any real doubts, they can always ask Iris Naylor what she saw.'

'That's not likely to happen,' Roscoe growled. 'It seems she had a heart attack on her way back to the nick and is in the ITU at Weston Hospital – not expected to survive.'

'So, Lupin has won in the end then?' Kate put in again.

Hennessey shook her head. 'Hardly. This is certainly not the way our obsessed killer would have wanted her vendetta to play out. Just before her heart attack, Mrs Naylor told the officer escorting her to the station that her niece had intended cutting off her head and sticking it on a spike on the roof, among the gargoyles, as a sort of message to the world.'

'Some might say that would have been quite an appropriate outcome,' Kate retorted drily.

Hennessey frowned. 'Surely you're not suggesting it would have been justified?'

It was Kate's turn to shrug. 'Not at all. George was an evil, cold-blooded murderess and she got what she deserved, but Iris Naylor and her sisters had a lot to do with the way she turned out. They made her what she was through their cruel, self-righteous fanaticism and furthermore, we still don't know what happened to the money Naylor was supposed to have invested in the so-called trust fund set up on George's behalf – probably never will now. So, don't expect me to weep for those wicked, hypocritical old witches. There are no innocents in this sordid case. No one is blameless—'

'Not even you,' Roscoe cut in again, his Mr Hyde asserting himself over his Dr Jekyll and obviously keen to have his pound of flesh, despite the inappropriateness of the moment. 'You went off at half-cock, as usual, didn't you? No wonder you're known as "Go It Alone Kate". You should have radioed in with the info on the nutter's location, not charged off on your own like bloody Don Quixote. If Dipstick here hadn't called in with the SP when he went after you, we would never have known where you were.'

Kate's lip curled. 'Fat lot of good calling in would have done. You arrived after it was all over anyway.'

But Roscoe was in full flood and ignored the remark. 'Then there's the small matter of the CID car you were using,' he snarled. 'I'm told you actually managed to write the thing off on the way here and dump it in a soddin' field. Got any more Inspector Clouseau tricks up your sleeve?'

'That's enough, Ted!' Hennessey rapped, conscious of several uniformed officers peering into the orangery through the open door. 'This is not the time or the place.'

Kate stared at him with undisguised contempt. She was still trembling after her near fatal ordeal and a numbing coldness was creeping up her legs and arms as the shock of it all finally began to set in. She hadn't expected praise from her boss for saving Iris Naylor's life or risking her own. In the police service, praise was a commodity that was in very short supply and in Roscoe's case it was unheard of. But an acknowledgment of what she had been through would not have gone amiss. Instead, it was just the same old cynical Roscoe, full of sarcasm, resentment and bitterness, and, after years enduring his coarse, misogynistic attitude, it was the very last straw for her in her present state of mind.

'Only one trick left, *sir*,' she replied in a tone of pure ice and, reaching into her pocket, she pulled out her warrant card in its small black wallet.

'You can stuff that as far up as it will go!' she said as Hennessey gaped at her. 'I'm done here.'

'My sentiments too, Mr Roscoe,' said Hayden, handing over his own warrant card with a grim smile. 'And I sincerely hope you enjoy the erotic sensation.'

*

It didn't take Kate long to clear out her desk when she and Hayden were driven back to Highbridge police station by a Traffic patrol and she dumped most of her paperwork in Roscoe's office. It took Hayden even less time to do the same thing, but as they both walked out of the police station for the last time, the tension between them was almost palpable.

'So, what do we do now?' Hayden asked a little too casually in the police station car park.

Kate paused by her car and shrugged. 'I'll move out and find a flat somewhere,' she said.

He shook his head firmly, flinching when he went to grasp her arm and she drew away from him.

'There's no need for you to do any such thing,' he said.

She sighed heavily. 'You … you saved my life, Hayd,' she said, 'and I'm grateful to you for that, but … but you and me – it's all over. It has to be.'

He shook his head again. 'No, it doesn't have to be at all. I have something to show you – someone I want you to meet.'

She stared at him, anger starting to burn inside her again. 'Someone you want me to meet? You're not thinking of introducing me to that bit of tail of yours, are you?'

He took her briefcase from her and opened the boot of her MX5 to dump it inside.

'Just humour me for half an hour, that's all I ask,' he said and, taking her by the elbow despite her protests, led her away from her car towards the far end of the car park. 'It isn't far,' he encouraged. 'We'll take my Jag.'

Shaking her arm free, she walked ahead of him towards the sleek red saloon.

'No need for the mystery act,' she snapped. 'I know exactly where we're going.'

But as it transpired, she didn't.

*

The blonde-haired girl in the bed of the local hospital's ITU had probably been pretty once, but the ghost-white face, just visible behind the oxygen mask, was now gaunt, almost skeletal, and there were so many tubes and wires connected to her body that she resembled a visitant from another planet.

'She hasn't long to go,' Hayden said quietly. 'Liver's packed up, you see.'

Kate stared at the girl and then back at him in obvious bewilderment and he gave a wry smile.

'My "bit of tail"', he explained. 'The other woman you were talking about.'

'*She's* the other woman? I don't understand.'

'My kid sister,' he qualified.

'Your kid *sister*?'

He nodded. 'Tragically, a cocaine addict. Apparently OD'd about the time we had that mishap on our way to Down End House, though whether she did it deliberately or by accident, we'll never know now. Paramedics were called by the staff at the hotel where she was staying, but too late. Almost everything had shut down by the time they got to her. Hotel manager couldn't get hold of me on the mobile number I had left with reception, so he sent me a text. Only just picked it up.'

Kate grimaced. 'What a bloody awful thing to happen. She looks to be so young. But … but I still don't understand, why didn't you tell me about her at the start? Why let me think you were over the side?'

He sighed and crossed to the window to stare out into the grounds of the hospital.

'I didn't want you to get involved,' he replied.

'Involved? Involved in what?'

He turned to face her again. 'Assisting an offender,' he said simply.

A nurse came into the room and inclined her head in the direction of the door.

'I think you should leave now,' she said quietly. 'There's a waiting room just along the corridor. I will call you if anything happens.'

Hayden nodded and gently ushered Kate out through the door. Fortunately, they found the waiting room to be empty.

'Assisting an offender?' Kate queried as soon as they were inside. 'What are you talking about, Hayd?'

He waved her to a shabby armchair and dropped into the one opposite.

'Her name's Jill,' he said. 'Just twenty-five years old. Always been a bit wild and some years ago she walked out on my mum and dad after a terrible row with my father over some junkie pusher she was dating. I was at public school at the time and when I got home, she'd gone, no one knew where.'

He took a deep breath. 'Then a few nights ago she turned up right out of the blue and confronted me in the nick car park, demanding my help. Heaven knows how she'd found me, but she was emaciated, barefoot and filthy dirty – as well as on a downer after her last cocaine fix. Furthermore, she had partially healed slash marks to both wrists, indicating that she had previously attempted suicide, and she swore she would finish the job if I didn't help her out.'

He studied her for a moment. 'So, what could I do? You more than anyone would understand the invidious position I was in after what happened to you during that old Firetrap operation a while ago.'

Kate knew exactly what he was getting at and she tensed. Her mind was already peeling back the years, to the night her own drugged-up twin sister, Linda, had appeared at her flat, seeking shelter – only to later end up a victim of the murderous 'Twister', when the maniacal killer the police were hunting mistook her for Kate.

'Go on,' she encouraged, a tremor in her voice now. 'There's obviously more.'

He bit his lip. 'I found a room for her at a private hotel in Uphill, bought her some new clothes from M&S and had her clean herself up, intending to get some professional help for her addiction at a clinic near Bridgwater—'

'Bit naive of you?' Kate interjected brutally.

He gave a short, humourless laugh. 'There's none so blind as those who cannot see, old girl,' he retorted bitterly. 'But in the event, she repaid me by stealing money from the hotel till to buy more coke from a local dealer she knew. Fortunately, the hotel was unaware of it and when I found out what she'd done, I surreptitiously put the money back from my own wallet. But that wasn't the end of it all. A short time afterwards she confessed to something much worse. When she had originally turned up outside the nick seeking my help, she was apparently already in breach of her bail conditions from Oxford Crown Court, where she'd been due to answer multiple charges of assault and shoplifting.'

Kate took a deep breath. 'But you couldn't have known that when you agreed to help her?'

'Doesn't make any difference,' he said. 'No one will believe me. They'll say, quite rightly, that I should have turned her in the moment I found out, so I'll just be hung out to dry for assisting an offender – together with anyone else involved with me, which is why I wanted to keep you out of it.'

Deep down Kate knew he was right, but she hadn't the heart to say so. Instead, tears welling up in her eyes, she reached forward and placed a hand on his knee.

'Oh, Hayd,' she said in a husky, hesitant tone, 'I'm so, so sorry for all the horrid things I've said and for the way I've treated you. I ... I had no idea about all this and I should have had more trust in you. I've been a bloody fool.'

'Hasn't everyone at some time or other?' he replied, cupping a hand over hers and squeezing it tightly. 'Problem is, people like Roscoe don't make allowances for human failure – and he certainly won't be inclined to be magnanimous with us after what we told him to do with our warrant cards.'

The suggestion of a smile broke through Kate's tears at the thought of their parting comments to the DI and, springing from her seat, she fell into his lap, throwing her arms around his neck.

'We'll get through this together, Hayd,' she choked. 'I know we will.'

Neither she nor Hayden heard the nurse's soft footfalls and initially her discreet cough went unnoticed too, but then Hayden looked up and squeezed Kate's arms in warning, prompting her to break away from him and turn to face the young woman, smoothing the creases in her coat with both hands as she did so in a gesture of embarrassment.

'I think you had better come,' the nurse said. 'I'm afraid the young lady has passed away.'

It was an awkward, unreal parting. Hayden was clearly upset at the loss of his sister, but there was no display of emotion as he stared down at the dead woman, just a resigned, almost relieved acceptance.

'I never really knew her,' he said after the nurse had tactfully withdrawn. 'We never got on as kids and then she upped sticks and disappeared while I was away. I suppose I helped her more out of a sense of loyalty than anything else. Does … does that sound bad, heartless even?'

Kate shook her head firmly, staring for a moment at the white face on the pillow, framed by its mass of blonde hair – now strangely relaxed and at peace in Death's embrace – and thinking of the loss of her own sister all those years before.

'She chose the path, Hayd,' she said. 'She must have known what the eventual outcome would be, though it's tragic the way things have turned out. At least you did your best to help her.'

He grunted, turning away from the bed. 'At what cost?' he replied.

Kate shook her head. 'She's gone, Hayd,' she went on. 'Nothing the authorities can do to her now – and that means you too. She's out of it and you and I can simply walk away.'

'Where to?' he said. 'In the hot blood of the moment, we appear, rather foolishly, to have burned our boats with the firm and are out of a job.'

She took his arm. 'To a new life,' she said simply. 'A new beginning.'

But as it transpired, their old life was not quite done with them yet.

Hayden saw the envelope stuck under one of the windscreen wipers of her Mazda MX5 when he ran her back to the police station car park in his Jaguar. Their two warrant cards were inside the envelope, still in their plastic wallets, together with a curt note from DI Roscoe. 'Cards would not fit the suggested cavity,' it said with dismissive sarcasm. 'Resignations not accepted. Debriefing at 1400 hours. Be there!'

Hayden raised an eyebrow. 'Good lord, a reprieve, it seems,' he drawled. 'And after all that we said to him? The man must have the skin of a rhinoceros.'

Kate nodded slowly. 'Even thicker than that,' she said. 'And I suspect it's the nearest our esteemed leader will ever get to admitting he actually needs us.'

'Oh, you mean we *do* have value after all? So, what happens now?'

She chewed her lip for a second, then grinned, handing his warrant card back to him.

'I suppose we do like the man said,' she replied. 'Attend the debrief at 1400 hours. The new life will have to wait.'

THE END

The Detective Kate Hamblin mystery series

Book 1: MURDER ON THE LEVELS
Book 2: REVENGE ON THE LEVELS
Book 3: FEAR ON THE LEVELS
Book 4: KILLER ON THE LEVELS
Book 5: SECRETS ON THE LEVELS
Book 6: DEATH ON THE LEVELS

Please join our mailing list for updates on DETECTIVE KATE HAMBLIN, free Kindle crime thriller, detective, mystery books and new releases.

http://www.joffebooks.com/contact/

Thank you for reading this book. If you enjoyed it please leave feedback on Amazon, and if there is anything we missed or you have a question about then please get in touch. The author and publishing team appreciate your feedback and time reading this book.

Please join our mailing list for free kindle crime thriller, detective, mystery, and romance books and new releases.
http://www.joffebooks.com/contact/

Our email is office@joffebooks.com

http://joffebooks.com

We hate typos but sometimes they slip through.
Please send any errors you find to
corrections@joffebooks.com

We'll get them fixed ASAP. We're very grateful to eagle-eyed readers who take the time to contact us.

Printed in Poland
by Amazon Fulfillment
Poland Sp. z o.o., Wrocław

54545579R00153